FOR KING AND CORRUPTION

Dark Maji Book Four

KEL CARPENTER

For King and Corruption

Published by Kel Carpenter

Copyright © 2020, Kel Carpenter LLC

Contributions made by Lucinda Dark

Edited by Analisa Denny

Proofread by Dominique Laura

Cover Art by Trif

Map and Graphic designed by Zenta Brice

 Created with Vellum

To Graceley

You wanted your name in this book. Now it is. Thank you for being the motivation to write it when I couldn't find anything else.

Changing is what people do when they have no other options left.

Holly Black, *Red Glove*

The Sirian Continent

N

THE CRYSTAL
CONTINENT

JIBREAL

N'SKARA

TRITOL

LIPH

ILVAS

VUSUT

CISEA

CISEAN MOUNTAINS

BANGRATAS

DUMAS

ZYBURN

SARI SARI ISLANDS

NORCASTA

TRIENE

LEONE

IAMONT

Of Heads and Heralds

"Trust, when hard won, is not easy to break."
— *Lazarus Fierté, soul eater, the contemplative King of Norcasta*

Heavy was the head that wears the crown.

That's what Claudius told him with his dying breath before declaring Lazarus king. Months had passed, and he didn't agree with the sentiment any more than he had on his coronation day. The truth of it was that the crown itself wasn't the least bit heavy. The stipulations of being king, while tedious, weren't unmanageable. He didn't mind the royal games when he was the hand that moved the pieces.

What weighed on him as more time passed was in the back of his mind, a woman in leathers with a wicked smile called him a fool. She'd told him that the crown wouldn't be enough. She'd declared that he would want more.

And she was right.

Lazarus shifted against the wooden boards, iron nail-heads prodding his thighs uncomfortably. His fingers curled around the metal armrests as he listened to the nobles before him, droning on about some circumstances they wanted him to fix. They were under the impression that he existed to cater to their needs. A glorified butler of sorts. Lazarus could thank Claudius' blood heirs for that. They were still making a strong claim in the north, even after his ascension to the throne. With tensions heavy and the nobles' loyalties split, he had to handle the southern lords delicately—until he found a way to deal with the three children stirring up discord in his country.

Once again, he found his attention wandering to a woman he hadn't seen in several, very long months. His fingers curled tighter around the iron rests.

Draeven stepped forward and coughed twice. "Your Grace, if I might suggest we adjourn with the public audience for today?" His left-hand stood with both arms behind his back and his expression neutral.

Lazarus nodded. "Very well," he said, appreciating the reprieve from the lord's incessant whining. He glanced over at the short man in question. He was rounder in the middle than a lord his age should be, his tunic fitting too tight in the stomach and too loose in the shoulders. From the raised platform of the throne, Lazarus saw more than he wanted to in the man's pale complexion—clammy beneath the chandeliers. He found the sweat dotting his brow nearly as repulsive as the high twinge of his tenor. "We'll continue this . . . another time."

The lord stumbled for a moment over his words before muttering, "Very well, Your Grace."

Lazarus waited the brief stretch of time it took for the man to leave. Draeven sent away the servants milling about soon after.

When it was only the two of them, his left-hand sighed, dropping away the pretenses of formality. "You're drifting again, Lazarus."

"I tire of bending to the whims of lesser men," Lazarus replied curtly, leaning back into the ancient chair. He was growing used to the stiffness of it. It served as a constant reminder of the throne he chose and the position he now found himself in.

"Those 'lesser men' are all that stand between Leone and the blood heirs. They have nothing more left to lose since their father gave his country to his friend and not his children," Draeven said in a stiff reminder.

"That's not quite true," Lazarus said. "They still have their lives."

Draeven stilled. "Even if killing them was an option, we don't have anyone that could get close enough to do the job." Lazarus lifted his brows, and Draeven amended, "Anyone that is presently *here*."

"She'll return."

"Perhaps," Draeven nodded, lowering his voice a fraction. "But when? It's already been four months and we've heard nothing more than the whispers that carry to our door. We hear of the things she's done, but where *is* she? And why hasn't she come by now— if she's going to at all?"

Lazarus grit his teeth, uncurling his fingers from the throne despite the urge to crush it instead.

"She'll return," he repeated. *She swore it.*

"That's fine and well," Draeven said, "but in the meantime, you have a country to run, and while you dislike listening to the lords, you're not exactly in a position to do otherwise. Regardless of the blood heirs, you need them to support you or you risk war— not just on you, but on all of us."

Lazarus looked away from his left-hand and friend —one of the only true friends he had. "Get the man whatever he wanted within reason. I can't grant every request, or they'll think me weak, but I can try to appease them . . . at least until this situation with the heirs is dealt with."

Draeven nodded, "I think that would be wise."

He moved to leave when a knock came at the door. Without waiting for a command, the heavy wood creaked open.

"His Grace asked to be left—" Draeven started.

"My apologies," Gulliver said, stepping into the doorway but not closing it. His dusty gray eyes looked wary, and his weathered hands shook slightly as they held a wooden box between them. "We received a message for His Grace, and I—uh, think that this one warrants immediate attention." The older man pressed his lips together in a flat line and awaited Lazarus' command.

"Who was the sender?" Draeven asked before Lazarus could get to it.

"The messenger didn't say. Only that His Grace would know it when he saw it."

Both Draeven and Lazarus exchanged a look.

There were few people on this continent that would send a package to the now Norcastan King and have the audacity to assume as much. All of them but one were rulers in their own right.

A heat spread through his limbs as Lazarus stood from the throne and beckoned his vassal forward. "Bring it to me, and close the door behind you."

Gulliver shifted, careful to maintain his grip on the box as the heavy oak door fell shut. His footsteps echoed in the empty chamber as he crossed the length of the throne room. Lazarus descended several steps, meeting him halfway.

His blood pumped heavily, the pounding of it making the other noises fade. Gulliver dropped to one knee on the sandstone steps, and presented the message. Lazarus reached for the golden hinge that kept the lid shut.

His lips parted for a moment as he took in what sat inside.

"What is it?" Draeven asked, striding forward. Lazarus reached in and grabbed the gift by its hair. He held it up in the light for them to see. "Is that a—"

"Severed head," Lazarus finished with a nod. The face belonged to that of a man, or a very ugly woman. It was difficult to tell with the sallow skin and empty eye sockets. Juices dripped from the neck. The smell it emitted was nothing short of stomach turning. It was clear the person this had been attached to had been dead for quite a while. Between its lips, a piece of parchment was stuffed.

Lazarus reached up and tugged the paper from its mouth. The jaw unhinged and several rotted teeth dropped out, clattering against the steps.

"That's disgusting," Draeven said, turning his head to cover his nose with the back of his hand. "I think I might be sick." Lazarus placed the head back in the box, and Gulliver shut it quickly.

"My apologies, Lord Adelmar," Gulliver said to Draeven. His left-hand waved him off, though his eyes were watering from the stench.

Lazarus used his thumbnail to break the wax seal and unfold the message.

Four words was all it held, but they were enough.

For the first time in months, Lazarus smiled.

"Well?" Draeven asked. "What's it say?"

Lazarus refolded the letter and slipped it into his pocket. He turned on his heel and took the steps to resettle himself on the oak and iron throne. The discomfort didn't bother him so much as it had minutes ago. He knew why, but that didn't matter for now, not when his months of restlessness were almost over.

"She's coming home."

A Wicked Return

"Some days it pays it be a person with power, but most of the time it is the ones without that have true freedom."
— *Quinn Darkova, fear twister, right-hand to the King of Norcasta*

One month later . . .

Her lips were chapped and her lungs were on fire, but despite the dry heat, Quinn was never so happy to see the gates of Leone. In all her time in Norcasta, she'd only visited its capital twice. The first time to be sold, and the second to be hanged, though she found her way out of that predicament, much as she always did. Still, the limestone bricks piled a good ten horses high weren't so intimidating when the guards atop the wall wore red and gold. Lazarus' house colors. The colors of the new king.

"The gates are closed," Risk said over the pounding of hooves as they approached. Her voice was muffled through the white cloth wrapped around her head to keep the sand and sun at bay.

"It won't be a problem," Quinn replied. A wicked smile graced her lips as they came upon the great wall and strolled to a stop. The two guards on the ground looked them over.

"The gates are closed for the evening. Nothing in, nothing out; King's orders," the one on the right declared.

"You must be mistaken," Quinn answered them in a cold tone. "I am the King's right-hand, and His Grace would never—"

Two howling laughs greeted her ears. Risk looked over, an uneasy expression crossing what little of her features were visible through the garb. Quinn narrowed her blue eyes in contempt. Her fingers tightened around the reins guiding her steed.

It was all she could do to not lash out.

"If you were really the King's right-hand—you'd know that *His Grace* has a big event tonight going on at the palace," the one on the left started.

"Event?" Quinn asked.

"Oh, yes," the one on the right answered. "Most

of the nobles from the southern region are here attending some ball. His left-hand saw it fit that no man, woman, child, or beast be allowed in or out of these walls while so many wealthy landholders are here." He let out a chuckle, and his stout build shook from it.

"So you see," the one on the left started again. "Right-hand or not, the left has deemed it so, which means the King has—and unless we're told otherwise—"

At that point, Quinn's patience ran out.

She released the reins on her mount and lifted both hands, calling forth their fear. Both soldiers collapsed instantly, their bodies shaking and shuddering in the dirt not so different from how they had been when laughing. Quinn grinned as shouts started atop the wall.

Risk merely sighed. "Was that necessary?"

"They were annoying me," Quinn replied, her eyes watching as an archer took aim. With a wave of her hand, an illusion manifested itself in their place as both Quinn and Risk took off down the wall. Arrows rained down where they'd been only moments before, harmlessly embedding themselves in the rocky ground.

How easily fooled the skeevs were. Quinn was going to enjoy this.

"What's your plan now?" Risk called, easily guiding her horse over to the shaded side of the wall.

"How well can you climb?" she called back. Several months ago, she wouldn't have dared try a stunt like this, but her sister was a fighter—just as she'd predicted. True to her word, Risk chose to live for herself above all else and threw her malnourished and weak body into intense training. Today was just another test in a long line that Quinn had put them through to make sure she was ready—body and mind —for the inevitable return to Leone.

Risk didn't disappoint.

With a huff, she spoke in low tones to the beast, guiding it right up beside the wall. She pulled herself up to balance on the creature's back, and trusting as it was with the young beast tamer—it let her. Her nimble gray fingers sought the cracks in the stone as she slowly began her ascent. Quinn watched her with pride, plucking a dappa fruit from her satchel to munch on while she waited. The guards were entertained enough with the illusion several hundred yards away. To them, Quinn and Risk hadn't left their spot at the gates, but somehow they managed to deflect the arrows.

It perplexed them as much as it amused her.

Risk reached the top of the wall, her hands growing claws that helped her haul herself up the last few feet. She pulled herself over the edge, and her body disappeared for a brief second before she popped back up. The white cloth wrapped around her face had fallen away, and in the sunset her onyx horns gleamed maliciously.

Quinn smiled as Risk pulled a length of rope from her satchel and tied it around one of the stone posts, releasing the other end. Quinn dismounted from her horse and slapped it on the rear to send it running in the distance, repeating the same action on Risk's. Her sister watched them go with a sad sort of understanding as Quinn strolled up to the wall and grasped the end of the rope.

Her wooden staff hung at her side, and the satchel carrying her only worldly possessions hung close to her side. She gripped the roughen strands, thankful for the months she spent as a gladiator in Jibreal. Ten horses was nothing to climb when she didn't have a windwyvern at her back, threatening to send her to her death with a single misplaced step.

Quinn dispersed the illusion at the gates and set to climbing. Her hands were rough and calloused, more than they'd ever been before. It made it easier to hold the rope as she dug the toes of her boots into the uneven mortar of the wall. Tiny filaments slipped from between the stone, sliding out beneath her boot to the ground now fatally far below.

Quinn felt no fear as she scaled the wall. Above her, the sounds of a scuffle quickened her pace. While Risk was clever and sure-footed, she still had a ways to go before she'd be able to beat Quinn in a duel. The only thing she had going for her in close combat was her panic.

Like a beast cornered, she lashed out under pressure.

It was the single thing that kept Quinn's own powers in check when she hauled herself over the top of the wall. Her stomach heaved from the exertion. Quinn was beginning to regret eating the dappa fruit while she waited, but all thoughts of queasiness fled her at the three bodies by Risk's feet. Claw marks slashed their chests as crimson bled onto the sandy stones.

She rolled over the edge and climbed to her feet, quickly assessing Risk's watering eyes and bared teeth. Quinn held both hands up and approached in slow, measured steps.

"You did good, Risk, but we need to go now." She spoke calmly, her voice not quite warm but at least not hard. She rested her palm over Risk's shoulder and tilted her head.

This was a big moment.

The first time it happened, the breakdown that followed had been soul-wrenching. She didn't desire to kill as Quinn did, but after months of being forced into similar situations, both knowingly and unknow-ingly, she was beginning to grow cold to it. Hardened.

Her bottom lip still quivered, but Risk pressed them together and sucked in a tight breath, blinking away the tears. Her unnaturally blue eyes rose from the bodies at her feet to Quinn's face. She nodded. "I'm ready."

Quinn didn't insult her by coddling. She was still growing a backbone. She simply nodded and pointed over her sister's shoulder. "The palace is that way. We'll need to jump from here," she motioned to the wall, "to there—and then take to the streets." Quinn mimicked the movements with her fingers, pointing to the flat roof they'd have to jump to.

Risk took a deep breath and released it slowly, nodding her head. "Alright," she said, "but this time you're going first."

Quinn quirked an eyebrow, the corner of her lips drawn up as she grasped two stone battlements and hauled herself up again. Standing at the top of the wall overlooking Leone, the only thing taller was the palace itself. In the center of the city, a building crafted from sandstone and slaves rose up. Whereas most rulers used marble or gold to show affluence, a past king chose elaboration to be what made it significant. It wasn't glittering like Ilvas, nor was it foreboding like the temples in Liph. Jibreal favored marble columns and scaffolding. Bangratas preferred a more straightforward approach; castles filled with riches instead of the buildings themselves being grand.

It was only here in Leone that she had ever seen a monstrosity as beautiful as it was terrible.

She looked on it for only a moment before flinging

herself off the height of the wall. The fall was a short thing. Her legs hit the hardened clay roof and bent, letting her roll the rest of the way so that she didn't hurt herself.

Quinn stood and brushed the orangish-brown dust from her leathers. She turned her chin up to see Risk's quivering form wavering on the ledge.

"Just jump," she called up. Her sister leveled her with a sour look before bending her knees and leaping. While small and fast, her legs didn't have enough muscle to put major strength behind the jump. Her boots skimmed the edge of the roof as she slid right over the side. Quinn's stomach leapt into her chest as she ran to the edge.

A gray hand with black claws had embedded itself into the side of the building. It was the only thing stopping Risk from falling. Quinn leaned down and reached for her other hand. The sweat from her palms and dirt on Risk's skin smeared everywhere as Quinn pulled her up from the ledge.

Risk flopped onto her stomach and let a grunt.

"Ugh," she groaned. "One of these days you're going to get me killed."

Quinn snorted, pleased the earlier melancholy from killing had already left her. She turned, covering her eyes to shield them from the dying sun. The skies bled crimson and violet as she pointed to the tops of the houses. "If we take each of these down, we can get to the ground before nightfall and go the rest of the way on foot."

"Sounds simple enough," she said, climbing to her feet. She narrowed her eyes at Quinn and then out over the city. "What's the catch?"

Quinn blew out a rough breath and walked to the edge of the roof. She flashed her a wicked grin and said, "The whole city will be looking for us."

Then she stepped off the edge. The drop wasn't nearly as steep, and she only needed to bend her knees, though the impact still jolted through her bones. Quinn repeated the action; Risk right behind her all the way down the side of the buildings to the roughly maintained streets below. Their footsteps were soft and sure as they snuck through the shadows of Leone, Quinn only bothering to mask them in an illusion when the palace stood before them.

They walked right through a group of guards, unseen to all. Risk clutched her hand and grit her teeth to keep from making a sound as they brushed too close to the men for her liking. Her irises had changed into cat-like slits, and black spots dotted the skin of her face in the lowlight.

They'd been close to men before. Quinn had made a point of it once Risk was well enough with a blade or her claws to defend herself. But the proximity always brought out the wild magic in her. This time it was the spots of a cheetah, and she no doubt would have speed beyond what even Quinn could keep up with if she chose to run. In the past, it had been other things. Wings. A tail. Claws. Hooves.

She'd never seen a beast tamer so strong that their very body changed around their fear, but it appeared that Risk was—because as surely as it happened, she also had zero control over it.

Quinn gripped her hand harder as they strode up the palace steps, filthy compared to the patrons milling about. Two wide double doors were open in a gesture of welcome, and while she knew it wasn't for her alone—she liked to think so.

Inside, colorful tiles painted in images of the gods spanned the entire ceiling—only visible from the thousands of candles placed throughout. Quinn's breath caught as she took in the foyer of the great palace—the eggshell-colored floors and dainty slippers that touched them. Every person in sight was dressed similarly, with rich fabrics fashioned in either dresses or tunic. She looked down at her own dirt-covered leathers and tugged the white cloth she'd worn around her own head away.

"We're here," Risk said. "Now what?"

Quinn slowly made her way through the nobles to come to stand between two immense doors. She recognized what lay beyond instantly.

The throne room.

"Now," she said, "we make an entrance."

Risk frowned, her eyebrows drawing together uneasily. Quinn pointed over to the corner of the room where food and drink were made available to the wealthy guests. Risk looked between her and it hesitantly.

"Are you sure——"

"Go. Wait over there and I'll catch up once I pay my respects to the King." Risk stole a glance across the room to the immense throne where a man of even greater power sat. She shuddered once and turned heel for the food, as Quinn knew she would.

It was only once Risk was out of her line of sight that she let the illusion masking her drop away. Several people who had been standing right next to her let out startled gasps. She let their surprise trickle through the room as whispers started, carrying to the throne rapidly.

Quinn looked up. Eyes black as Mazzulah's heart and heated as the very sun looked upon her. The room was filled with people, nobles and servants, vassals like herself, and courtesans—and yet as she slowly made her way across the wide expanse—it was only them.

In the midst of the frivolity and merriment, a dark king looked upon her once more, and Quinn felt an echo of that unnamable emotion swell in her chest. Heart racing and blood pounding, she came to the bottom of the steps and started her ascent without waiting for permission.

He watched her, his face a cold mask of indifference—though his eyes told a different story. They told of the savage creature lying beneath, writhing to meet her in the middle. Her magic stirred, and when two guards attempted to intercept her she did nothing more than twist her fingers. Eyes still locked on him, she didn't watch as they fell to their knees, gasping their pleas of forgiveness.

She ascended the steps to stand before him, and while the room had gone silent, there was a pounding in her ears that drowned it all out.

Her heart rioted in her chest, but her movements were still.

Five months had passed since she left him to do what she needed to do, and she'd returned to a different man. She'd returned to a king—to a crown.

Quinn sank to one knee—allowing Lazarus to decide what it was he wanted to do. A moment passed where no one said a word as he stared at her with the weight of the things they had done and left unsaid. He was wearing gloves now, but she saw the shadows of his souls struggling beneath the hem of his cuff. She doubted anyone else would notice, but that small slip in control was all she needed to know that nothing had changed.

"Your Grace," a faceless, nameless voice called out from below. "Who is this woman?"

The corners of Lazarus' mouth turned up as a cruel expression of sick delight crossed him. Lazarus extended his hand for her to kiss the golden insignia upon it. Quinn raised an eyebrow, pausing just long enough for him to know this act of subservience was only that. An act.

As her lips pressed against the cool metal, Lazarus spoke.

"Rise, Quinn Darkova, right-hand to the King."

Mercurial Dispositions

"Everything is a game. You only lose when you think the game is over."
— *Lazarus Fierté, soul eater, King of Norcasta*

The moment he saw her, everything in their vicinity vanished.

Like a bloodlion on a scent, his entire focus was on the woman dressed in leathers. Her lavender hair was pulled back in a haphazard braid, stiff ends sticking out where mud had hardened and cracked. Her skin, what was visible, had been covered in a light sheen of orangish-brown dust. She must have crossed the desert to return to him, which only piqued his curiosity about what exactly she'd been doing on the other side of the continent. Above all, it was her eyes that he focused on. She wore a skin of cream and ice and all things light, but even in the blue of her eyes there was an unmistakable darkness.

She was *saevyana*.

His cruel woman.

She drifted through the throne room without a care for how her appearance stood out; so stark in a place of rich fabric and bright colors. Without asking permission, she ascended the steps, disarming his guards without any effort at all. Magic wafted from her skin, midnight weeds and damp petals assaulting his senses. He inhaled, embracing the cold bite of fresh snow and brutal winters that always made him catch his breath.

She stood before him, and then, with a grace that was all her own, she dropped to one knee.

It was that single action that cemented something in him.

He'd known from the moment he laid eyes on her, beating a nobleman with his own whip, that he'd never let her go. *But this* . . . this was a different kind of feeling. Though she was the one on her knee, he felt leveled. It unsettled him how much power he'd not just handed over to her, but how much she'd taken —because he felt something far greater than possessiveness for the creature before him.

Lazarus extended his hand. Her eyes flashed, the blue illuminating the power she hid within. When she leaned forward to kiss the insignia on the ring, his groin stiffened.

"Rise, Quinn Darkova, right-hand to the King."

She did as he said without turning to greet the eyes of the noblemen and women he had gathered tonight. Typical of Quinn. She had no desire to play games outside her own.

"It's been a while, Lazarus," she said, her gaze sweeping up to the hand-painted ceiling. She put one hand on her hip and the other came up for her to tap her bottom lip with her index finger. "I like what you've done with the place," she added after a moment, only briefly turning those calculating eyes to the room beyond before settling them back on him. Lazarus remained silent, his hands gripping the armrests of his throne while he took in her movements.

She'd told him she was coming home a month ago.

It was uncanny timing that she picked this night of all nights to actually return.

The woman knew how to make an entrance.

"Quinn," Draeven said, stepping out from the crowd and striding up the steps with a strong yet hurried gait. "We weren't expecting you," his left-hand started.

She turned, a wide smile spreading across her face. It was wicked, as always.

"My Lord Sunshine," she declared. "I did send a

messenger ahead of me, you know." Several noblemen glanced up from the base of the stairs. A string of snickers made Draeven stiffen, and Lazarus noted the way her smile only grew.

Cruel, cruel woman . . .

Draeven's eyes cut toward him. The stiff set of his lips said a great deal. "Draeven, if you could please entertain our guests. I think my right-hand and I need to have a word in private."

The brief flash of annoyance morphed into steady resignation as Draeven nodded. "As you wish, Your Grace."

Quinn looked between the two of them, her gaze growing shrewd. She didn't say anything as Lazarus rose to his feet and placed a hand on her lower back, guiding her down the side of the stairs. Nobles stepped out of the way, and he couldn't tell if it was from her expression or his own that they lowered their eyes as he passed by.

"Interesting company you're keeping these days," she said, eyeing a particular man who had a courtesan on each arm. They wore the golden collars of slavery. Her eyes turned glacial as her feet started to roll to a stop. Lazarus wasn't a fool, and kept pushing her along to the very end of the hall. Her neck was craning back to watch the man with his two pleasure slaves when Lazarus opened the door to his study and ushered them both in.

It clicked shut, and with a snap of his wrist, the lock bolted, preventing anyone from entering.

She shook him off and started a slow perusal around the space. Her motions were that of someone curious, if casually so. Her eyes revealed the beast within.

"You left."

She lifted an eyebrow. "I also came back." Her nails trailed over the smooth wood surface of his desk as she stepped around it. The large cloth chair drew her attention as she settled into it, crossing her legs and resting her arms on the sides. Her fingers steepled together as she regarded him with indifference.

"After five months," he replied.

She shrugged and then motioned to the door behind him. "You've clearly been keeping busy. I had things to attend to, and I returned when they were dealt with—just as I said I would."

Lazarus' blood heated from her attitude. He strode forward and put both hands on the desk, leaning forward. "Five months out of a five-year contract is a long time, Quinn. I'm adding it to your serving agreement."

She lifted both eyebrows and said, "Is that so?"

"You don't make the rules here, and while I might let you bend them, in the future, you need to seek permission before galivanting off to the other side of the continent." She snorted. The pads of his fingers pressed down, curling slightly in agitation.

"I'm still doing work in your name, Lazarus. You know that, otherwise the firedrake's magic would have killed me before I could set foot out of Liph." She released her hands and instead chose to lean forward, uncrossing her legs.

"You disappeared without a word. Five months, Quinn. I'm not yielding on this," he said. "You will not do so again." She watched him intently for a moment before getting to her feet and leaning across his desk. Her nose brushed his as the barest hint of her lips grazed the corner of his mouth. From another woman, it would have been a daring move, but for Quinn it was chaste.

She breathed softly, the scent of her skin and magic filling his nostrils. Lazarus' fingernails dug into the desk to stop himself from reaching for her.

"Are you sure about that?" she whispered. Her teeth trailed up his jaw. Warm breath fanned the inner shell of his ear as her tongue wet the lobe. The breath hissed through his teeth, and she bit down. Hard.

He groaned, and she released him, but he could feel the smile on her face as she pulled away.

Crimson dotted her lips.

His length stiffened further.

"Five months," he replied. She smiled. It was anything but kind.

"Are you upset with me, Lazarus?" she asked, her voice taking on a dark edge. She slowly pulled away, walking the rest of the way around his desk again.

"I was," he told her. She tilted her head, stopping before him. It was as if she hadn't expected the truth. "I no longer am, but that doesn't change my demand."

"Hmm," was all she said, leaning forward. She put one hand to his chest, and his heart began to beat wildly. "For it to go into effect, I have to agree—because I technically didn't break your contract. Did I?" Her hand slid down his chest, over the muscles of his stomach, heading down further. He reached out, catching her by the wrist. She stilled.

"What are you doing?" he asked her, cursing himself for the huskiness that clogged his throat. Desire laced every fiber of his being.

Quinn tilted her head back to look him in the eye as she said, "You wish to punish me for it. The least I can do is make sure it's a punishment we both enjoy."

His breath halted in his chest as lust and longing pushed him closer to the edge.

"I never said this was a punishment," he replied through gritted teeth.

"You didn't need to," she answered. Her other hand slipped between them, coming to rest over his shaft. She rubbed up and down slowly, applying not near enough pressure for the torture she was inflicting on him.

"Five months," he repeated, though his resolve

was weakening. He'd rehearsed how this would go for months, and yet within minutes of her return, she'd pushed him to the edge. Anger flared in his veins. He opened his mouth to speak when she arched on her toes and pressed her lips to his.

Her mouth opened as she kissed him, her tongue darting out to twine around his. She stepped closer, flattening her palm against his shaft. Quinn stroked up and down while kissing him with a fierceness that blew away his memories of that night.

She pulled away just as suddenly and whispered, "I have a better idea." Her impish little tongue darted out, wetting her lips. "I take you between my lips and let you have your wicked way, and we call it even."

Lazarus groaned. "I can't negotiate with you like this, Quinn."

"Why not?" she asked. "You have before. A punishment is a punishment, Lazarus."

"I never said it was a punishment," he bit out sharply, stepping away from her wandering hands. He turned away, trying to calm the racing of his heart. The ache in his shaft was becoming more pressing by the second.

"I see." Her voice was icy. Cold. It stirred up the rage in him as much as the desire. "You're a king now. It was okay to take me when you were simply a nobleman, but now you let the expectations of *lesser men* guide you. How . . . pitiful."

Lazarus whipped around, his fists clenched and

jaw set as he regarded her closed off form. She leaned against his desk, watching him, both arms crossed over her chest.

He had to remind himself that there was no way she could know how close to the truth she really was. It was as if she plucked the thoughts from his very mind.

He despised it. He despised her.

An even greater desire rose up in him.

She might very well get what she asked for.

"I am King now. I bend to no one. I yield for no one. Not even you, *saevyana*," he growled in a rough voice. Her expression didn't change, and it only served to piss him off more.

"I come back after five months and you're holding a party for all of those pathetic skeevs. They flaunt their slaves and wealth in your halls, and you pay for them to do it. The man I knew didn't bend a knee for anything less than what he was getting in return." A ghost of a smile graced her lips and it didn't take him long to realize where her mind had gone. "So tell me, Lazarus, how you're above all else when the metal on your head keeps you bound to their whims?"

"You come into this palace and mean to insult me—"

"I don't mean to, Lazarus. I am. But what do I know? I'm just a vassal." Her eyes dropped to his erection and then rose back to his own. She held them for several seconds before turning to leave, and he wasn't sure what did it then. Whether it was the audacity with which she mocked him, or the way in which she meant to dismiss him.

Her arm brushed his, and his fingers snapped out, curling around her bicep.

Quinn paused.

"Get on your knees."

He could have sworn there was a hint of a smile as she turned back around and kneeled before him. The position of her beneath him filled Lazarus with a sick sort of joy as he tugged at the laces of his trousers. There was a pounding in his head as he pulled his length free.

"I've told you before that insulting me is unacceptable. I am King—and no one, not the lords, not the ladies, not the Gods themselves, and certainly not my vassals will stand in the halls and talk to me as you do. The five months was not a punishment. It was payment for the five that I gave you. This—this will be a punishment. Do you accept, Quinn?"

Quinn looked up at him, her blue eyes sharp and clear as she reached up to grab his shaft. The palm of her hand was warm against him as she stroked.

"No," she breathed. "I don't."

Shock radiated through him. Her lips parted, and she pulled his shaft to their welcoming plumpness. At the first lick of her tongue, his hips arched. She quirked an eyebrow up.

"I please you because I wish to. I came back

because I chose to. You punish me because I let you. This isn't a punishment for me, Lazarus. I know what I desire. This is for you."

He buried his fingers in her braid roughly, getting a firm grip on her head before thrusting forward. Her mouth opened further to allow entry as she took him in. Lazarus breathed harshly. He hadn't touched a woman since her, despite the many that came to him within the court before, and more so now that he was king. He had no intention of telling her that, nor would he admit that she was his very weakness.

He pulled back and pushed forward, burying himself deeper in her. She choked once, saliva coating him and making the warmth of her mouth now as slippery as her heat. His hips started a rhythm, pushing and pulling and thrusting into her—all the while Quinn watched him take his pleasure between her lips.

She somehow managed to look like she was still winning this power struggle between them, even without words. That infuriated him, and Lazarus pushed further, burying himself to the hilt. She choked again, her eyes watering, but not once did she try to pull away as he held her fast. Within minutes, his release was upon him. Sweat dotted his brow as Lazarus groaned, pumping shallowly into her warmth. The pounding had reached an all-time high as all noise was blocked out by his own driving desire to dominate her. With one final thrust, the dam in him burst as he let go. His liquid flooded her mouth, but Quinn swallowed it down and kept swallowing until his motions grew still.

Half limp, but still burning inside, Lazarus pulled his shaft from her mouth and turned to tuck it away. When Lazarus looked back, she was already on her feet, arms crossed over her chest. "While I was away, I arranged for both the leaders of Bangratas and Jibreal to send ambassadors to hear you out. The head I sent was a messenger from Amelia Reinhart, the late King's first-born child. They'd been in the process of negotiating an alliance of their own when the messenger disappeared." Lazarus stood, stunned. Anger fizzled through his veins as she continued. "Contrary to what you've convinced yourself, I still acted in your best interest. I left with the promise to return, and I have." She sighed, stepping toward the door, and this time he didn't stop her. "You're angry, but you'll get over it. I have a vested interest in this court, but an even greater one in its king. Draeven has convinced you to give too much. I am back to remind them that you *are* king."

Quinn reached for the lock on the door, and Lazarus asked, "What exactly is that supposed to mean?"

She looked back at him, as arrogant as she'd been when she made her entrance before.

"You wanted me to become a monster, and I have," she said, the corner of her mouth turning up.

"What remains to be seen is whose monster I will be. Yours," her eyes slid sideways toward the door, "or theirs?"

Lazarus didn't say a word as she stepped out of his study and into the hallway beyond. He had wanted her to come back, but he didn't think to predict the damage that would be left in her wake.

Quinn reveled in destruction.

Now he had to find a way to ensure it wasn't his own.

A Wary Encounter

"Each man will have a reckoning. Some in the form of tasks, others in the form of people."
— Draeven Adelmar, rage thief, left-hand to the King of Norcasta

Quinn had returned. Lazarus' eyes lit up like the fires of the dark realm had taken hold of him as she strode through the ongoing party—one of many the new King had thrown to appease the spoiled, petulant southern lords of Norcasta. Draeven sucked in a breath as she approached and bent low, bowing her head with a wicked grin upon her lips. He shook his head. The woman was a menace, but still, Draeven was glad she was back. Her return would surely mean that Lazarus would stop his incessant sullenness. Besides, things were always a bit more interesting when Quinn was around.

Brameer, a nasally country lord, was the first and only one to break the silence that had befallen the room as he inquired to who the woman was. Who was the woman who walked through them as though she saw nothing but Lazarus? Who was the woman that smelled of blood and decay and smiled with a dangerous gleam in her eyes?

Lazarus answered the questions in the minds of all those present as he spoke. "Rise, Quinn Darkova, right-hand to the King."

Eyes widened around him. Several of the lords looked to him for confirmation, as they often did when Lazarus' actions or words confused them. Draeven sighed and nodded, and their eyes returned to the King as he rose from his seat and reached down for the fear twister that had done more than twist him up inside.

Lazarus' expression hardened as Quinn rose and looked to him. "Quinn," Draeven said. "We weren't expecting you."

"My Lord Sunshine," she said, a twisted smirk on her face. "I did send a messenger ahead of me, you know."

Draeven scowled, remembering with shuddering horror. His nostrils still burned at the scent of the severed head. With a strained look, Draeven frowned at her. A few snickers erupted behind him, but he paid them no mind.

Lazarus placed a hand on the small of Quinn's back and leveled his left-hand with an intent look. "Draeven, if you could please entertain our guests. I think my right-hand and I need to have a word in private."

Bowing his head slightly, he replied. "As you wish, Your Grace."

Draeven turned as Lazarus nodded before urging the lavender-haired demon away—out of the room, no doubt to a more secluded area in which he would punish her. Draeven snorted to himself, knowing the truth. No matter how angry the man was at her, he doubted there was anything he could do or threaten her with that would truly frighten her. Draeven doubted that the woman was afraid of anything at this point. She seemed beyond fear. He wondered if it came from her magic, or if her magic chose her for that reason.

Once Lazarus was gone from the room, the lords and even the ladies accompanying them converged on him.

"Who was that woman, Lord Adelmar?"

"She was N'skari, was she not?"

"I've never seen an N'skari this far south. I wonder . . ."

"How long has the woman known the King?"

"Is she blackmailing him, perhaps?"

"The repulsiveness of her looks, can you believe . . .?"

"I swear I've never seen such an uncouth entrance . . ."

Draeven huffed a breath, hating Lazarus and Quinn for leaving him to deal with the noblemen and women, before plastering a fake smile on his face and whirling to answer their questions.

"Ladies and gentlemen, please calm yourselves," Draeven said with a pleasant tone. "Lady Darkova is the King's right-hand, as you heard. She has been away several months on a mission of the utmost importance." *A mission in driving his master insane,* he thought. But Draeven didn't voice that little tidbit.

"But she—!"

Draeven lifted a hand and stopped the next onslaught of questions and hurled confusion as he spotted a creature several paces behind them all. Had he not been standing facing her, Draeven might have missed her for a wallflower—one of the many plain-faced young ladies who stood in the background, too shy or unwilling to enter the fray before him. But she was no simpleton.

Draeven nodded for Lorraine, who stood—as she usually did—within calling distance. "Please calm yourselves, my lords and ladies," Draeven said as Lorraine nodded and came forward. "Enjoy the festivities. Drink and dance to your hearts' content.

I'm sure that on the morrow, His Grace will answer all questions."

Some seemed to take his words at face value, nodding and moving away. For the few who were less than appeased—Lorraine stepped forward with the perfect distraction.

"Ladies and gentlemen," she announced with an easy smile on her face—one much more genuine than Draeven's own. "His Grace has elected to gift all attendees this evening with a show. Please follow me to the gentlemen's lounge for an enticing display of unusual arts."

"Unusual arts, you say?" Brameer repeated, firmly bound by curiosity as Lorraine led them away.

Unusual arts, indeed. Lazarus had invited a small party of acrobats and magicians from Dumas to attend to his guests for this party. They had just been about to announce it before Quinn's arrival. Draeven sighed in relief as Lorraine and the others disappeared from the room, following her to the setup the group had prepared beforehand.

His attention switched back to the woman he'd noticed from across the room, but she was gone from the place he'd spotted her before. With a small frown, he shifted through the remainder of the crowd, heading for the last area he'd seen her. She wasn't hard to find again, her gray-toned skin and onyx horns marked her as different from the rest.

Those that noticed her backed away with confusion and more than a little fear. Draeven knew exactly who this woman was, despite the fact that he'd never actually seen her before now. It was Quinn's sister, the half-raksasa. The tainted.

"Excuse me, Miss——" Draeven reached out, intending to halt her as she moved through the crowd, avoiding touching anyone.

One moment he had his hand outstretched, reaching for her shoulder, and the next he was bent over, his arm yanked behind his back.

"*No touching*," the woman hissed in his ear. Her hands trembled against him as she held his arm bent at an awkwardly painful angle. Then, just as suddenly as he'd been grabbed, he was released.

Draeven straightened, blinking in confusion as he rotated his shoulder, urging feeling back in the limb of his arm. "My apologies," he said as he lifted his eyes and froze.

Twin pools of ice-cold frost met his gaze. Impossibly light, with just a hint of blue, the woman's face centered around her eyes. They spoke of darkness witnessed and experienced, of pain felt, of a rage so deep within that there was no way——even with his own power——he would be able to steal it all.

"You're Risk Darkova?"

The woman paused as she backed away from him, narrowing her gaze on him. "Who asks?" she demanded.

Taking in a breath and forcing his eyes away from

hers as he took the rest of her in, Draeven gestured to himself. "I'm a friend of Quinn's," he said. It seemed the safest explanation of who he was. "I'm Lazarus' left-hand. We've never met, but I've heard of you."

The suspicious look in her eyes didn't lessen. Not even a little bit. "What do you want?" she asked.

Draeven watched the way she moved. It was clear that she was uncomfortable with his nearness, so he took a step back before speaking. "I saw you from across the room," he explained. "I assume you came with Quinn?" She nodded, her eyes tracking him with distrust. When one of the guests passed behind her, she whirled sharply, but they were already well on their way—not even aware of the glint of wildness in her eyes that had her turning abruptly back to him and moving even further from him and the throng of people at his back. "You're not comfortable around crowds, are you?"

"No." She glanced to the side, looking for exit, he assumed.

"Why don't I take you to Quinn's chambers?" Draeven offered politely. "Lazarus had them prepared months ago for when she'd returned. We weren't sure if you'd be coming with her, but it's large enough for both of you until—"

"Will it get me away from here?" she demanded, interrupting him.

"Yes, her chambers are on the other side of the—"

"Fine. Let's go. You can lead the way." She gestured for him to move, wary as she watched him. Draeven got the distinct impression that she wouldn't trust him behind her, so he simply nodded and moved ahead.

Quinn's suite was far from the ballroom where they'd left the court musicians and Lorraine to entertain the guests. As Draeven walked along, every once in a while he'd glance back, noting that Risk watched him with a focused, serious gaze and one hand on her side, fingers clutched right over the hilt of a dagger.

Gray spots danced across her knuckles as she tightened her hold.

Draeven turned back, but not before he saw the way her spots had grown, more cropping up along her wrist and forearm. *Very interesting*, he thought. He hadn't met another beast tamer since his friend Haspati.

"Here we are," Draeven finally announced, pivoting with a flourish and gesturing to the grand oak door. Beyond it was a suite style room, large enough for a Queen, not that Quinn would ever take that position or admire the lavishness. But as Draeven lifted his eyes to meet Risk's once more, he wondered if her sister would appreciate it.

Risk glared at him as she sidled past. Before she could open the door, Draeven remembered his manners. He'd been far too caught up in her eyes. He jumped forward and turned the knob, only to realize that Risk had her dagger out and pressed to his throat.

That wildness in her eyes turned to slitted fury. The blue morphed into a cat-like gold as she hissed at him. Draeven went still, judging her nearness to insanity. Raising his hands as slowly as possible, mimicking the gentling nature that Haspati had taught him with animals, Draeven released a quiet breath.

"It's okay," he said. "I'm not a threat. I mean you no harm."

Glaring at him, Risk pressed her blade up even further until the edge of it just nicked him. He felt the warmth of blood ooze from a tiny sliver of a cut—barely larger than anything he might have done while shaving. Then the blade was gone, and she was on the other side of the door.

"Perhaps I could—" he started.

The door slammed shut.

His whole body sagged ,and then with a curious smile, Draeven lifted his fingers to the bead of blood that had welled up at his throat. He chuckled again.

"Another time," he whispered as he turned and walked away.

Penchant for Peril

"Trust is rarely, if ever, freely given. Everything has a price."
— Quinn Darkova, fear twister, right-hand to the King of Norcasta

"This heat is stifling," Risk said as she sat by the window. A flat rock scraped against her dagger, base to tip, as she scowled into the courtyard below.

Quinn cracked her neck and stretched, wondering where Lorraine would be at this time of day. "Perhaps you should go out, then," Quinn suggested. "Get out of the room. You've been in here since we got here. You're going to need to eat at some point."

"You brought me dinner," Risk replied. "I wouldn't eat anything you didn't bring me anyway. I don't trust these people." Her scowl deepened as she saw something beyond the glass pane that seemed to irritate her further. Quinn paused and lifted a brow at her sister as she accidentally nicked herself on her own blade. "Blast!" Risk stuck her thumb in her mouth, keeping her eyes trained on whatever was happening outside.

"Distracted, are we?" Quinn finished her stretches and moved over to the window. Before she could peek over her sister's shoulder, Risk quickly got up— shoving Quinn back a bit as she circled around her. Eyes wide with surprise, Quinn's gaze glanced to the courtyard, but whatever had been there before was gone now. Turning back and eyeing Risk speculatively, she said, "What was that?"

"What was that?" Risk asked as she found the water bowl on one of the ornate dressers across the room and washed the blood off her hand.

"You know what," Quinn said.

Risk merely cast a look at her that she'd gotten quite used to. It meant she wouldn't be getting anything out of the girl unless she wanted to use force, and Quinn was still treating her with kid gloves, so the only thing left to do was drop the issue.

Shaking her head, Quinn headed for the door. "I'll be back later," she called over her shoulder. Risk merely grunted a reply as the door closed behind her.

It wasn't far from Quinn's chambers to an open archway that looked out past the center gardens, and Quinn found that easily enough, stopping a servant scuttling by with arms piled high with freshly laundered sheets. "Where is Lorraine?" she demanded.

The servant, a wide-eyed young woman, jerked her gaze down and mumbled her response before hurrying away, but she didn't care. She'd gotten her answer. The east wing library. Though Quinn had never been to the palace before, she found the east wing rather easily. A little while later, and a few more stopped servants, she managed to find the library as well.

Lorraine stood atop a rickety-looking ladder, leaning heavily on the shelves before her as she wiped down the edges and then retrieved a book from one of the stacks. Quinn paused with a small smile and crossed her arms and ankles as she leaned against the doorframe, watching the other woman work.

"Have you been demoted to librarian in my absence?" she asked after a little while.

Lorraine jumped, teetering dangerously on the ladder before she caught herself with one hand on the shelves and the other curling around one of the rungs of the ladder. The book that had been in her hands fell the ten feet or so to the ground, smacking the hard, wooden floor with a loud thump, a musky plume of dust rising from between its pages.

"Quinn!" Lorraine looked back in surprise and hastily descended to the ground. "Where have you been, you ridiculous girl?" The moment the older woman's feet touched solid floor, Quinn uncrossed her ankles and arms and stood up straight, blinking in shock as Lorraine hurled herself at Quinn and hugged her to her bosom.

"Er . . . Lorraine?"

Lorraine released her and clicked her tongue as she brushed spots of the desert dust from her skin from where her water bowl wash hadn't been able to reach. "You're filthy," she said with a frown. "Where have you been? You were gone for so long."

When Lorraine turned her worried eyes to Quinn's face. Quinn let her shoulders lift in a shrug. "Here and there. I had some business to take care of. I traveled to Jibreal and Bangratas on Lazarus' behalf." Extracting herself from the woman's arms, Quinn moved across the room and bent to retrieve the fallen book.

"Hmmmm," Lorraine hummed. "And was Lazarus aware of the business you were conducting on his behalf?" she asked with a raised brow.

Quinn grinned over her shoulder. "He's aware of it now."

Clicking her tongue once more, Lorraine shook her head. "You're going to drive that man to the brink."

Quinn knew she'd already done so, time and time again. She smiled thoughtfully to herself because she knew there would come many more times where she did so again, but she didn't voice those thoughts as Lorraine came and took the book from her hands, cupping her cheek in a motherly fashion that had Quinn stepping back in discomfort.

"You're back now—to stay, no less—and that's what matters," she said with a decisive head nod.

Quinn moved past her, finding one of the library loungers. She dropped to sit on it and reclined with her hands steepled behind her head and legs kicked up on the low table before the settee. "It was a long trip," Quinn admitted with a half-yawn. "I'm glad to finally be off the road."

"Yes . . ." Lorraine drifted off as she fingered the edges of the book in her grasp. "And . . . I assume your sister has rejoined you here?"

Quinn peeked her eyes open, shocked to realize that she'd gotten so comfortable that they'd closed all on their own. "Rejoined?" she parroted. "No, Risk was with me the entire trip."

"She was?" Soft footsteps sounded and Quinn lifted her eyelids all the way to see Lorraine circling the lounger across from where she sat and dropping down upon it to lean forward. "How is she, then?"

Quinn blinked at the concern in the woman's voice, but then reminded herself that Lorraine was a mother, and that was as much a part of her identity as anything else. The need to nurture and care was ingrained in her. Sighing, Quinn unlaced her fingers and sat up.

"We left Liph the night before the rest of you," Quinn said, "and from there, we traveled to Vusut in

Jibreal. The road was hard, especially that first month. Risk . . ." Quinn drifted off as she recalled the exhaustion that had pulled both her and her sister down so much so that they had drooped and fallen asleep mid-ride far too many times to count. Risk's nightmares had been intense, and because they'd been so close, Quinn hadn't been able to help being pulled into them. "She's a lot better now," Quinn finally said.

"The dear girl . . ." Lorraine whispered, worrying her lip.

Quinn snorted. "You may not call her that now," she replied. "Five months of freedom, food, and training have given her a new personality."

"It has?"

"Well, perhaps not a new personality so much as it has given her true personality time to flourish," Quinn amended. "She's a wild one. The animals that followed her around . . . some nights, I had to beat off the creatures just to get some decent sleep only to wake the next morning to find a mountain cat protecting her like its kit. They can't help themselves. They're drawn to her."

"She's a beast tamer?" Lorraine asked, curious.

"She is." Quinn nodded. "She's more at home in the wilderness than she is in the palace."

"I'm sure she is," Lorraine agreed. "Palace life can be stifling to those not used to it. It's confining."

"Yes . . . I don't suppose you'd know a beast tamer that lives within the city, would you?" Quinn asked.

Lorraine blinked and sat up straighter. "No, I don't recall ever meeting one myself. Draeven or Lazarus might know of something, though."

Quinn nodded. She supposed they would. Silence fell between them. Lorraine caught Quinn's expression just before Quinn shoved to her feet and circled the lounge away from the other woman.

"Quinn?" Lorraine's curious voice sounded across the room, and Quinn stiffened for a brief moment before forcing her muscles to relax. "What is it?"

Quinn ran her pale fingers down the spines of books, dust coating her skin as she did so. It was so very hard to ask something like this. Perhaps it wouldn't be to someone else, but for Quinn . . . Risk was her responsibility. It felt wrong to ask for assistance, but Quinn could not be with the girl all hours of the day and night. Now that she'd returned, she doubted very much that she'd have the time necessary to help Risk. She'd come a long way in the five months they'd been gone, but she still had an even longer path ahead.

"I have a favor to ask of you," Quinn said softly.

"What is it?" Lorraine's voice had grown closer since she'd turned her back. Quinn knew the woman had stood up from her place and was likely following Quinn as she circled the room—needing something to look at, to touch, to keep her mind busy as she asked for the other woman's aid.

"Risk is still wary of people. She cannot stand to

be touched, and now that I've returned, I expect Lazarus will have plans for me. I cannot be with her all the time, not as I had been while on the road. She's unwilling to leave my chambers as of yet, and I worry—"

A hand closed over Quinn's wrist as she reached out to pluck a book from its shelf. Looking down at Lorraine's understanding eyes, Quinn shifted uncomfortably and tugged her limb free, letting it fall back to her side. "Yes," she said.

"Yes?" Quinn repeated.

"I will watch after the girl in your stead."

"I only wanted to ensure that she was fed. She will not take food from anyone but me, she says, but she has met you, and I thought, perhaps—"

Lorraine shook her head, cutting Quinn off once more. "There is no reason to worry. You can trust me, Quinn."

"She needs to eat," Quinn continued. "She has training, and her body requires that she continue to eat in order for her to keep gaining muscle—"

"You don't need to explain it to me, dear," Lorraine said with an amused smile.

Quinn let out a tight breath, and her muscles uncoiled. "Thank you."

"Of course."

Quinn waited a bit, but when Lorraine merely smiled at her, she decided she had best get to finding the man of the palace. "I should go look for Lazarus," she said by way of explanation as she headed for the door.

"He's probably in the throne room at this time of day," Lorraine called after her.

Quinn lifted her hand behind her in goodbye as she left. Stepping into the corridor, she shook off the strange feeling assaulting her. *Trust*, Lorraine had said. She could trust her. It was not something Quinn was used to. Giving, or receiving.

Shaking that away, she made her way to the throne room. Guards stood on either side of the doors, and as she approached, twin spears blocked her path. Pausing, Quinn took in the sharpened spears for a moment before looking to the guards faces. When their eyes met, the men had the sense to keep their faces forward as the one on the left spoke.

"Do you have a scheduled meeting with the King?" he asked in a gruff voice.

Quinn looked from him to his partner, who swallowed around a nervous throat. With a chuckle, Quinn reached forward and grabbed onto either end of the spears and lifted them without much strength. When the guards realized that she meant to bypass them without answering, they turned on their heels and—fell to the ground in a heap as whispers of darkness touched them.

Rolling her eyes, she stepped over their shivering bodies and shoved the throne room doors open. When she had passed through the archway, she released the guards from her powers and they blinked, glancing up as she waved and shut the doors in their faces.

"Quinn." Lazarus' deep voice echoed across the large elegant room.

"Your Grace," Quinn said, stopping to bow slightly when she saw another lord stood before Lazarus. Had they been alone, she wouldn't have pretended such etiquette.

The doors behind her opened, and Lazarus jerked his gaze up, narrowing his eyes as the guards paused just outside, likely intent on retrieving Quinn. "You may leave," Lazarus rumbled, and Quinn grinned when she heard the doors slide shut once more before standing and walking the rest of the way.

Draeven stood to his left, hands folding at his front. "Lord Sunshine," Quinn nodded as the man rolled his eyes. She took her spot along Lazarus' right side with all eyes following her movements. Lazarus didn't ask why she'd arrived. He merely returned his attention to the man before him, a rather tall fellow with a thick, full auburn beard and glittering brown eyes.

"I apologize for the disruption, Lord Callis. You were saying?"

"Please, Your Grace," the other man held up his hand with a wide smile. Gold rings glittered from each of his fingers. "There are no apologies necessary. I trust this is your vassal from last night? Quinn Darkova?"

"I am," Quinn answered.

"My, it is a wonder why the King has been hiding you away. Your beauty is beyond anything I have ever beheld." He bowed slightly.

Quinn pursed her lips, but didn't say anything more. And she wouldn't have had she not noticed Lazarus' furious expression. Of course, by the time Lord Callis raised his head, Lazarus had hidden the ire in his gaze. But Quinn had seen it, and it left her feeling rather curious.

"You flatter me, my lord," Quinn replied, drawing all of their attentions—even Draeven, who looked at her as though she'd grown a new head.

"No flattery necessary. Merely the truth."

Quinn hummed her reply as Lazarus growled low beneath his breath, so quietly she was sure only she and Draeven had managed to hear it. Lord Callis returned his consideration to Lazarus and bowed low once more.

"I came to you today to propose a hunt for the court. I thought perhaps it would be the perfect time for us to discuss our mutual interests in the kingdom."

"A hunt?" Quinn tilted her head to the side, curiosity catching her tongue. "What is that?"

Lord Callis smiled at her indulgently, thinking her a rather dull-witted woman despite her appearance— both the night before and now, as she stood before him in her leathers. It no longer surprised her how some men tricked themselves into thinking they were the more intelligent sex, ignoring even what their own eyes warned them was dangerous.

"It's a sport where the men of court ride out at dawn and often spend a full day or two hunting wild game to bring back," the lord explained patiently.

"A sign of your prowess, no doubt," Quinn nodded, hiding the grin that threatened to come forth as Lazarus' scowl deepened. "It sounds exciting." It sounded like the perfect opportunity for Quinn to get Lazarus alone outside of the palace. The perfect moment in which she could ask him about finding a beast tamer for Risk. She turned to Lazarus and eyed him innocently. "I trust you'll agree, Your Grace? I would love to see such a hunt."

Lazarus gritted his teeth before replying. "A hunt is acceptable," he said to Lord Callis. "However, a hunt is comprised of men. Therefore—"

"We should invite your vassal, Your Grace," Lord Callis interrupted. "If only to show her your own prowess."

"I think that's a wonderful idea," Quinn said with a smirk. "Thank you, Lord Callis. I accept your offer."

Lord Callis, oblivious to Lazarus' rising anger, smiled and nodded. "I shall have to make the arrangements. Shall we say, tomorrow at dawn?"

"Tomorrow at dawn," Quinn agreed with a smile,

watching as the man nodded, bowed, and then left the room.

As soon as the doors were closed behind him and they were left alone, Draeven sighed and pinched the bridge of his nose. Lazarus was out of his seat before Quinn could take a step down. "What are you doing?" he demanded.

Quinn looked up at him, working to keep her face passive. "I don't know what you mean."

"Whatever game you are playing, Quinn, I'll not have it."

"Were you not going to agree to a hunt?" she asked.

Draeven stepped forward and clasped Lazarus' shoulder. "Perhaps you should take a moment, Lazarus," he suggested. "You've been listening to the Lords of the Court all morning."

Lazarus growled, the sound vibrating up her chest as she met his intense gaze. He looked like he wanted to both strangle her and fuck her at the same moment. Quinn quirked a brow and waited, but he merely pivoted and stormed away.

Draeven sighed. "You do so love to irk him," he said, glancing back at her.

"No," Quinn replied. "I simply love to remind him that he isn't as all powerful as he likes to believe."

"That is a dangerous endeavor," he reminded her.

"I'm well aware," she replied. It was a fact she so enjoyed about him. She doubted anyone else could handle her penchant for peril. The hunt, however, was a means to an end, but she'd let them think it was merely another of her whims, one of her many ways to drive the dark soul eater past his breaking point.

He had never reached it, but she so desired to see it. Craved to see just what he would do when she drove him over the edge and not just to the sharply pointed tipping point.

A King, A Tyrant

"Power lies in small things. A kiss or a blade—both can kill."
— *Lazarus Fierté, soul eater, the irritable King of Norcasta*

T he scent of fresh hay and horse dung permeated the air as Lazarus strode into the manger. Stable hands hurried out of his way as he stormed down the aisle, looking for—he stopped just outside the end stall, narrowing his sights on the woman he had come for. She stood with her back to him, her long lavender hair pulled into a braid that hung almost to her mid-back. It had grown these last five months. Dark trousers molded themselves to her hips, drawing his unwilling eyes.

"You should return to your chambers. You won't be needed this morning," he said.

Quinn didn't even start. She merely continued to brush the hay from her horse's hair. It seemed in the months since they'd been apart, the beast had calmed somewhat at her presence. Or perhaps, it realized that there was no use in fighting her. She was far more powerful than the creature ever could be.

As if sensing his thoughts, Quinn turned and set the brush aside, reaching for a treat that she handed the horse, letting it eat from her palm. "Risk taught me a lot while I was away," she said quietly. "At first, I thought I was the teacher—training her, helping her learn how to survive, be independent. But she has a way with animals, and she showed me how to approach them."

Lazarus shook his head. He did not care for her knowledge of animals. He was here for a very specific reason, and that was to ensure she did not disrupt his meeting with Lord Callis again. "Did you hear me?" he demanded, his voice a low growl.

Quinn chuckled quietly, finishing what she was doing with the horse and turning to face him. "You know what I found to be the most surprising lesson?" she asked instead of answering him. Quinn took a step toward him, tilting her head to the side as she looked up, meeting his gaze. "You have to be gentle with beasts; make them think that they are in charge. Give them the illusion that they are completely in control. Once she taught me that . . ." Quinn drifted off, moving even closer. Lazarus stiffened. "Well, they weren't so hard to handle anymore."

Lazarus narrowed his eyes on her face. He had the distinct feeling she was no longer talking about animals. "You should leave," he said around a throat full of tension.

"Why's that?" she replied.

She was teasing him; pushing him to the brink. She always did. Quinn seemed to think playing with his anger was like a child's game. She didn't shudder or shy away from him. No, she danced with Mazzulah willingly and let the madness consume her and shove them both to the very edge of a fine-pointed blade.

"Lord Callis has something that I desire, and I don't want anything interrupting my meeting with him. It is imperative that all goes well today."

"What do you want from him?" Quinn asked.

Lazarus scowled. "It does not matter what it is. The fact is I need it, and therefore, I need you to stay here."

She shook her head. "No, I think I'll be of far better use to you on the hunt. You're not getting rid of me that easily." She turned away from him and for a brief moment, he felt air refill his lungs. He hadn't realized that merely being so close to her was changing him. He had held his breath, if only to stop breathing in her enticing, dark scent.

"Quinn, this is nonnegotiable." He watched as she

picked up a wool blanket, folded it, and placed it over the back of her horse before returning for her saddle.

"What do you need from him?" she asked again. "I'll ensure you get it."

Lazarus folded his arms across his chest. "As simple as it would be to torture what I need from him, unfortunately, it is not something so easily attained."

Quinn finished doing up the buckles on her horse and twisted back to reach for the horse's harness. She fixed the harness upon the beast and then offered a bit to its mouth, settling the reins around its head. "So, it's not an object, then," she said.

"No."

"Then it's not his wealth or his estate? Not a person?" she pressed. "Is it his influence?" Lazarus stiffened, but didn't reply. It didn't matter, though, because he'd already given her the answer. She nodded as if he had, in fact, spoken. "Then you're simply playing a game with him because you want him to swear fealty to you, yes?"

As she reached for the reins, intending to lead the horse from its stall, Lazarus dropped all pretenses and reached for her. His fingers closed around her upper arm, drawing her to a halt. "This is important, Quinn. Lord Callis is one of the most powerful Norcastan lords. His family has been close with the royals for a long time. They were once stewards to Claudius' ancestors. His support is a necessity if I'm to avoid a civil war."

"Avoid a civil war?" Quinn froze at his touch, a hard note entering her voice. "What do you mean? You're King."

Lazarus shook his head and then backed her further into the stall, lowering his voice on the off chance one of the stable boys was nearby. "I am, yes," he replied, "but Claudius' children—the blood heirs—"

"The ones who had you followed to the Cisean Mountains and then Ilvas," Quinn said with certainty. "Amelia Reinhart and her brothers."

He nodded. "They will not readily give up what they feel is theirs by right of birth."

"And you need Lord Callis' support in order to . . ." She quirked an eyebrow, prompting him.

"I need his support and influence to silence, or at least tamp down, the worst of my subjects rallying behind the Reinharts," Lazarus finished.

"You would win a war," Quinn pointed out as she tugged herself free of his grasp.

Lazarus released her, not because she wanted it, but because there was no longer a reason for him to hold her. No reason for him to touch her. "I would," he agreed with a nod, "but I would be a tyrant and not a king were I to force my reign upon the people of Norcasta."

He did not care for the way she eyed him. "You want to avoid bloodshed, Lazarus? A king and not a tyrant?" Her lips twitched in amusement. "For some reason, I feel as though that goes against your very nature."

Perhaps it did. Perhaps he enjoyed the taste of blood and darkness on his tongue. Perhaps he wanted to lift the violent little mauve-haired creature that had been tormenting him for months and dive between her legs and find out if she tasted just as wicked.

"Either way," she said when he didn't reply. "I am going on this hunt. I have a request to make of you, anyway."

Lazarus moved back to the edge of the stall. "What is this request?"

He didn't notice the shake of her head as he glanced out of the stall, searching out for one of the stable boys. Eugene, a young sandy-haired stable hand froze when he spotted the King, and when Lazarus lifted his hand and gestured, the boy got the gist. He nodded and turned, scurrying away. His horse would be readied post haste as it appeared there was no talking Quinn out of coming along.

"Your request?" he prompted once more.

"We will talk about it while on the hunt," she said, taking the reins of her horse and leading him out into the aisle. It followed at a sedate pace, keeping pace at her side.

Instead of pressing her, he narrowed his eyes on her form. "You will behave yourself?" Though it had been meant as a command, it came out as more of a question.

"Don't I always?"

"Quinn." His voice held a multitude of warnings.

"I will behave," she replied, and then, as if she couldn't help herself, the woman had to push him a bit further. She continued with a quiet, breathy, "for now."

Lazarus felt fire enter his eyes, a burn that stretched up his back and chest as the souls beneath his skin squirmed and made themselves known at last. It was a wonder how they hadn't before now. Whenever he seemed to get close to the little fear twister, he felt their silent limbs reach through his veins, sending rockets of pleasure sliding through him.

"Your horse, Your Grace." Eugene had returned as Lazarus and Quinn reached the edge of the stables. The boy held Lazarus' horse's reins in hand, and he quickly passed them to the King as he bowed and scurried away.

As Lazarus exited the manger with Quinn just behind him, he saw that Lord Callis and his entourage had already arrived and were waiting in the front courtyard. The other man laughed gaily as he regaled the other stuffed lords with a hunting story of his past. Lazarus knew the moment the lord spotted Quinn, for his back straightened and he tugged the reins of his horse to allow him to face both of them as they approached.

"So glad you could make it, Lady Darkova," he called.

"Just Quinn, Lord Callis," she replied, bringing a low growl to Lazarus' throat.

"Ah, then you must call me Artan," Lord Callis replied.

Lazarus glared at the man, but said nothing as he waved away an approaching stable boy carrying forth a small step ladder, and grabbed ahold of his horse's saddle, swinging himself into the seat.

"Shall we be off to the hunt, then?" Lazarus said, drawing Lord Callis' attention.

"Oh, but surely, we must wait for—" Lord Callis slid his gaze back to Quinn only to pause. Lazarus didn't have to look behind him to know that Quinn had done the same. She had likely refused the ladder as well, and though her stature was much shorter than his own—she was tall for a woman and even stronger than most men. "Well, Quinn, you are full of surprises, aren't you?" Lord Callis laughed as Quinn trotted by Lazarus, throwing a smirk in his direction.

"You have no idea, Artan," she said pleasantly.

Lazarus' scowl deepened even as he caught a glimpse of Dominicus astride his own steed, maneuvering through the others and heading his way. No, the soft-bellied nobleman didn't. He had no clue the level of danger the woman he was presently eyeing presented to him—or even Lazarus, himself.

The Hunt

"The good hunter is one that knows her prey as well as she knows herself."
— Quinn Darkova, fear twister, right-hand to the King of Norcasta

Dogs raced ahead, their snouts pressed to the ground, their tails stiff and straight at their backs as they tracked their prey. Quinn sat astride her steed with Lord Callis on one side and Lazarus on the other.

"Tell me, Quinn, you're N'skari. Are you not?" Lord Callis started.

A faint smile of amusement crossed her lips as she said, "I am."

"Why would you move to Norcasta? I heard your people were quite attached to the north," he continued, leaning over the side of his horse toward her.

Quinn laughed, the sound tinkling and false even to her own ears. She could feel the way it made Lazarus stiffen in his seat. The man hadn't relaxed once since he had come looking for her in the stables and as they had set out on the hunt. He'd only grown more agitated the more she spoke to Lord Callis.

"That's true," Quinn replied to the man's words. "There was a time when I thought I'd never leave my place in the north."

"Why did you?" he pressed.

Quinn smirked. She could practically feel the burn of Lazarus' glare in the back of her head. "Unexpected circumstances brought me to Norcasta," Quinn answered vaguely. "And since meeting His Grace," she paused, "well, where else would I go?"

Lord Callis smiled. "Too true, I suppose. Once you've found an appropriate master, there's really no getting away, is there?"

He laughed as though he'd made a joke, and Quinn forced herself to smile despite her irritation. Quinn had no master; not even Lazarus. Perhaps she was willing to follow him, fight for him, kill for him . . . but no man was her master. Not any longer.

Quinn shifted upon her saddle and cracked her neck as Lord Callis called out that the dogs had found something and raced ahead. Several of the following lords bounded after him, clicking their heels against the sides of their horses to hurry them along even though it was useless in the heavily wooded area.

As the others moved ahead, Dominicus urged his horse in front of both Lazarus and Quinn, allowing the two of them some privacy. "You play with fire, Quinn," Lazarus grunted with irritation as they trailed the others at a more moderate pace.

"Yes, I suppose you're right," Quinn replied without looking his way. "But I can't seem to help myself, especially when it hurts so good."

A growl came from him in response, which only served to make the corners of her mouth tilt up even more. "Lord Callis is not to be trifled with," he said.

Quinn waved her hand through the air. "I'm not concerned, but I did want to talk to you about something." When he didn't reply immediately, she took that to mean he was willing to listen. "While I was away, Risk developed some rather unique skills. You recall I mentioned she was good with beasts? Well, it's not just an inclination."

"She's a beast tamer," Lazarus surmised.

"She is," Quinn replied. "I was hoping you would know of an experienced beast tamer. Perhaps, someone in the capital? She needs a trainer."

Lazarus nodded. "I'll have Draeven look into it."

"Thank you."

He nodded.

They were catching up to the others fast. Lord

Callis and several others had made it into a clearing and were urging their horses in a circular motion as the dogs barked and growled. They had caught a mother fox between them and as one pulled a bow from his side saddle and aimed, Quinn and Lazarus stopped at the edge of the clearing. She turned and looked toward Lord Callis just as he released his arrow, and the yelp of the wild fox ricocheted up into the tops of the trees.

Interesting enough, the man's gaze was steady, his eyes alight with pleasure as he snatched another arrow from his side quiver and took aim once more. It appeared he had only wounded the animal. Quinn nudged her horse further into the clearing as the others came to a standstill, some calling out encouragement, others booing him for taking so long. Lord Callis smiled as he released his next arrow, and Quinn looked to the creature on the ground, noting that the first arrow had caught it in the left hind leg. The next, however, pierced the flesh above its heart, and with a sag, the creature collapsed.

As Lord Callis put his bow back, one of the accompanying squires leapt from his mount to hurry over and retrieve the animal—yanking the arrows from its body to hand them back to the lord.

"Well done, Lord Callis," Quinn said as she pulled up alongside him.

"I told you, Quinn," he replied, shooting her an

easy grin. "Call me Artan. And it's a fine creature. I hope to have it skinned and made into a neck scarf."

"For your wife, I suppose?" she asked.

"For my mistress," he replied honestly.

"Oh?" Quinn quirked a brow, but kept her face otherwise impassive.

Lord Callis sighed as the rest of the troupe moved back into the woods, setting the dogs on yet another trail that they followed. "I hope you do not think less of me for admitting what every man here knows. We all have mistresses. Some are more tangible and pleasurable than others." Quinn frowned, and he noted the confusion in her expression. Before she could ask, he answered her unspoken question. "A man's work is often his mistress. I am lucky enough to call a woman mine," he said. "I do so enjoy the pleasures in life."

"I see," Quinn replied, watching as Dominicus took the lead this time. Lazarus, however, remained a ways behind. Though he refused to glance back at them, she knew he wanted to be nearer to her so long as she was with Lord Callis. "May I ask a question?"

"Of course," Lord Callis replied, his interest piqued as he pivoted in his seat and leveled her with the full weight of his attention. "I welcome any and all questions you may have. Is it about the pleasures a man finds with his mistress?"

Quinn forced back her true feelings, but she could feel the strain in her features as she gave him a small smile and shook her head. She could tell where that conversation would have led. His eyes had already strayed far too many times to her hips and to her breasts, pressed together by the tightness of her leather clothing as she sat upon a saddle. She would let him look his fill. It did, after all, serve a purpose—to draw him in for her to examine and dig deep into his words as she analyzed just what kind of man—ally or foe—he could be. "Regrettably, no, it's not. It's about the fox you just shot."

"Oh?" He looked perplexed.

"You were so close to it. One arrow would have sufficed. You don't seem inexperienced with a bow. Why did you use two? Why make it suffer?"

Lord Callis stilled for a moment before shooting her an unabashed and rueful grin. "As I said before, Quinn, I enjoy the pleasures that life has to offer." With that, he kicked at his horse and sent the creature galloping forward, catching up quickly with Dominicus and the rest of the group.

Quinn let the facade on her face drop as she ambled up next to Lazarus. "What did you learn?" he asked, noting her expression.

"That your Lord Callis is a dangerous man," she replied. Another woman—or even a man—might have been confused by the lord's answer, but not Quinn. She was not naive, and she knew how to recognize someone of similar interests. Lord Callis enjoyed delivering pain and suffering. His jovial attitude and quick smile hid a much darker persona than his fellow lords probably knew of.

Lazarus glanced from her to ahead where the others had once again caught a trail—this time a fawn. "Do you think he will be amenable to my reign?" he demanded.

Quinn nodded. "There's nothing yet to suggest he wouldn't be." *So long as he had the room to take from the pleasures of life, as he had so eloquently put it,* she thought.

Lazarus nodded, and together they once again hurried to meet the others, watching from the sidelines as another lord pulled his own bow and arrows as they tracked the fawn through underbrush. Quinn split off from Lazarus and rounded the sides of the group, watching as small woodland creatures—little rabbits and other fluffy tailed creatures—darted out of the way of her horse's clomping hooves.

The lords weren't concerned with them, though. They were more focused on other prey. While they trailed the fawn, she trailed Lord Callis. Watching him curiously as he laughed and joked with his fellow noblemen. She wondered what other things were hiding beneath his surface. Every once in a while, he would turn his head and catch her looking. Mistaking her interest for a different interest of sorts, he would flash her a roguish grin.

As the hunt drew to a close, though, she once again found herself in his close proximity. He urged his mount close to her own, letting several of the others pass them as they headed back to the palace.

"So, Quinn, what did you think of the hunt? I assume you've never been on one."

"Why do you assume that?" she asked.

"You didn't bring a bow," he pointed out.

Reaching into her boot, she withdrew a wickedly long blade. "I prefer a closer kind of hunting," she said, twisting the blade so that a ray of sunlight as it descended beyond the treetops glinted over its metal surface. She let him examine it for another moment before slipping it back into its place. "But you would be correct. I've never been on an *official* hunt before."

Lips twitching in amusement, Lord Callis hummed. "Fascinating," he replied. "Did you not care for it, then?"

"No," Quinn answered as they broke free of the tree line and spotted the palace in the distance. "It was quite informative."

"I'm glad," he said. "You'll have to come to my estate outside of the capital. We have much larger game there."

"You don't live inside Leone?" Quinn twisted her head toward him, blinking thoughtfully.

He shook his head. "I keep a townhome within the city walls, as do most noblemen, but I have a large estate about a half a day's ride away. Would you come visit me there?"

Quinn noticed Lazarus drawing near as Lord

Callis asked his question. "I would be delighted," she replied readily as Lazarus halted alongside them.

"Delighted for what?" Lazarus inquired, watching them both suspiciously.

Quinn turned a smile his way. "Artan was just telling me about his estate outside of the capital. He invited me there for another hunt. I told him I would be delighted to visit."

"Yes," Lord Callis agreed. "You're both invited, if you like, Your Grace. I'd be honored to have you as my guest—provided, of course, that you bring your lovely vassal along with you."

"Flattery, Lord Callis?" Quinn shook her head as they came to a stop in the courtyard. Throwing one leg over her horse, she slid to the ground and sent a plume of dirt up around her legs. "I'll have you know that doesn't work on me."

"Oh no?" Lord Callis did the same, leveraging one leg over the side, and dismounted just as quickly. "I shall endeavor to entice you with something more interesting. Perhaps something different than a hunt when you come to visit me."

"I look forward to it," Quinn replied.

"See that you do, Quinn Darkova," Lord Callis said with smirk as he led his horse away, dropping the reins into the waiting hands of a nearby stable hand.

Quinn watched him go, studying the way he moved from his stride to his confident air.

"Good work," Lazarus said gruffly, sounding as

though the words were being pulled through a throat made of broken glass.

Quinn flicked him a smug look, and taking up the reins to her own horse, she turned her back and headed for the stables, calling over her shoulder as she walked away, "Know your prey, Lazarus. Know your prey well, and maybe you might catch them."

Bizarre Happenings

*"It's easy to hate what you don't understand, just as it's easy to
fear what you do."*
— *Mariska "Risk" Darkova, beast tamer*

S weat slicked her skin from beneath the stiff
burlap shirt and loose-fitted trousers. While Risk
was finely boned, she dressed in a man's clothes—
much to her sister's chagrin. Quinn had offered her
leathers, such as her own, but Risk hadn't batted an
eye at those. Instead, it was the ill-fitted things that
drew her attention—because it wouldn't draw anyone
else's.

That was before they'd crossed a desert in the
godsforsaken heat.

Before they'd moved into a literal palace, where

their rooms were on the top floor and the blasted heat rose to greet them. Risk turned away from the window she dared not open. Not when the creatures of the north and the night followed her like a plague.

She paced the length of the long chamber. That animal-like restlessness stirring within. The urge to fight or flee was great these days, in equal measure. She loved her sister for what she'd done for her, but these people—this place—it was Quinn's.

Now it's yours too.

She told herself the words Quinn had spoken time and again, but without her sister here saying them, even her own thoughts rang hollow. Deep down, she disliked this place. She didn't trust its people. The cold, terrible, truth of it was that she disliked and distrusted any*one* as well as any*place*. She could pack up and leave now, she knew. Quinn wouldn't stop her, but there was nowhere to go. No one to run to.

Everything she had was here because Quinn was here.

And so, much as she entertained the thought of leaving this place behind with its judgmental eyes and bastard heat, she wouldn't. The fight drained from her, gone as quickly as it had come on. It didn't help that her sister had been gone for more than half the day, and the way she'd left things between them . . . it didn't sit well with Risk.

After everything she'd done for her, Quinn didn't deserve her attitude, but still she found herself unable to help it. Months of travel had done little to soothe her nerves around people. Now here, her otherness was stark. If not for her beast tamer magic, then her half-raksasa blood would mark her as different. No matter the garments she wore, she had horns, and unlike her sister—she couldn't simply make them disappear.

Risk sighed and repeated another of her sister's mantras.

"Let them hate you. Let them love you. Let what they think matter not. If they try to end you, we'll crush them all," she whispered the words, but again, the comfort that they provided on the road was no longer there.

Here it was not about them ending her. It was about them accepting her. Not that Quinn would ever understand that. She cared not for acceptance, and her advice would be for Risk to do the same.

Risk took another deep breath and looked at the door, longingly.

She'd done it a hundred times by now, but this time, she was committed to do something about it. Regardless of her appearance, they would never accept someone they did not know. If she wanted them to see her as something other than raksasa, she needed to go out.

The pounding of her heart hammered in her ears as she approached the door. Her fingers were clammy as she gripped the handle, sliding over the smooth metal. She wiped them on her shirt and tried again, stilling as her own resolve began to fumble.

Risk grit her teeth and twisted. The door swung open, and her heart plummeted from her chest to her stomach. She took a deep breath, counting to ten.

And then she stepped outside.

One short walk, she told herself. *Then we don't have to see anyone until Quinn gets back.*

She nodded to herself and began taking short, stilted steps. She was halfway down the hall when it occurred to her that she'd left the door open. She turned to double back; the movements coming easier now, though it helped that no one was around.

Risk closed the door firmly and paused.

She could go right back inside. It was still an option.

"No," she breathed. "You'll never get better if you don't try." It was another saying Quinn loved to tell her, but this time it did the trick. Risk turned with her back straight and head high.

"Who ya talkin' to?"

Risk jumped, her claws unsheathing instantly as she whipped her head around and cast a wild glance back. A young girl, no bigger than herself, stood holding a dead rat in one hand and bloodied knife in the other.

"No one," Risk said, shaking her head. The child quirked a red eyebrow and tilted her head.

"Why were you comin' out of Quinn's room?" the

girl asked. Risk breathed a little easier that this person at least knew her sister. That boded well for her.

"I'm sharing her room with her," Risk said. The girl's eyes went wide, a scandalous smile spreading across her face. Two gold teeth glinted, drawing Risk's attention.

"I thought the hussy was with the King. Well slap me silly and—"

"No, no," Risk interrupted, shaking her head. "I didn't mean it like that." She sighed. "We're sisters."

A look of understanding crossed the girl's face as she drawled, "Ohhhhhh. I see." She seemed to consider this for a moment, while Risk stood there, feeling more self-conscious by the moment. "You sort of look like her with the whole dark magic thing goin' on. Your horns are way cooler, though."

Risk blinked and straightened a little. "You think?" she asked hesitantly.

"Oh yeah," Axe grinned. "I could hang so many rat skulls from those things." She tapped her chin with the tip of her bloody knife, considering the prospect.

Risk grimaced, unsure how to respond to that. "I suppose you could."

A door opened at the far end of the hall. Voices filtered through, though Risk didn't know any of them. The distinct maleness of them made her wary. Her fingers tightened around the door as the idea of turning to her and Quinn's chambers tempted her.

The girl had a different idea.

She took off down the hall, only pausing for a brief second to look over her shoulder. "You comin' with?" she asked.

"I . . ." Risk fumbled, her gaze darting back to where the voices were coming from, and to the girl in front of her. "I didn't realize I was invited," she settled on.

The child shrugged and wiped her nose with the back of her hand holding the knife. "Do you know how to keep quiet?"

Risk's eyebrows drew together as her expression became wary. "Yes . . ."

"Then you can come." Without realizing it, her fingers had already slipped from the handle. She started toward the girl, a light feeling settling over her as they moved down the hall together. She was still trying to name the sensation in her chest when they reached the furthest end of the hallway. The girl cast her a side glance and grinned slyly before finagling the door open while maintaining her hold on the knife. The knob twisted and the wooden panel fell open.

She stepped in, surveying her surroundings when the door shut. That light feeling in her diminished as she turned to look at the girl who was already pushing her aside. She froze, shocked by the contact. The girl seemed to have no idea what she just did as she laid the dead rat next to two others on a bed. Risk had only barely recovered when the child turned and said with a firm nod, "*This* will show that rat bastard."

"Who?" Risk asked, her voice sounding a little breathier than she would have liked.

"Vaughn," the girl scowled. "He's my nemesis."

Both Risk's eyebrows rose toward her hairline as voices echoed down the hall, drawing closer.

"Quick," the girl scrambled forward. She thrust open the wardrobe doors beside her and motioned for Risk to get in.

"I'm not sure—" Risk started, her heart beating fast. The voices neared, and that fight-or-flight instinct took over. She jumped into the wardrobe and the child followed behind her, pulling both doors closed with a click.

They waited in the shrouded darkness as men approached. One of them had an accent, much like her own, except it wasn't N'skaran. Just close.

The blood coursing through her veins pounded heavily in her ears as she tried to calm her racing heart. Her nails had turned into claws once again. She closed both fists tightly, letting them bite into her skin. It was better to keep them hidden than accidentally stab the girl as they both waited with bated breath.

Finally, the door to the room creaked open. Risk peered through the crack in the wardrobe doors. In walked a man of considerable size. Dressed in leathers, not so different from her sister's, Risk watched him. A feeling of dread settled in her, snuffing out all happiness at being included.

He approached the bed and paused. She waited for the fury that would follow at such a thing. She only now realized her folly in helping the girl, but it was too late. He saw the three dead rats and then, without further delay, let out a full-bellied laugh.

Her jaw went slack as her mouth dropped open. *Laughing? Why in the world is he laughing?* The dread in her gut settled out, but it was quickly replaced by confusion. She'd been gone from the world for a long time, but surely these weren't ordinary people. They were her sister's friends, and that in itself should have told Risk a lot.

Still, she couldn't hold back her surprise as he called out, "Well done, little pirate. Your prowess in hunting the vermin of the palace is admirable. You will make fine she-wolf one day."

The wardrobe doors flung open as the girl beside her stormed out.

"You idiot!" she screamed. "The rats aren't a gift, you thick-necked mongrel—they're a warning—an omen—" The man approached the girl, and despite the smile on his face as he looked down at her, Risk's claws curled further. She wavered where she stood as he grabbed the girl with one arm and lifted her up in a . . . hug. His other hand came out to snuzzle the top of her head, mussing her fiery-red hair into an even greater mess.

"Little pirate is growing into woman. It's normal to bring your guardians gifts in preparation of learning how to woo your mate." He let out another laugh, and the girl huffed in frustration, sinking her teeth into his arm.

The man's grip slipped on her, and she dropped to the ground and rounded on him, punching into his big chest. Despite the girl's aggression, the man only laughed, holding up his hands in surrender. "Come now, little—"

"Arghhhhh!" she screamed, launching herself at him. She tackled him head-on, sending the man sprawling back in bed as she jumped on top of him and continued to deliver blows. "You," she gasped. "Will—" she picked up a pillow. "Fear," she growled as she began beating him with it. "Me!"

Risk stared on at the scene unfolding before her with wide eyes. She'd never leave a woman undefended, but in this case, it was the girl beating the man, and after all her blows he'd yet to even lift a finger against her. "Yes, yes, little pirate," he coughed, trying to hide his laugh and failing. "I fear you greatly."

His words did nothing to dissuade the child, and Risk took that as her permission to leave. She stepped out of the wardrobe without either of them noticing and slipped out the door, letting it click softly behind her.

Risk leaned back and inhaled deeply, letting the

breath go. Her nerves calmed significantly with that one act, but Risk had decided she'd firmly had enough interaction for one day. Perhaps she should take Quinn up on meeting her friends with her around. She'd be able to explain the nonsensical thing she'd just saw.

Slowly, she pulled away from the door and started back down the hall. Too late did she notice the person walking toward her, though he was hard to miss. His sandy blond hair reminded her of the people in Bangratas, but his violet eyes—they were something uniquely his own. She'd never seen another with eyes that color. She wondered if he was different for it, or if she was simply untraveled.

"Lady Darkova," he said in greeting. She purposely stepped to the side, closer to the wall and further from him. If he noticed her attempt to steer clear of him, he didn't say.

"I'm not a Lady," Risk bit out. Some of her temper coming to rise again.

He looked her up and down once, and she shivered in fear. There was nothing heated or lustful about his watchful eye, though, and it kept her from lashing out.

"Would you prefer to be known as Lord?" he asked, completely serious.

Baffled into an answer, Risk replied, "No. I'm no Lady or Lord. I don't want or need a title. I simply am." He regarded her again. The steadiness of that gaze; it beguiled her.

"What would you wish me to call you, then?" he asked.

She blinked, again, not expecting his question. It went without saying, because there was one name she could stomach to be known by. "Risk."

The man opened his mouth to say something, but a war cry erupted from the room she'd just left. An amused expression crossed his face as the door itself came flying off its hinges and into the hall. The red-haired girl came storming out behind it, followed by the man, Vaughn. He tried to console her, but that only seemed to make the child angrier.

"Until next time, Risk." He nodded once, making no move to touch her before striding off toward the bizarre scene. Risk shook her head and hurried down the hall.

As she reached her room, she couldn't help herself from taking one last look over her shoulder at the three people she'd already met in her time here.

While strange and unlike anything she'd ever known, perhaps they weren't the absolute worst thing ever, if a bit odd.

She went inside and closed the door behind her, feeling a little bit better than when she'd left.

Letter from a Lady

"Keep your friends close, and invite your enemies to dine at your table. All the better to poison them."
— *Quinn Darkova, fear twister, right-hand to the King of Norcasta*

Quinn bit into a purple-skinned fruit, watching Risk with raised brows as her sister recounted her adventures from the day before.

"And then she bit him," Risk said. "And he didn't hit her. He just laughed, or rather, he tried not to laugh, but he couldn't seem to help himself. The more he laughed, the angrier the girl got. She said his name was Vaughn. But I can't recall if she gave me her name. The man—Vaughn—called her a pirate.

Do they sound familiar to you? She said she knew you."

Quinn sighed and nodded. "That would be Axe."

Risk's eyes bulged. "That's her *name*? She was named for a weapon?"

Quinn smirked. "Yeah, you could say that. It's complicated. She's not a Maji, but she . . ." Quinn trailed off, unsure how to explain the creature that was Axe.

"She said she should've known that we were sisters," Risk said. "That our Maji auras were . . . well, she acted like she could *see* them. I've never heard of someone being able to do that."

"Axe is a bit different," Quinn said, finishing off her fruit and standing as a knock sounded on the door across from them. Probably Lorraine back to retrieve the tray that Quinn had taken from the kitchens for breakfast.

"Different is a bit of an understatement," Risk muttered as she bit viciously into a loaf of bread and chewed.

Quinn opened the door and blinked to find Draeven there instead. Behind her, the scrape of Risk's chair against the stone floor sounded. Quinn glanced back, taking in Risk's narrowed eyes and stiff shoulders. Her sister stood with a hand on her hip, where her dagger would have been had it not been sitting on the nightstand behind her.

Looking between them, Quinn tracked the way

Draeven's eyes traveled to her sister and then returned to her almost forcefully as he spoke. "I apologize for intruding, but Lazarus has called for you. He's meeting with his council of advisors, and as his right-hand you're expected to make yourself present."

Narrowing her eyes on the man, she nodded. "Alright." Turning back to Risk, she spoke in low tones. "I'll be back later today. Will you be alright by yourself?"

Risk's shoulders lowered, and her hand fell away from her side as she straightened. Looking to the table, she nodded. "I'll be fine," she replied.

Quinn waited a moment, eyeing her, but she didn't want to hover, so she merely nodded and turned back to Draeven, stepping out into the hall and letting the door close behind her.

"Is your sister getting used to the palace?" Draeven asked as they made their way down the hall.

Sliding a glance his way, Quinn murmured her reply. "She's getting along fine."

"Lazarus told me you asked for a trainer for her," Draeven said. "I've arranged for an old friend to make the trip here. He'll be here within a day or so, and he'd be happy to train her."

"Risk still isn't comfortable around men," Quinn warned.

Draeven nodded and turned to her with a grin. "I doubt she'll truly think of Haspati as a man. He's not much more than a mass of darkened wrinkles and age spots at this point." He laughed. "But I would say that you should warn her of his coming, so she's not startled. I'll be arranging it and overseeing their sessions."

Quinn nodded, making a note to talk to Risk. She'd be happy to have a trainer, but not about the gender—regardless of age. Quinn stroked the skin just beneath her left elbow and felt a twinge from the creature beneath it. There were ways around the discomfort. Things she could do to make Risk feel more secure, much to Draeven's chagrin.

They arrived at a small chamber of sorts a few moments later. Draeven reached forward, hands closing around the ornate handles to a set of double doors, turning them and pushing them inward, revealing a room full of familiar and unfamiliar faces alike.

"Dominicus," Quinn greeted the man who stood to Lazarus' side.

Dominicus grunted his greeting, moving away as Draeven entered, turned to close the doors behind him, and then moved to Lazarus' left side. Quinn stopped by Lazarus' right and turned, facing the men surrounding the long oak table where Lazarus sat at the head.

Of the four others surrounding them, Quinn only recognized one. Lord Callis smiled her way, and she returned the notion, eliciting a quiet frown of disapproval from Lazarus, which only made her smile widen.

"Now then," a tall, gray-eyed, older man said, coughing as he called everyone's attention to himself. "If all members of the King's council are present, shall we proceed with this matter?"

Lazarus nodded and waved his hand, gesturing for the man to continue. It was Draeven who stopped them.

"Actually, perhaps we should go around the table and introduce ourselves. I know most of you haven't yet met His Grace's right-hand, Quinn Darkova," he interrupted before the man could continue.

The lord shot Draeven an annoyed look, but grumbled an agreement. "Very well," he said. "I am Lord Langston. This is Lord Brameer—" He paused, gesturing to the slightly younger man to his side, and then pointed across from him as he continued. "Lord Callis and Lord Northcott." Quinn nodded, and he took that to mean that his duties of introduction were through. "We're here to discuss the letter His Grace received from Amelia Reinhart requesting an audience."

"Is it just Lady Amelia?" Lord Callis inquired. "Or will her brothers be joining her?"

Lord Langston coughed as he reached for a piece of parchment set on the table before him, lifting it up as he withdrew a set of spectacles from his pocket and fixed them upon his nose and glanced through it. "By the sounds of it, her brothers as well."

Quinn watched as Lord Callis smirked. "She

rarely leaves them behind," he said with a knowing nod.

"Right," Lord Langston replied, turning to face Lazarus. "Then, should you decide to agree to her request, you'll be agreeing to hosting the three of them."

Lazarus nodded. "Understood. Do you think I should agree, then?"

"They're the blood heirs." Quinn stated. "Why would you invite your enemy to your home? This is no longer their right."

"Lady Darkova," Lord Langston blustered, his face growing red beneath his glasses. "You were invited here as a vassal to His Grace, but it is clear you know nothing of these circumstances."

Quinn leveled the man with a dangerous look. "Oh, no?" she replied. "Then perhaps you might be willing to explain them to me."

"What Lord Langston means, Quinn," Lord Callis said, "is that the Reinharts are not enemies. They are highly respected nobles; the late King Claudius' own children."

"Who no doubt would love nothing more than to see Lazarus removed from what they consider *their* throne," Quinn replied stiffly.

"You obviously don't know how court is run," Lord Brameer said with a nasally scoff. "Why His Grace would allow an uncouth woman in his council is beyond me."

Quinn felt a rage boil up within her, and she took a step forward as if to show the pathetic worm of a man just how much of an uncouth woman she could be. Draeven, however, chose that moment to move around Lazarus' chair and grab her arm as he lifted his head to address the others.

"I think what Quinn means is that she is only concerned for King Lazarus' safety," he said gently. "It's no secret that history has seen trouble for new rulers when there is an abrupt power shift. There are those who would prefer to see Claudius' children on the throne rather than his chosen heir."

Quinn let Draeven's arm stop her, but that didn't keep her from glaring at Lord Brameer with the promise of violence should the little prick irritate her further. Lord Brameer, for his part, appeared uncomfortable as he adjusted in his chair and looked away from her intense gaze.

"That's quite insightful, Lord Adelmar," Lord Callis said, clapping his hands. "And it's quite noble of Quinn to want to keep her master safe."

Quinn stiffened at that word once more, leaving off staring at Lord Brameer to take in Lord Callis' pleasant expression. She shrugged off Draeven's arm, though the man stayed at her side, nonetheless.

"Do you have a particular way you want this to play out, Your Grace?" Dominicus asked, directing his attention to Lazarus.

Lazarus frowned, leaning forward to prop his

elbows upon the table and steeple his hands as he considered his words carefully. Silence stretched through the room as he thought long and hard. Everyone else remained mute as they waited with bated breath to see Lazarus speak his desires.

Before he had a chance, however, the quiet came to an end when the only man in the room who had yet to speak, gave his answer.

"Whether or not you want to amend to Lady Reinhart's request, Your Grace, I do not see how you have much of a choice."

Lazarus looked up as Quinn did, both of them fixing the dark-haired lord with a serious expression and giving him their sole focus. "What choice do I not have, Lord Northcott? Speak up," Lazarus commanded.

Lord Northcott lifted his head, his expression unchanging as he took in his surroundings. Quinn got the distinct impression that this man had seen danger and was intelligent enough to weigh the pros and cons of anything he said or did. When his eyes settled on her and remained briefly, her suspicion was proven. He knew danger when he saw it.

"If you do not acquiesce to Lady Reinhart's request, then she or her family will surely use it as an excuse to prove that you mean to cut them out completely of what many argue is their inheritance by birthright. It would behoove you to allow her an audience and at least see what she has to say."

"No," Quinn argued immediately. "He doesn't have to do anything. He is King. He makes the decision."

"Yes, he will make the ultimate decision, Quinn," Draeven said. "But Lord Northcott has a point."

Northcott nodded, but he sent Quinn a wary glance, especially when she pivoted abruptly to look at Draeven as though the man had lost his mind. "What in the dark realm are you talking about?"

"His Grace should agree to Lady Reinhart's request. It is better to hear them out and understand their demands than assume and make a blunder that could hurt not only his reputation, but his rule."

"You—"

"Then it's decided," Lazarus said, cutting Quinn off. "We will have a vote."

"A vote?" Lord Langston sounded confused.

"Yes," Lazarus answered. "I, of course, will still make my decision regardless of the results of said vote, but I am curious to know how many would prefer I agree and who would argue that I shouldn't concede to this request. Draeven?"

"Yes, Your Grace." Draeven straightened as Quinn pressed her lips together and glared her displeasure, splitting her anger between Draeven and Lazarus. "Those in favor of agreeing to Lady Rein-hart's request, raise your right hand." Hands lifted. Draeven, Lord Langston, Lord Callis, Lord Brameer, Lord Northcott, and . . . Quinn blinked in surprise as Dominicus' hand remained down. "Those in favor of declining her request, raise your right hand."

All other hands lowered as Dominicus and Quinn lifted their palms. She looked at the weapons master with a small form of respect. At least not everyone in the room was a complete fool.

"Thank you, you may lower your hands," Draeven said, turning back to Lazarus. "Your decision?"

Lazarus nodded. "I think Northcott has made a good point. Lord Langston, you will arrange for a messenger to deliver my acceptance?"

Lord Langston bowed as Quinn gritted her teeth against her frustration. "As you wish, Your Grace."

"They are in northern Norcasta, are they not?" Lazarus asked.

Lord Langston blinked, seeming a mix of surprised and confused by the question. "Why . . . yes. They are, sir."

Lazarus nodded. "Send one man on horseback. He'll be much faster that way. In the correspondence, let Lady Reinhart know that I expect her presence immediately. I want no time wasted."

"It'll be a stretch to expect her in anything less than ten days," Draeven commented.

"Ten days it is, then," Lazarus said with a nod. "You're all dismissed."

Quinn scowled as she stomped past Draeven,

tossing him a disgusted glare as she slammed out of the chambers.

"What a reckless young woman. . ." one of the men commented as she left. The voice was that of Lord Langston, but Quinn didn't care. If they thought her reckless, then they were weak-bellied creatures.

Men. The fool of the species.

A Point to be Made

"Ignorance is not bliss, just as bravery is not a good thing. Teach people the brutal truth, and perhaps they won't be susceptible to the beautiful lie."
— *Quinn Darkova, fear twister, right-hand to the King of Norcasta*

Heat pounded through her veins as she stormed down the halls. Guards looked on from their posts, servants scuttled to the side, but not a soul dared say anything to Quinn when she was in a mood such as this. She made her way across the palace in half the time it had taken her and *Lord Idiot* to walk. Her hands trembled from rage as she grasped the metal handle and twisted sharply. The door to her rooms swung open, and Quinn stepped inside, slamming it behind her.

Risk jumped up from the window seat and looked her over. "What happened?"

"The blood heirs happened."

Risk blinked and slowly started toward her. "What do you mean, 'the blood heirs happened'? They can't be here," Risk paused, looking back to the window behind her. "Are they?" Quinn shook her head, her fists clenching hard enough she might actually be able to crack stone.

"No, not yet." Quinn curled and uncurled her right hand. Wisps of black floated off her skin.

"Then I don't understand—"

"They will be," Quinn interrupted. Her eyes flashed as she looked from the wisps at her fingers to her sister. "Amelia Reinhart sent a letter asking for an audience with Lazarus, and like the fool he is—he accepted because his blasted council deemed it the 'right' answer."

Risk nodded slowly, her expression wary. "You don't agree, I take it."

"No, I don't," Quinn said through clenched teeth. She paced the length of the room and back. The action was doing little to settle the anger inside her; bubbling, seething to get out.

"Why?" Quinn paused. "Why don't you agree?" Risk asked.

"The blood heirs believe they deserve the throne,

and there's a decent portion of Norcasta that agrees. Lazarus knows this, and still he is inviting them into Leone—welcoming them into his house like this is any other noble and not the people that most want to see him dead." Quinn pivoted again, pacing the room once more. Risk seemed to consider her words for a moment.

"Surely they can't be that dangerous," her sister started. "This place is armed with guards at every entrance."

Quinn laughed, and it was a cruel thing.

Risk shuddered.

"Guards?" she asked her sister. "You think they could really prevent an assassination in any way?"

"Well, they're there for a reason—" Quinn held up her hand, not even letting Risk finish that thought. She motioned with her fingers for her sister to follow as she turned for the door.

"Let's take a walk."

The wary expression on Risk's face only deepened as she looked on with distrustful eyes. Still, she followed Quinn out of the room and down the hall.

"Is there a reason for this walk?" she asked as they came to the foyer. Quinn continued on, past the guarded entrance, toward the wall around the palace. "Or are you simply tired of wearing a path into bedroom floors?"

Quinn paused, and Risk followed suit. "Look there," she pointed. Risk did as she said. They both

watched as the guard standing post chatted animatedly with the other. "How difficult do you think it
would be to take them out?"

Risk shifted uneasily. "Not very, but they might be
Maji—"

"Maji?" Quinn repeated, lifting a brow. "You
think any of these pathetic skeevs could be Maji?" At
that, some of the other guards milling about started to
take notice.

Quinn laughed again. Risk grimaced.

"There's no way to really know. . ." her sister
started, eyeing the men distrustfully.

"You're right," Quinn said. "You're completely
correct." Risk blinked, not expecting Quinn to agree
so readily. "That's exactly why the heirs shouldn't be
allowed within the walls of Leone *ever*." Realization
dawned on Risk's features as she pushed her lips
together, but made no move to comment. "Who's to
say how powerful they are? Who's to know if their
guards are Maji?" Quinn turned back to the palace,
glaring at it with vehemence. It wasn't the palace itself
that incurred her wrath, but the pointless rules and
maneuverings that Lazarus was attempting to play
within. As if he were a lesser man. "Certainly not the
council that voted to invite them as guests and not the
traitors that they are." Her last words had been spoken
softly, but a hush settled over the courtyard between
the palace entrance and its wall that sectioned it off
from the rest of the city.

"Quinn, I think we should go back inside. We're starting to draw attention." Risk pulled at her sleeve, and Quinn went completely still, her sister following suit. The beast tamer in her knew when to recognize a threat, and slowly she backed away as Quinn warred to take hold of herself. The dark magic in her veins was humming, striving for a way to break free.

"You should listen to your sister," one of the guards said.

Quinn slowly turned her head. The man in question stepped forward. He wore a gold chest plate, but the cloth had been dyed red. His hair was short and uneven, as if someone had chopped away at it for utility and cared not how it looked. The dirt beneath her boots was the same color as his currently harsh eyes. Quinn noted the golden pommel of the sword hanging at his hip, and the insignia laid into it.

Lazarus' crest.

"Why is that?" she asked, taking a single step forward. Several hands went to their waists at that moment, not even disguising their mistrust.

Quinn was alright by that. She made no attempt to disguise what she was. Not anymore.

The man continued forward. "Because those are mighty big words to come from a woman. Right-hand or not, these soldiers act at the King's behest—just as you."

Quinn took a single sweeping look around the courtyard. What she saw, she found . . . lacking.

She raised a single delicate eyebrow, making that observation known.

"I'm sure you lot do the best you can," Quinn said. He nodded as if finding that amenable, but Quinn continued. "However, a single Maji with enough power could walk right through you. You're well-suited for managing citizens, but a real threat—a true assassination attempt?" Quinn laughed again; the sound as lovely as it was horrible. Risk stepped away, her lips pressed together in a grimace. "Lazarus would be just as well off to leave children at the gates. At least the enemy might have moral conundrums in slaughtering them."

The sound of metal sliding along metal reached her ears, and a full smile bloomed. Quinn looked over at the young guard that had drawn his weapon.

"Do you think you could slay me with that, boy?" she asked, her voice dripping with condescension. The entire courtyard held its breath as she stepped forward, not toward the man with the weapon, but the one that had thought to dismiss her to begin with. "Do you think you could stop me from doing what-ever I wish?" she asked him, still looking at the man only feet from her. The one with the uneven hair and hardened gaze.

Quinn extended her hand, and though she held no weapon the boy with his rushed forward.

A single twist of her palm and snap of her fingers was all it took.

Black wisps they could not see shot forth, rooting the child playing hero where he stood. His weapon clattered to the ground. Quinn grinned.

"Tsk, tsk," she murmured. "I did warn you."

The guard who should have held his tongue walked forward, and Quinn leaned in, blowing a breath of black air in his face. He stumbled and then halted. His eyes went glassy, and his fist uncurled into claws. A sweat dotted his brow as his bottom lip trembled.

Quinn tilted her head to the side and said, "You fear us Maji for what we are. You know deep down that there is nothing you could do in a real invasion. I find it interesting that you fill these boys with hope." His teeth chattered, doing everything he could to stay on his feet. "Instead, you should instill them with fear. Make them cautious. Make them careful. Don't fill their head with false dreams of glory. Their ignorance might mean not just their king's life, but theirs as well."

Quinn reached for her dagger. Not a man stepped forward to stop her, though; not when she dispatched two with such ease. They were learning, or at least that was how Quinn justified it to herself. She turned her hand over and offered the guard the handle.

"Take it," she whispered. Fingers shaking, he reached forward and grasped the leather grip. "Now lift the knife—there—yes, just like." He held it with the tip pointing toward the sky, but not toward her own person. "Now touch the tip to your temple." A cold chill broke across the courtyard as the guard did exactly as she directed him. Tears leaked from the corners of his eyes, but Quinn didn't let up.

The metal touched his skin, and his hand trembled. She knew he feared what she would make him do. They all did.

"Slowly push the blade in."

Blood welled as the edge of the dagger broke skin, and just as she'd told him, he slowly began to push.

"Stop," the voice behind her made Quinn blink. She held up her hand and the man paused. He didn't withdraw, but he didn't keep going. "Stop it. They didn't ask for this."

Quinn turned, leveling Risk with a cool glare. "Ask for this?" she prompted.

"They didn't ask to be toyed with. It's not . . . right."

Quinn lifted both her eyebrows. "Right?" Risk stared back in defiance. "What is right or wrong doesn't matter. It's what will keep all of us alive— what will keep Lazarus alive—that matters."

Risk shifted side to side. "How does torturing them keep anyone alive? You came out here to make a point—which you have," she quickly added. "Now let them go. They realize their folly."

Quinn clenched her jaw. "Lazarus doesn't. Hurting them will—"

"Enrage him," Risk said. "Sister, you know I hold

no love for men, nor do I care for this court or its politics. Please, take the knife and let's go back to our room. You've made your point. He will hear of it."

Quinn teetered on the edge. Part of her wanted to punish them. To show Lazarus what true punishment was. To make him see that he's playing at a position he already held.

But Risk also had a point.

Hurting them would only enrage him. And to what gain?

Quinn cracked her neck and then extended her hand. The guard lowered the knife, hilt first into her waiting palm. "Consider yourselves lucky," she snapped before striding back toward the palace entrance. Risk followed on her heels.

It was only when they got back to their room that her sister finally spoke. "Why did you do that, Quinn?"

Quinn walked toward the window and stared down over the city of Leone.

"They do not respect me, and they never will. I am a woman in a man's world. Something I was reminded of today." Quinn looked over her shoulder, back at her sister. Risk was still not great at hiding her emotions, and the troubled expression on her face said much. "Lazarus doesn't listen when I behave, perhaps reminding him of what I am will do the trick."

Check

"Wild dogs cannot be tamed; just as wild women cannot be caged."
— *Lazarus Fierté, soul eater, the frustrated King of Norcasta*

"She's a menace. My men were made a mockery of in that courtyard today. You must do something about her. Whether she is your vassal or not, as King, you have a duty to—"

"That is enough!" Lazarus snapped, lifting his voice sharply.

Captain Barbaro stilled, his angered face lessening in its redness. His eyes went to the floor as Lazarus fixed him with a particularly cruel look. "You will not lecture me what I am and what I should do. Is that clear, *Captain* Barbaro?" Lazarus emphasized his title, reminding the little, insignificant man what his role was here in the palace and how easily he could be removed from it.

"Yes, Your Grace," the man said as he went to his knee—the formal greeting of a high-ranking military soldier to his King—one he had forgotten when he had first come barreling into Lazarus' throne room, ranting and raving about Quinn's behavior. "Forgive my insolence."

Lazarus sat back against his iron seat, taking a breath to dispel the frustration that was currently building within him. "I understand you're upset, Captain Barbaro," Lazarus said, "and I will ensure that my right-hand is dealt with accordingly. I have already dispatched a servant to retrieve her and bring her to me."

The Captain's head snapped up. "She's coming? Here? Now?" The man did not look so happy. In fact, he appeared very much like a frightened fish, ready to swim away at a moment's notice. Lazarus released another breath and reached up, rubbing the bridge of his nose with two of his fingers.

"This would be the place that I have requested her to meet me, yes," he said. "Is there a problem with that, Captain?"

"N-no, of course not, Your Grace. I apologize for my rude behavior earlier. I'm sure you know how best to deal with your vassal. Thank you for—"

He was interrupted by the sound of the twin

doors opening behind him. He stiffened, realizing just who was behind him. Lazarus fought off the smirk forming on his face. The man may be respected by the palace guards, but he would have no chance against a creature such as Quinn. Something that he obviously knew, given away by the paling of his skin.

Draeven came to his rescue. "His Grace will speak with you later, Captain Barbaro. You are dismissed."

He nodded and quickly got up from his position on the floor. Lazarus watched as the man realized that to get out of the room, he would have to walk by the very woman he had been scorning just moments ago . . . and that Quinn was no fool. She knew exactly what he'd been doing. She lifted her chin as she followed behind Lorraine, and when she and the Captain passed each other, while the man's head went down another notch and his legs sped up, she merely lengthened her stride and smiled, acting as though she were on her way for a leisurely stroll through the gardens.

Closing his eyes, a dull pounding began to start up behind his eyelids. Lazarus took a moment to collect himself before reopening them and settling the woman who so loved to torment him with a cold glare. Even as he kept his gaze to Quinn, however, he spoke to Lorraine. "Thank you, Lorraine, you may go now. I appreciate you running that errand for me."

Lorraine smiled under the praise and curtsied politely. "It's always a pleasure, Your Grace."

With that, Lorraine turned and headed back the

way she came. Lazarus didn't speak again until the doors had closed behind her. "You know why you're here," was all he said.

"Of course," she replied.

They looked at each other—Lazarus with a deeply rooted frustration and perhaps a small measure of amusement, and Quinn with a wicked grin fixed upon her face. Draeven was the first to break the silence.

"What happened in the courtyard with the guards cannot happen again," he stated flat out.

It took a while for Quinn to shift her gaze from Lazarus to Draeven. When she did, however, the grin on her lips only intensified. "It's not my fault they're weak and needed me to prove it to them," she said.

"You were going to make one of the guards stab himself in the head," Draeven said.

She shrugged. "I can assure you; he probably would have been much more useful after I was done."

"As what?" Draeven said, shocked, "A pin cushion?" He shook his head. "The only reason you stopped at all was because Risk was there with you."

Quinn's eyes hardened, and her lips fell into a flat line. Lazarus watched on with curiosity. "And just how would you know that, Draeven?"

"Because I'm not an idiot," Draeven replied blandly. "When they said that a woman with you—one with *horns*—stopped you, who else would it be?"

"You're not an idiot?" Quinn laughed, the sound sharp and biting. "You could have fooled me earlier."

"Is that what this was about?" Draeven asked. "You were angry about what happened in the council meeting."

"I'm not angry, Draeven," Quinn replied, her voice calm. "I'm furious."

"Why? Because you didn't get your way?" Draeven snapped. "This is a kingdom, Quinn, and you are in the King's palace. You have a duty to Lazarus—"

"My duty is to keep him safe, and it seems as though I'm the only one who is actually working to do so," Quinn interrupted him.

Draeven shook his head. "You are out of control. There are rules here. Laws that we must abide by."

"Who cares about rules?" Quinn spread her arms wide. "Lazarus *is* the law, Draeven. He doesn't have to care what anyone says or thinks. Certainly not those pathetic lords."

"It is your kind of thinking that will get him killed," Draeven argued.

That dull thudding behind his eyes was beginning to grow into a steady roar, Lazarus noted with displeasure as he finally decided it was time for him to step in. "Enough with the squabbling," he snapped, halting the both of them and drawing their attentions. "You are acting like children."

"And you are acting a fool," Quinn shot back

immediately. She took a step toward the throne, her stance strong and ready. He could feel she was brewing for a fight.

It had not gone unnoticed that she had—once again—called him a fool. It seemed to be the insult she loved to throw his way, and he would not have it. Without looking at Draeven, Lazarus let his voice drop low. "Leave us," he commanded.

Draeven may have hesitated a moment, but sensing Lazarus' precarious emotions, he nodded once and then took his leave, striding down the steps of the throne and passing Quinn on his way out. Lazarus did not wait for the doors to close as he rose to his full height, forcing Quinn to crane her neck back to keep her gaze glued to his own.

By the time he descended the steps, Draeven was nothing more than a whispered memory in the room. "What have I said about calling me that?" he asked casually, as if he were asking for nothing more than the time of day.

Quinn straightened her shoulders. "I do not listen to fools," she replied coldly. "When you are not acting like one, I will not call you that."

"I am King," he reminded her.

"Which only makes your foolishness more disturbing," she said.

"If you are to remain here as my right-hand, you need to be more inconspicuous," he warned. "Making an enemy of the soldiers who watch the palace is not wise. While powerful, you can't be everywhere or alert at every moment. If I am a fool, then so are you."

Quinn froze, her muscles bunching as though she wanted to punch something, but Lazarus had her backed into a metaphorical corner. He knew it, and so did she. He stopped in front of her, waiting for her reply.

"Draeven would have you cater to those around you," she said through clenched teeth as her fists tightened at her sides.

"Draeven has his points," Lazarus said.

She shook her head vehemently. "If you are King, then they should cater to you. Not the other way around, Lazarus. You are the ruler here, are you not? Tell me, am I your right-hand, or theirs?"

She pointed at the hall behind her, and Lazarus drank in the violence in her eyes. He listened to the sweet music of her words. All the while, a war raged within him. On one side, Draeven's voice whispered in his ear of keeping the peace, of giving a little to receive much more. And on the other side . . . Lazarus could not dispute that he preferred Quinn's way of thinking. Though he understood the political way of the world—it was not his nature to cater to others; to appease them as if they were worth more than the dirt beneath his shoes. Few people were.

Quinn was one. And as she stood before him, urging him, fighting with him as she was, he couldn't help but stop and admire her.

"You are right," he finally said. "I am the ruler, and you are my right-hand, which is why you will respect my decision. Draeven is right. What happened in the courtyard today is not to happen again, do you understand?"

Quinn gritted her teeth. "I will make no such promise."

"Quinn," he growled out her name, but before he could truly say anything more, there was a heavy knock upon the door. His head lifted over her shoulder as she pivoted.

Who dared to interrupt them?

"Your Grace, Lord Callis wishes an audience with you," the guard outside announced.

"Send him in," Quinn called. Word must have spread of her run-in with the other guards, for the man opened the door before Lazarus could form his own reply.

Glancing down sharply at the wicked demon in front of him, he stared at her neck with a fiery ire, wanting nothing more in that moment than to wring her little neck.

"Your Grace; Quinn," Lord Callis said in greeting, drawing his reluctant attention up as the other man hurried through the throne room. "How splendid that both of you are here. I came on behalf of my earlier offer. I was hoping I could entice the two of you to come visit my estate outside of Leone for another hunt. Tomorrow, perhaps? Or the next day if it's more convenient."

Quinn took a step forward—a step away from Lazarus—a smile on her face as she welcomed the man. "That sounds wonderful, Artan," she said in a blithely ignorant voice meant to lure Callis in.

Lazarus scowled.

"So, you will?" Lord Callis stopped before Quinn, taking her hands in his. "I would so love to show you my estate."

"His Grace and I would be glad to take you up on your kind invitation," she replied happily, shooting a conniving look at Lazarus as he seethed in his silent fury.

"Excellent." Lord Callis looked up to Lazarus. The smile slowly faded, and he released Quinn's hands at once, but the trifling twit didn't have the sense to realize that he should take back his invitation as well. Instead, he backed away nonchalantly toward the door. "Oh, I do apologize. Were you in a meeting? I assumed when they opened the doors that I was allowed to enter."

"It was nothing." Quinn laughed softly, waving the man's legitimate concerns away. "We were just finishing up. You came at the perfect time."

He could not kill her, Lazarus reminded himself. She had more than four years left of their contract to serve. Granted, he could kill her and nothing bad would happen to him, but . . .

Lazarus shook his head and realized that the two of them—Quinn and Lord Callis—had moved away. Quinn was leading the man out of the throne room as though she had already been dismissed from his presence. Shock ricocheted through him. The vile little maruda.

Just before she disappeared with Lord Callis through the twin doors, Quinn turned and settled him with a particularly calculating smile. Her mouth opened, and Lazarus narrowed his eyes as he read the silent word that formed around her lips.

"Check."

Lord Sunshine

"Sometimes those who understand us the greatest come from the most unlikely of places. After all, it is not where we have been, but who we are that matters."
— *Draeven Adelmar, rage thief, left-hand to the King of Norcasta*

He raised his hand to the door and rapped his knuckles twice.

A shifting on the other side told him she was there. The lock clicked and the handle turned before the wooden door swung open. Draeven stepped back.

Standing in men's clothing with Quinn's purple scaled basilisk was Risk. The slight girl lifted her head and brushed a stray silver lock from her face. Her eyes narrowed in distrust, but she didn't slam the door on him. That, at least, was a win.

"I've come to take you to your trainer. Quinn mentioned she'd let you know that I was overseeing it.
. ." His voice trailed off as the snake lifted its serpentine head and hissed. The girl lifted her hand and caressed the creature without a care. Draven's jaw tightened, but he resisted the urge to back away in fear—instead fixing the creature with a glare of defiance.

"She told me," was all the girl said. She stepped into the hall and closed the door shut behind her. It took all his will power to not react to the beast curled around her small frame. Of course Quinn would leave the damned basilisk with her.

He wondered if it were just to mess with him. After their argument yesterday, he didn't doubt it. She was cruel.

"Very well," Draeven said. He started to motion for her to go ahead of him, but then thought better. Stepping forward, he started down the hall. Risk walked beside him, albeit keeping five feet of distance between them.

"My sister doesn't like you much, does she?" Risk asked, never losing pace. He almost stumbled over his own feet, surprised that she was even speaking with him. Draeven glanced sideways and her open-expression almost immediately shut down.

"Sometimes. We don't see eye-to-eye on many

things, and for Quinn that can be a deal breaker on whether she respects you much at all. Why do you ask?" He worked to keep his tone conversational, and the suspicion in her eyes lessoned.

"She told me your name is Lord Sunshine," Risk answered. He choked, masking it as a cough. "I'm not very well versed in who is who around here, but I had a feeling that wasn't the truth." He turned the hall, leading them out into the courtyard. Several of the guards took notice, and her posture became more guarded, not able to tell the difference between curiosity and what she assumed was hostility. *Or perhaps,* it occurred to him, *the reason matters not. Their attention in itself is too much.*

"Lord Sunshine is what Quinn likes to call me when she thinks I'm too cheerful or optimistic. Lord Idiot is the less kind name she reverts to when she's angry, so if she's still using sunshine, I can't imagine I've crossed her too badly." A laugh, like the peal of windchimes, drifted through the air for too short a moment. He glanced over again, and this time Risk was grinning, although she tried to hide it.

"Well, she's used both a decent bit, truth be told," Risk said. "She's quite angry about the decision to allow the blood heirs into Leone. Her show in the courtyard was to get the King's attention." Her jaw clicked shut, as if she only just realized who she was talking about. That perhaps she said something she thought she shouldn't have.

"I'm aware," Draeven said, turning off the path to walk toward some of the only foliage you'd find in all Leone. He pushed the palm frond to the side. "Do you know what it means to be a hammer?" he asked her, careful not to look her way too much or trail behind. Though she eyed him with wariness, she continued walking through the plants as well.

"Everything is a nail?" she replied.

"Precisely," Draeven replied, pleased that she'd picked it up that quickly, though he couldn't understand why. "Quinn is a hammer, and to her, every problem is a nail."

"She doesn't understand the need to keep the peace because she herself doesn't understand peace. Only war . . ." Her words trailed off as they entered the gardens. It was the most secluded part of the palace. There they wouldn't be interrupted by prying eyes or chatty servants. In the center, sitting upon a flat rock, was the man that would be her teacher.

Risk tilted her head in a way that was eerily like the woman they spoke of. With sunlight filtering through the leaves, illuminating the thoughtful—instead of calculating—expression on her face, Risk Darkova was nothing like her sister.

No, in that single moment, Draeven thought that even with the horns and gray-tinted skin, she was quite possibly one of the most beautiful things he'd ever seen.

She continued walking, and he jerked, blinking

twice. The movement snapped him from his reverie, and Draeven followed, careful not to be too close behind her.

"Hello . . ." Risk began, looking back at Draeven and then to the withered old man atop the rock. He sat with his leg crossed, one bare foot poised on his knee. He wore a simple set of brown robes and stared out with unseeing eyes. Beside him, a baboon that had never grown to its full size sat atop a tortoise that rivaled the size of some sea turtles from the western coast of Bangratas.

"Take a seat, child." Haspati spoke with a deep thrum that resonated in Draeven. The accent of his childhood; of smoked peppers and mulled wine, of late nights in the humid summer pushing his body past its limits. It was the voice of the man that helped bring him out of his first rage. The voice of patience beyond any soul he'd ever known.

Risk settled on the flat rock across from him, her knees locked together and back straight. Draeven walked around the side, standing off to where she could see him easily. She relaxed slightly.

"I was told you're going to help me master my magic," she began in a voice that didn't betray what her face showed she was feeling. It amazed him how different she and Quinn were. While they shared a lineage, dark gifts, and the same facial structure, that was where the similarities stopped.

"In due time," the ancient beast tamer replied.

She blinked, her face falling as she looked from the blind man across from her to Draeven. He shrugged, hoping that his suspicion about her was right.

"Alright," she drawled. "What do you want me to do first?"

The old man cracked a grin, and her face completely blanched. "Settle in and sit still. Focus on the world around you." She did as he asked, or at least tried to. Every time her razor-sharp focus started to drift, she snapped back to attention. "Are you doing it?" he asked her in a way that implied he knew she was not.

Risk let out a huff. "I'm working on it."

"Very well," Haspati told her. They lapsed into a comfortable silence for the following hour, upon which Risk never asked what to do next. Draeven only knew how much time had passed from the sundial in the garden. That and his own memories of his old friend's teachings.

When Risk finally managed to relax into the world around her for more than a minute, the old hermit said, "Tell me, what do you feel?"

"I feel . . . " she paused, grasping for words. "I feel the wind in my hair and the sun on my skin. I feel Neiss lying over my shoulders." Draeven frowned. He hadn't known that Quinn named the thing. Neiss, no less. He wondered what the god of fear thought of that, but then shook his head, suspecting that if the gods were indeed real, he'd probably be pleased.

Draeven continued listening as Risk's answers became far more particular. "I feel the distending of claws in my fingers, and the heaviness of wings between my shoulders. My skin prickles like it's going to grow fur and—" She stopped abruptly. Just as in the courtyard earlier, she blinked and paused as if realizing what she was saying. The old man simply smiled.

"What you are feeling is magic. It's in the air. In yourself. It's all around us. Few beings have the ability to harness and control it, but you—you feel it inside." Risk's brows drew together as she eyed the man across from her.

"I'm a beast tamer. Of course I feel it inside."

"When you feel it—do you associate the touch of that magic with any emotion?" Haspati asked her. Risk opened her mouth and started to form a dismissal when her eyes landed on him. Draeven quirked an eyebrow and gave her an encouraging smile.

"Panic," she murmured so softly he barely heard it.

"Ah," Haspati said in a tone equal parts understanding as it was frustrating to him when he was in her position. She looked as if she felt the same. "I see."

"Well, I don't," she snapped. "I thought you were going to help me learn how to control my magic, not have me sit here for an hour just to tell me what I already know." Her eyes narrowed as he started laughing, revealing a row of perfectly white teeth despite his age. Not even fifteen-year-old Axe could boast that. They stood out stark against his brown skin.

"Tell me, when you panic, does the magic within you react?"

"Yes," she answered, almost begrudgingly.

"And if you don't panic, can you access it then?"

She narrowed her eyes at him, leaning forward. "Why would I want to do that?"

Draeven wanted to turn and sigh, but he knew this was neither the place nor the time for that. He understood all too well what she was dealing with, and it relieved him that his gut choice on instructor had been right.

"Child, how do you think you'll ever learn to control magic without practicing? A painter does not wake up one day and become a master. A blacksmith does not work in the forge once a moon and expect to create a masterpiece worthy of kings." Her eyes glowed blue for a moment as she stared at the old man. There was a fierceness in her features that hadn't been there before, and he suspected he was seeing the other side to Risk. The darker one, still wavering where it belonged.

"If it was as simple as practicing, why would I need you?" she asked him in a tone reminiscent of a certain fear twister.

Without so much as a twitch, the baboon leapt off

the tortoise's back like it meant to strike her. Risk jumped back, landing squatted but on her toes. Neiss perked up but didn't strike. Claws, deadly and as sharp as knives, grew from her fingers. The skin of her face changed, taking on the glint of scales.

"Stop the magic," Haspati said.

She looked at him as if he'd grown a third eye.

"It's not that simple," she hissed.

He smiled. "Focus on the world around you. What do you feel?"

She eyed the baboon skeptically, but did as he said. Her eyes fell closed, and within minutes the tension had drained, though interestingly, the magic had not.

"I feel the weight of my claws and the itch of scales across my flesh. I feel the blood pounding in my ears as magic hums through me. I feel . . . alive." She grimaced with her eyes closed, as if unsettled by the statement. Draeven scrubbed a hand down his jaw, watching her intently.

"Calm the magic as you would an animal."

Her brows puckered and sweat dotted her forehead as she squeezed her eyes shut. She breathed low even breaths, and after several minutes, the claws slipped back beneath the skin as if they were never there. The scales on her face faded into smooth, unblemished skin. Risk blinked down at her hands, lifting them to examine.

She looked between them and her trainer, a begrudging respect in her gaze.

"How did you know that would work?" she asked him.

"I didn't," he shrugged. "Much of teaching young Maji is learning as they do." Haspati chuckled to himself, and the baboon followed suit, making her roll her eyes.

"But you're a beast tamer," she said. "Shouldn't you know how it works?"

He reached up and scratched his chin. "A beast tamer can be a Maji, but not all Maji are made the same."

"That makes no sense," she grumbled, kicking her legs forward to slump onto the rock. She leaned back on her bare palms, her chest rising and falling in exertion.

"Not much does in this world," he said. "You are a beast tamer, but you are also other. There is much to learn in that. Much to see." She squinted at him, her lips pressing together like she wasn't quite sure about that. Draeven didn't disagree.

"You can't see," she pointed out. Many might think it rude to point out the obvious, but her inflection was that of confusion.

"Perhaps not with my eyes," he nodded. "But I can with theirs." He motioned to the baboon and the tortoise. She turned, regarding the two creatures with renewed interest. "You will learn when you find your familiar."

"How do you know that Neiss is not mine?" she asked.

Clever, Draeven thought. *She's clever, but not cruel.*

"The basilisk is bonded to another." Risk glanced back to Draeven, as if questioning how much he told the old man. He shrugged. In truth, he'd told Haspati very little about the girl he'd be training. The man had a way of figuring it out all on his own. "You've also not yet reached your ascension. Your familiar will make itself known then."

Risk blew out a breath and tucked a stray lock of silver hair back in her braid. "What's an ascension?"

Draeven's lips parted. She was even more clueless than Quinn had been in that regard, but at least she wasn't a dark Maji. Not really. Like him, she landed somewhere in the gray.

"It's different for every Maji," Haspati said. "Yours will be unlike mine, which was unlike our young lord, which was unlike numerous others. The ascension in itself is the gods testing your strength—to see if you're ready and able to hold the full might of the power gifted to you. Your time is not yet for a while, though."

Risk opened her mouth to ask another question, but Draeven chose that moment to step forward and interrupt. "I have business on behalf of our king this afternoon. Why don't we pick this up again tomorrow, shall we?"

Risk glanced up, her blue eyes as endless as the ocean as she peered up at him. She wasn't thrilled, he could tell, but she was also letting it go.

"Alright," she said, getting to her feet. Risk nodded, almost awkwardly. Whereas Quinn knew every proper response and chose to dismiss them as beneath her, the girl before him seemed to be at a loss most of the time. He supposed after the life she's lived, at least what snippets of it that he'd heard, he probably would be as well were he in her shoes.

"Until next time, old friend," he called over his shoulder. Haspati merely smiled and started humming to himself.

They turned and went back the same way they'd come, crossing through the courtyard. One of the guards saw her and started forward, despite the shake of Draeven's head.

"Excuse me, my lady," the man said. Draeven didn't know him by name, but he could only guess what this was about based on his tone. Not that Risk noticed. She froze up, taking several steps back.

"W-what?" she asked. Draeven wanted to run a hand over his face and laugh all at the same time, but he did neither.

"We wanted to say thank you for the other day," he said sincerely. "For stopping her."

Risk's lips parted, and she blinked. "Oh, it was nothing—"

"You saved at least one man's life. That's not nothing."

She pressed her lips together, staring at him, but not seeming to have words. Draeven touched the guard on the arm and nodded. The man stepped back, and turned to go back to work. Risk watched him the entire way, and then they continued onward in silence.

It was only when they reached her door that she finally looked at him and said in a whoosh of breath, "If your name is not Lord Sunshine, what is it?"

He smiled. "Draeven. You can call me Draeven."

She nodded once, and though there was shyness in the movement, things were easier than they'd been before. Slowly, she was getting used to him. Risk reached for the knob and whispered, "See you tomorrow."

Draeven opened his mouth to reply, but the door was already closing shut.

Ignoring the clench in his chest, he smiled and walked away.

Courting Darkness

"Idiots have a habit of dying from their own foolish actions, but still, far too many inhabit the world of the living."
— *Lazarus Fierté, soul eater, King of Norcasta*

The carriage rattled over the uneven terrain as Lazarus sat straight-backed with his arm folded across his chest and a dark shadow cast over his face. Quinn merely swung her legs with a small smile twisting at the corners of her mouth, unaware—or more likely, uncaring—of his displeasure.

Check, indeed, he thought with restrained ire. He had intended to take Lord Callis up on his invitation to visit him at his estate—alone. Without a certain thorn in his side there to tempt him away from more immediate matters that required his concern. Lazarus grit his teeth as the man's large countryside mansion came into view just outside the carriage window.

"When we arrive, you would do well to keep your temper in check," he said, speaking for the first time since he'd arrived to find her already prepared and ready for the half a day's travel.

She turned to him, lifting one elegant brow. "Am I the one who really needs to keep an eye on my temper?" she inquired.

Narrowing his eyes at her impetuousness, he replied, "Lord Callis is important, Quinn. He is not to be used as a pawn during one of your tantrums. I know you are still upset over the impending arrival of the blood heirs, but you will come to understand my decision. And if you don't, then that's unfortunate. I am King, as you so eloquently put it yesterday, and you are my vassal. You serve me. Not the other way around."

Quinn's small smile stretched and blossomed into a darker version of itself. She leaned forward, and in the small space provided by the cramped quarters of the carriage, her hands landed on either side of his thighs. She flicked a strand of hair from her chest, her pale breasts pushed up by the tightness of her leather top.

"I live to serve, Your Grace," she bit out. Perhaps she meant for him to be reminded of the last time she'd been under him so readily, serving him in a manner that made him feel more powerful than a mere king. With her lips wrapped around his shaft, he hadn't felt like a king. Oh no. He'd felt like a god. But her current condescension was yet another puncture in his otherwise pristine reserve. A lesser man would have none of the fortitude it took to handle Quinn on a daily basis.

Lazarus tilted his head so that he looked down his nose at her, mimicking her haughty tone—if only to irritate her—he replied, "See that you do."

She sat back up, that smile dimming a small fraction, changing into one of anticipation as she too looked out the window and saw the building they were nearing. The tall arching structures—twin towers on the far east and west wings of the mansion bore the flag of the Callis clan. The crossing of two staffs, one made of ornate gold and the other of a solid wood over a shield bearing the crest of Claudius' reign. Lazarus narrowed his eyes. Unsuspecting eyes would think nothing of it, but Lazarus knew what that crest meant. Lord Callis—or his family at least—still backed the blood heirs. Hopefully, his continued visits would change that.

Lord Callis himself was not a loyal man. He was conniving, greedy. A glutton for self-satisfaction. Though Lazarus kept his face turned to the window, his eyes slid to the side. Uncertainty assaulted him. Perhaps he had been a fool to have allowed this. From the information Dominicus had gleaned upon his many observations of Lord Callis, the man had . . .

particular appetites that would, no doubt, prove disagreeable in Quinn's eyes. He could only hope that she would heed his warning to keep herself in check while they were here.

His lips twisted as the carriage passed through the mansion gates and rounded to the front entryway where Lord Callis stood with his steward, awaiting their arrival. The carriage came to a grinding halt, and before Lazarus could reach for the door, Quinn beat him to it.

Tossing the door open and stepping down, she looked up at the mansion before fixing her gaze on the man hurrying down the stairs toward them. Lazarus scowled as he followed after Quinn, leaving the carriage door hanging ajar as his long legs ate up the distance.

"Quinn," Lord Callis took Quinn's hand and bent over it, pressing a chaste kiss to the back of her knuckles. "It's lovely to have you here. Welcome." Lazarus stopped just behind her, and Lord Callis tilted his head back with a small smile. "Your Grace, welcome to my home. I hope you'll find your overnight accommodations comfortable." He released Quinn and bowed.

"I want Quinn placed in a room near mine," he said. Quinn cast him a look that spoke volumes; one intending to provoke him, but he would not rise to her challenge.

"Oh, I had her placed in the east wing, near my

own chambers—for in the event she needed anything. The west wing, however, has beautiful decor and a wonderful view of the forest toward the back of my property. I thought you would enjoy the wild imagery," Lord Callis said quickly.

With a cruel smile of his own, Lazarus shook his head. "I'm afraid you'll find that Quinn enjoys wildness far more than myself. Perhaps she would be more comfortable there."

"I'll be comfortable anywhere, Artan," Quinn said. "Please don't concern yourself with my comfort."

Lord Callis' lips pursed in displeasure as he took in Lazarus' expression. "Well, perhaps my steward can find a suitable room somewhere else in the east wing and have it aired out," he finally conceded, nodding to the older man at his side.

Interesting, Lazarus thought. He was so unwilling to have Quinn far. The man was infatuated with his little fear twister. It was unfortunate, then, that if the man so much as touched Quinn in the ways he no doubt wanted to, Lazarus would severe his arms from his body.

"I've had a late luncheon prepared. Shall we adjourn to the dining room for our meal?" he asked, nodding to the open front doors as he held his arm out for Quinn to take.

Without hesitation, she did, moving with a grace that befit a battlefield more so than a noble's dining chamber. Lazarus trailed behind the two of them, fantasizing about when he could take her alone into a room and deliver a series of blows upon her backside that would no doubt do nothing for her temper, but would at least assuage a miniscule amount of his frustration. Barbarian that he was, he enjoyed the idea of her bending before him once more.

Callis' dining room was the picture of elegance and dignified heritage. Murals decorated the walls on either side of the long table. One of them depicting a man in ceremonial robes, bowing before the pillars of the gods; statues representing the council of divine beings that had created this world and the next. Turning his head, he took in the second mural, which showcased a brilliant shining white knight riding into battle with a horde of soldiers at his back and a fierce dragon at his front, breathing fire down upon them. Lazarus' mouth curled in amusement. If asked which he pictured himself, he would say that while knights were noble and respected——he was more akin to the dragon.

"What do you think, Your Grace?" Callis asked as he sat himself at the head of the table with Quinn taking her seat on the right. Lazarus waited for a servant to pull out his own chair and sat as he nodded to the murals on the wall.

"Beautifully crafted," he replied.

Callis, obviously pleased, nodded. "Yes, I thought

so too. I had the one on the left commissioned with an artist that hailed from Jibreal."

"And the other?" Lazarus inquired as a line of servants appeared, carrying trays leaden down with a feast that was far too much for the three of them. Lazarus did not comment. Luxury and overindulgence was something he knew the nobles of any region were well versed in.

"I don't know actually," Lord Callis looked up at the picture of the knight and dragon. "It was found in a centuries-old toppled temple, and it has been in my family for many generations. I was told by my father and his father before him that it was a gift from one of the Reinhart kings of generations past."

"Hmmmm," Lazarus hummed, a non-reply as the coverings were removed from the platters of food and they began their meal. Small talk filtered through the dining room as Callis tried hard to win Quinn's affection. Lazarus watched the two of them with a combination of annoyance and indifference, fighting for the latter, though the previous continued to crop up.

"That was a lovely meal," Quinn said, wiping down the corners of her mouth as the food was carted away, more than half of it still on the plates.

Lazarus slid his eyes to Callis. "When shall we take to the forest for our hunt?" he asked.

"Oh, the hunt is already prepared," Callis said, standing and gesturing for the door. "Let me take you outside. Normally, I wouldn't suggest hunting after a particularly filling meal such as that one." He paused and patted his stomach with a satisfied smirk on his face. "But I've had my hunt master prepare something more enjoyable for us."

Quinn frowned, but didn't say anything as she followed behind. Lazarus kept his eyes trained on the back of the man's head as he led them both outside to a veranda that looked out over the long stretch of land that made up Lord Callis' estate. Just beyond the flattened grassy plain, a wall of trees awaited.

Callis led both of them down the side stairs and out where one man—the hunt master, Lazarus presumed—stood with his grip on a young boy. Lazarus sensed the moment Quinn realized what was happening. His arm snapped out, his fingers closing over her forearm as she strained. Callis, unrealizing, tramped onward, leaving them several paces back, his smile still in place. The fool.

The complete and utter idiot.

Lazarus cursed under his breath even as Quinn spoke up. "What is this?" she demanded, gesturing to the obvious slave—a young sandy-haired boy with big eyes and hair shorn so close to his scalp that there were obvious nicks and cuts where the blade had cut too close.

Callis paused and turned back, shock on his face at the clear vehemence in her tone. "It's a slave hunt," he replied nonchalantly. "I find it somewhat more challenging than hunting animals. Slaves have some brain power and can think for themselves. A bit harder to kill, perhaps—" The slave boy's eyes widened, and he began shaking as tears welled within the depths of his gaze. "But that's why I had a boy brought out and not one of the men or women. Adolescents are a little easier, and I didn't want you to be dissuaded by difficult prey."

"Quinn . . ." Lazarus warned, tightening his grip upon her arm. Her muscles tensed, and her veins began to darken and turn black.

"He's human," was all Quinn said, the quiet in her voice an ominous warning.

Callis laughed. "That's debatable, but I suppose if you want to be technical. Yes, the slave is human."

"You've hunted slaves before?" The uncanny stillness of her form gave away what Lord Callis was too foolish to see.

"Not as much as I wish, but. . ." the idiot prattled on, unaware of the violence he was feeding. Lazarus could feel it, though. He turned, quickly cutting off the man as he stepped in front of Quinn.

"Go inside," he ordered. Quinn didn't move. She didn't even appear to hear him. "*Quinn.* Go inside, *now*," he repeated.

"I want to kill him," she whispered, too low for Callis to hear, though the man was watching them with confusion.

Lazarus shook his head. "I will deal with him. Go inside."

"The boy—" she started.

"Take him," Lazarus said quickly. It would give her a reason to stay away. She wasn't the maternal sort, but she understood the child in a way no one else in the vicinity could.

"Excuse me, what seems to be the problem?" Callis approached, and Lazarus felt Quinn tense. She bared her teeth—not that the foolish Lord could see with Lazarus blocking him. Black wisps slipped from her fingertips and lifted, tickling Lazarus' senses. The souls within him stirred for her.

Lifting a calloused hand, Lazarus gripped Quinn around the throat, turning her attention back to him —at least somewhat marginally. She was so focused on Lord Callis that she hardly reacted to his rough handling. That concerned him. Ordinarily she would have griped or pushed or done anything she pleased to either force him to unhand her or push him closer.

Quinn did neither. Her blue eyes reflecting wisps of darkness through them like shattered glass.

Lazarus tightened his hold.

"*Take the boy*," he enunciated each word clearly as he leaned down next to her ear. "And go inside. Once you've seen him fed and back with the servants, find someone to take you to your room and remain there until I come for you."

"Your Grace?" Lord Callis was almost upon them. "Quinn?"

Lazarus released her, and they moved in sync,

Quinn sliding past them as he turned and blocked Lord Callis once more. Lord Callis noted Lazarus' frown and then glanced back as she went to the hunt master, snatching the boy from his grip and storming away. The child cried out, terror clear on his face, and Quinn paused, bending briefly to say something to him that neither he nor Lord Callis could hear. The boy nodded, confused, but allowed himself to be lead away as Lord Callis turned to Lazarus.

"What's the meaning of this?" he asked.

"Quinn does not hunt slaves," Lazarus said. "In fact, you should be aware that slave hunting will become illegal the very moment I return to the palace on the morrow and have a seal placed in my hand."

"What?" Shocked, Lord Callis stared at him as though he'd lost his mind. The man had no clue how very close to losing his life he'd come.

"Quinn's past is a private matter, but she does not condone the use or possession of slaves. You will refrain from discussing the matter with her. Is that understood?" Lazarus spoke with authority, unable to stop a small amount of malevolent intent from entering his tone.

"Your Grace . . ." Lord Callis looked at him curiously. "You don't mean to outlaw slavery in Norcasta, do you? These actions are not the actions of a man who wants to keep from . . . inciting a series of riotous events in the country." Lazarus eyed him coldly at the underhanded remark. The southern lord's intent was quite clear. "Slavery is an age-old means of servitude. It has been around for centuries. To rid the country of such a trade—it would devastate the economy and no doubt turn many noblemen against you."

Lazarus didn't care for slavery one way or the other, but this rule had little to do with him. In his mind, everything was merely a means to an end, and though he hadn't considered it before, he knew that were he to outlaw the practice of slavery, it would strengthen Quinn's loyalty all the more. Perhaps even cut the outbursts down against his own house; something he very much needed with her back in the country. However, he needed to reply to Callis' indications very carefully. He hadn't yet made any decisions, but he needed to make his point as crystal clear as possible, lest the idiot unintentionally give Quinn yet more cause to come for him. He still needed the man, much as his mere presence was beginning to be a problem. Lifting his head and glaring down at the lord before him, Lazarus folded his arms over his chest.

"Lord Callis, you misunderstand me," he said. "I have not outlawed the practice, nor the trading of slaves," he paused, letting the unspoken *yet* hang in the air before continuing. "But it would behoove you and your health were you not to speak of it in Quinn's presence. Do you understand?"

Lord Callis took a step back, cold dissatisfaction making its way into his expression. "As you wish, Your Grace," he said.

Lazarus let his glare stretch between them for a moment more before he turned and strode back to the mansion. He glanced above, noting the stretch of the afternoon sky. Though it wouldn't have been too late for a short hunt in the nearby woods, it was far too late to try and head back to the palace. Darkness would soon fall, but the moment dawn broke, he and Quinn would be well on their way back. He needed to get her as far from Lord Callis and the man's slaves as quickly as possible.

In Cold Blood

"The vermin of the world should be extinguished. It is the only way humanity can thrive."
— *Quinn Darkova, fear twister, right-hand to the King of Norcasta*

Q uinn paced across the room she'd been shown to after she'd taken care of the slave child. Hours had passed since she'd nearly lost her mind and killed Lord Callis on the back lawn of his estate. She paused at the four-poster bed, one hand going to the elaborately carved footboard. Her fingers curled into the wood, nails digging in until she felt her own blood run wet against her fingers.

Hatred, vile and cruel, filtered into her thoughts.

She had thought Lord Callis cruel. She knew he enjoyed pain. But this . . . this was much worse. He wasn't simply a man taking whatever pleasures he sought in life, twisted or not. He was a slave owner. A slave *killer*.

The footboard beneath her grip groaned and cracked with her strength as a fissure worked its way up from the bottom. If she held on any longer, she'd break the two-inch-thick wood in half. Quinn would have much preferred Lord Callis' throat to be in her grip.

Damn Lazarus, she thought. She'd been nearly out of her head with rage, on the brink of murder. She regretted it now, not killing the Lord. She could easily find him. She considered it as she turned toward the room. He would have no clue. She could sneak into his bed and should he awake, he would welcome her with open arms. He'd made his thoughts on Quinn's presence in his chambers quite clear. She'd slide between the sheets, pin him to the mattress, and watch with a smile as the life drained from his eyes as she'd slide a blade right into his heart.

Quinn shuddered with desire. How she wished to make that dream a reality. Lazarus, however, would have her head. She shook the image she'd built of the kill from her mind.

Outside, darkness had fallen. She moved to the window, thinking back on what Lazarus had come by to tell her after leaving Lord Callis. They would leave at first light. He'd also told her that upon his return to the palace, the hunting of slaves would be banned. It wasn't nearly enough. She wanted Callis' head on a platter. Or better yet, his heart. She wanted to carve it into a thousand tiny little pieces and feed those pieces to the rats.

A knock sounded upon her door, and she froze, her hand on the pane of the window. Surely, Lazarus wouldn't—

"Quinn?" Her eyes widened with shock. Instead of Lazarus, it was Lord Callis' voice that filtered through the wood.

Sucking in a breath and holding it for fear she'd march across the room, throw the door open, and stab the man through his groin and up into his intestines, Quinn counted down the seconds in silence before the man spoke again.

"Listen, I was hoping we could talk," he continued. Her chest burned with the effort she was expending to keep absolutely still. "I'm aware that you were upset by today, and I was hoping that I could ease your concerns." When still there was no answer, she heard him sigh. "I'll be in my study if you change your mind," he said. "It's just down the hall. I'll leave the light on for you. I . . . hope you change your mind."

Oh, she was changing her mind, alright, she thought as

she listened to him move away from the door. Her breath came rushing back into her chest. The air fueling the wildfire within. Though she craved desperately to kill him, she knew she couldn't. Lazarus had instructed her, quite specifically, to stay put until he came for her. He would not come for her again until morning. But Callis—dear, foolish Callis—was dangling a carrot before her nose.

Twisting back to the window, Quinn grit her teeth. *You can't kill him*, she told herself. She repeated it in her head. *You cannot kill him.* He was a pawn; Lazarus' pawn.

A battle raged within her. If she left this room, she feared what she would do. The door was flimsy in comparison to her power, but the door itself was not the issue. It was a symbol; a reminder of what she was. She was under Lazarus' command, and no matter the vileness of the man that owned this mansion, she needed to somehow curb her dark cravings. She needed to—Quinn scowled at the irrational thought—make peace with him.

Dark tendrils wafted from her skin, curling in her hair, caressing her cheeks. It was as if her own power disagreed. She knew that she herself was not wholly in accordance with the knowledge of what she needed to do. It felt as though Draeven had sunk into her mind. Peace was not a concept she enjoyed. In fact, she hardly understood its meaning. Lazarus had done well to angle her attention elsewhere this afternoon. He'd kept her from committing what would be an atrocity in the eyes of the nobles—and justice in hers.

Instead of peace with Callis, she would create an illusion. One guaranteed to keep him under wraps, at least until Lazarus gave her the go ahead to kill him. She would weave Lord Callis into a web that would hold him hostage. Oh yes, she liked that idea. There was something to be said for the breaking of a man. Some were shattered instantly. Others took a bit longer. She wanted to make her torture of Lord Callis last. Perhaps, she'd first feed him nightmares. Never-ending horrible nightmares that would shake him to his very core. Drive him to the brink of insanity.

Quinn straightened away from the pane of the window and turned to the door. She could wait for his death, she decided. She was sure that once Lord Callis served his purpose to Lazarus, he'd allow her the opportunity to remove the beating organ that kept the vile man alive. A slow grin spread across her face. Yes, he would. And in the time Lord Callis borrowed in Lazarus' will, she would plan for the man's death. It would be far more glorious than what it might have been this afternoon. She'd been too rash. He would keep breathing, for now, and when his time came, she'd make him suffer before she let him leave this world. She'd take him straight to the edge of madness —as she'd done with her sister—and then she'd end the man's miserable existence.

Quinn's feet carried her to the door, and she turned the handle, slipping into the hall. He said he'd be waiting in the study. Pivoting on her heel and easing the door shut behind her, she took off in the direction she'd heard him go. The man was a fool. All it would take were a few simple, fake words of apology for her reaction this afternoon. She let her legs take her to the end of the hall and on the right, she spotted the flickering of candlelight from beyond.

Quietly rapping upon the door, she reached for the handle and turned it, letting herself in before she could be turned away. Lord Callis stood from his desk as she came in. He looked surprised, but also pleased to see her.

"Quinn. . ." He looked her over. She had not changed from that afternoon and was still dressed in her leathers. Blinking and turning his gaze back to her face, he sighed. "I was afraid you would not come."

"Yes, I wasn't sure I should." Quinn congratulated herself on her calm exterior.

"Would you like to have a seat?" Callis gestured to one of the lounges as he rounded the desk.

Quinn didn't even look as she stepped to the side, moving to the wall of books that decorated the study. "No," was all she said.

Callis paused in front of his desk. "Quinn," he started. "His Grace told me that your past was private, so I will not ask it, but I know you were upset today. I don't understand why, but I'd never want to upset a lady of your standing."

Quinn chuckled, the sound a rasp in her throat. She was no lady. And any standing she held was not built on blood and bones.

"I accept your apology, Lord Callis," she said.

"Artan, please. Quinn—"

"Did you know that the N'skari people do not believe in slavery?" she asked, cutting him off as she trailed her fingers down the spines of books.

He stared at her from across the room. "No, I was not aware. I don't know much about the N'skari people," he admitted. "In fact, you're the first of your kind that I've ever met. Is that why you were upset today?"

She shook her head, letting her hand fall away from the books as she pivoted to look at him. "No," she said.

"I'm sorry if the presence of slaves offends you, Quinn," he stated. "But here, in Norcasta, slavery is a tradition. It is a staple in our very economy."

"And yet you treat your slaves as though they were less than mere objects," she countered, speaking softly. There was deceptiveness in her tone that the Lord wouldn't see. Not until it was too late.

"I treat them like animals," he said with a shrug. "It's what they are."

"You, yourself, admitted that they were human," she replied.

He sighed and then leaned back against his desk, holding his arms out as he gestured and spoke. "I said that was a technicality. They are merely slaves; nothing more, nothing less. I assume Lazarus told you —as he told me—that slave hunting will now be banned?" From the tone of his voice, his disapproval was clear.

"Yes." The word was grated out from between her lips. The rage that she had pushed down was pushing back now. Quinn was too far in the room to make it back to the door, though her eyes shot there for a brief moment of contemplation. This had been a mistake.

"Well, I hope you understand that the banning of slave hunting will not be met with approval by many of the nobles. I know that the King wants to keep the peace, but he is making changes he has no business making. Regardless of your N'skari views on slavery, slaves are property—and I can do with my property what I wish."

Something within Quinn snapped. She was across the room before she even realized it, and by the look of utter shock upon Lord Callis' face, he finally understood that he'd said too much. Her hand went to his neck, gripping him hard enough to jolt the man back in horror, but her fingers held firm—squeezing just enough to cut off his airflow.

"You can do what you wish?" she hissed in his face. "Yes, I suppose you can, but allow me to show you

that doing as you wish comes with severe consequences."

Quinn pulled him toward her and then flicked her hand, sending the lord crashing into his own desk. His back met the surface, the wood cracking and splintering beneath him as the desk snapped in half. Lord Callis slammed into the floor and was stunned to stillness for a beat as Quinn unleashed the black tendrils that had been squirming to get out.

Eyes wide as fear assaulted him, the man crawled backwards, waving one hand before his face. "No!" he yelled. "Stop! Get it away from me!"

Quinn stalked forward—all of her well-laid plans for the man's future torment erasing with each step she took. The wisps slithered over Lord Callis' arms and legs, pinning him to the ground as Quinn reached down and retrieved the dagger that was strapped to her leg just inside her right boot. Callis didn't see it. He was far too concerned with the illusion that the wisps were trapping him in.

The man squirmed and wiggled upon the floor like the worm that he was. Quinn struck with the speed and ferociousness that boiled within her blood. He screamed as she sank her blade into his stomach and twisted, cutting across his gut. His screams were a beautiful symphony in her ears as she reached into the man's stomach and yanked out his intestines as she withdrew her dagger and raised it above her head.

She stabbed downward, and the next scream he

emitted was interrupted by the bubbling of blood from his throat. She stabbed and hacked so quickly that as she yanked the blade from Callis' flesh, a strip of blood came with it and slapped her across the cheek. Blood leaked out from his wounds, but she was nowhere near finished.

Quinn had finished with the blade and dropped it to the side. In the distance, she heard the stomp of booted feet as she reached into Callis' chest, grasping for his heart. Her hand squeezed around the organ, and with a violent jerk, she ripped it from its cage of bone, breaking a few of his ribs in the process.

The rage she had felt before—like fire in her blood—cooled. There was no more of a burn within her veins, instead it was ice. Frost beneath her flesh as the thing in her fist pumped once against her palm— or perhaps it was her own heart thudding in her ears, slow and even—and a purge of blood of the darkest red color slipped from between her fingers. Quinn stood as the door behind her was thrown open. She clenched the heart in her hand as she stared down at Lord Callis' face, twisted forever in the agony of his death. She couldn't even recall when he'd stopped screaming. *Had it been when the heart was ripped from his chest, or was it before?* she wondered idly.

"Quinn!" Lazarus snapped from behind her. "What have you done?"

Turning, Quinn met Lazarus' furious eyes and held up the heart of Lord Callis. She crushed the deflated piece of muscle until the bloodied juices of its existence dripped onto the rug beneath her feet.

"I did what I always do," she said coldly, letting him see the perverse detachment on her face. "I did what was necessary."

Boundaries Crossed

"It wasn't the words spoken, but in the silence where things lingered that you should listen."
— *Lazarus Fierté, soul eater, the exhausted King of Norcasta*

S ilence.

It spread between them with things unsaid. It became a yawning chasm that divided him and *her*. As the carriage dipped and jerked along the night road, they said nothing to each other. Not a word since they'd left Lord Callis' study. Her fingers were still sticky with the late lord's blood. It splattered her face, her hair, and soaked into the pores of her skin.

Not that you'd know it when she wore a thick cloak despite the summer heat.

Lazarus had pulled it from Callis' own quarters and handed it over wordlessly.

Quinn . . . for all her japes and difficultness, hadn't complained once. It was like she knew that she'd finally done it. She crossed the single line that couldn't be overlooked.

He couldn't undo what she had done.

Lord Callis was dead, and with his death, Lazarus' hold upon the throne was going to be even more difficult to maintain. Once the council learned of what she'd done . . . he shook his head. That was a problem for another day. It couldn't wait past tomorrow, but another day still.

She sat as stiff as the fabric of her trousers, legs crossed and arms folded as she looked out the window. She hadn't glanced at him, not even once. Lazarus supposed that was probably a good thing. Hers weren't the only emotions running high this night.

She had crossed a line, but he had to ensure that whatever he did next didn't shatter the line completely.

He had to remind himself that, though much had changed in the months prior, the girl that he'd seen in the market was still there. That who Quinn had been before she met him was still who she was now. That young woman that nearly beat a noble to death with his own whip was still there. Refined certainly, but not completely eradicated. Lazarus might have smiled at the thought, had her actions not cost him so deeply.

That day he'd found it amusing.

Entertaining.

Fascinating even.

And now . . . now he understood the warnings that had been there all along. He'd thought he'd read the writing on the wall. That he understood Claudius' words those six years ago.

His old friend had called upon him because he saw a vision.

The future, Claudius had called it.

Or really, two versions of it.

In an infinite sea of possibilities, the old king told Lazarus that should he come to power, it would all hinge on a single woman. N'skari born, but dark of magic, she would bear gifts unlike any the world could remember.

True gifts from the gods.

That she alone would either cement his empire or be the destruction of it.

Lazarus shook his head, running his calloused palm along his jaw. For the first time, he wasn't so certain which of the two Quinn would turn out to be. In the past, he'd had minor doubts. Those had been easily pushed aside, though. Her shows of loyalty as they traveled the eastern side of the continent made him so certain that he knew what she would come to be. *Who* she would come to be.

Now, however, Lazarus wondered.

The lights of the city flashed through the side windows of the carriage, making the last leg of the journey blend together. Only when the carriage finally came to a total stop did Quinn pull away from the window, but she didn't move to unlatch the door and get out.

Voices drifted from outside the carriage, and Lazarus reached for the door, exhaling a heavy breath as he opened it before Gulliver could.

"Your Grace, I—"

"Find Lord Adelmar and tell him to meet me in my study," Lazarus said. His long-time driver nodded and hurried away without further questions. Lazarus turned back and motioned for Quinn to come out. She stood, and he couldn't help but stare as she stepped out of the carriage with such lethal grace. She was neither heavy of foot nor clumsy, but more akin to a blade in the dance of swords. Lord Callis had liked that about her; the mystery, the edge of darkness that any man could taste, but few would ever be privy to truly know as Lazarus did.

Quinn might have killed him, but the man chose to dance with a sword, and that was a fault all his own.

"Come with me," he told her, turning heel to enter the palace through an entrance that was less trafficked at this time of night. They crossed the grounds and cut through the gardens, Quinn trailing behind him like a shadow the entire way.

Lazarus entered his chambers, not pausing to look behind himself. Not sure he wanted to see the apathy on her face. Quinn loved her games and wore her masks beautifully, but this particular one was not a mask he was well acquainted with, and he never wished to be.

He exited through his room, finding Draeven already waiting at the end of the hall.

"Lazarus? Quinn?" he asked, rubbing the sleep from his eyes. His hair stuck up unevenly on one side, and while his robes befit a noble, they'd been thrown on in haste. "I thought you two weren't returning till tom—"

"In my study," Lazarus said, cutting the man off. Draeven blinked and peered past him. Lazarus knew the moment when he realized an inkling of what had gone on as his eyes widened, and his training took over.

"Very well, Your Grace," Draeven said, opening the door for them. Lazarus went around his desk and took a seat in the overstuffed chair, exhaling heavily. The lock clicked shut.

"Take off the cloak," Lazarus told her.

He leaned forward, resting both elbows on the desk as Quinn silently slid the fur-lined garment from her body. Tufts of brown and black clung to her arm where the fur had touched the blood while wet, and stuck when it dried. In the dim light of his private study, the red was no longer shining, but instead a molted, flaking brown. She looked as if she'd rolled in clay instead of having just killed a man.

"Myori's wrath," Draeven cursed. "What in the dark realm did you do?"

"Lord Callis is dead," Lazarus said, answering for her. Draeven paled further, his gaze swinging between them. "I need the situation handled . . . swiftly. Discretely."

"That's it?" Draeven asked after a heartbeat. "She *kills* one of the wealthiest lords in the southern region —one on your council, no less—and all you're going to do is—"

"Draeven," Lazarus snapped. "This isn't the time." His old friend pressed his lips together, and while his face revealed how much he disagreed with Lazarus, he didn't say a word. "Quinn, go to Lorraine's room and have her help you clean up. Tell her the cloak is to be destroyed, burned preferably. I'll send for you in the morning."

Without a word of goodbye, his right-hand picked up the cloak and pulled it back on. She tied it around her shoulders and then turned away. She opened his door, and it was only when she was halfway out that Quinn turned back. He could have sworn there was something other than apathy there.

Something almost like . . . guilt.

She might not regret it, but he got the impression

she was sorry all the same.

Quinn didn't say those words. She merely pivoted back toward the exit and walked away, closing the door softly behind her.

"I told you that she was going to be a problem," Draeven said. "She's too impulsive. Too violent. Too—"

"*Draeven*," Lazarus repeated, harsher this time. "I'm well aware of who and what Quinn is, but I'm afraid this time I might be just as guilty as she."

His friend turned, his lips parting. The words came out in a rush. "How do you figure that?"

"Lord Callis invited us on a hunt, but so *skillfully* managed to leave out what we were hunting," Lazarus said, casting him a meaningful look. Draeven swallowed and looked away.

"Slaves."

"Indeed," he nodded. "He had a child—a boy not yet a man. Quinn went into a rage, but I chose to remain the night, thinking it better we head back in the morning. She'd walked away. I didn't think he'd ignore my order to leave her be and now the man is dead."

Draeven ran a hand down his face, pinching the bridge of his nose.

"Many mistakes were made, it seems," Draeven said. "I can understand her abhorrence and what sent her into such a state, but Lazarus—this is a country that we are fighting to keep. A kingdom we're trying to prevent from going to war. As soon as the council hears of this—"

"I plan to gather my vassals in the morning to figure out how we're to handle the council. In the meantime, I need this mess cleaned up and to be left alone for the remainder of the night," Lazarus said. He leaned back in his chair, and Draeven sighed.

"I'll get Dominicus. Consider it done."

Draeven turned to leave, and Lazarus said, "Thank you . . . my friend."

He paused, his hand on the doorknob. Draeven looked over his shoulder and said, "I have followed you for nearly a decade knowing where it would lead. I'm not going to let Quinn throw that away for any of us, but you will have to decide what you want most . . . the woman, or your crown."

Lazarus didn't respond, and Draeven didn't wait for one.

They both knew the truth.

They both knew the price.

But above all, they both feared.

It was a terrible place to stand, being the hand that honed her, and the King that couldn't smite her because fear herself had learned the truth as well.

Freedom was already hers to claim.

Whispered Truths

"There are consequences to every action, both good and bad."
— *Quinn Darkova, fear twister, right-hand to the King of*
Norcasta, uncertain murderess

She walked the halls of the palace, hoping her footprints were no longer bloody. The heat was stifling beneath the heavy winter coat, but she kept it securely around her shoulders as she headed toward Lorraine's room.

Draeven was right to be angry.

Never in a thousand years would she tell either of them that.

But in this instance, she understood.

Her rage had consumed her, and now the consequences would fall upon them all.

His only true command since she'd returned had been to behave in regard to the southern lords. To not touch the prized sheep, for they were what stood between Leone and the other wolf's den. It was all he had asked of her.

And, in a way, she'd betrayed that request.

Quinn swallowed the lump in her throat as she lifted her hand to Lorraine's door and rapped twice. There was a stirring on the other side. Footsteps approached. The bolt unlatched, and the door creaked open.

"Dom?" a feminine voice whispered.

"I'm afraid not," Quinn answered. The door opened further. Lorraine stood in a silken nightgown, long and decent, but not unflattering in the least. She held up an oil lamp, and the crinkles around her eyes were illuminated.

"Quinn, what are you. . ." Her words fell silent as she took in the heavy cloak and stained hands that were peeking through it. "Come inside."

She stepped back, and Quinn followed her in. The door shut behind her, and Lorraine lowered the lamp. "I did something," Quinn said, trying to swallow whatever this emotion wreaking havoc inside her was. She'd never felt it before.

"I can see that, dear. Tell me everything."

Quinn began speaking as Lorraine busied herself with lighting the lamps around the room, casting them both in a soft but entirely visible glow. Only when Quinn was finished did she return to stand before her. Both women looked at each other.

"I killed him. I killed Lord Callis." Quinn's words fell out from between her lips as a whisper.

Lorraine peered up at her, and despite the admission of her cold-blooded act, there was warmth in her gaze as she placed a soft palm against Quinn's cheek.

"Do you know what it means to be the right-hand, Quinn?" she asked her.

"I thought I did. I'm beginning to wonder."

Lorraine nodded as if she'd suspected as much. "It means being the hand that strikes. Draeven is the diplomat. He's the smooth talker that keeps Lazarus out of trouble, and councils him with a level head. You—you're the one that makes the calls no one else will." She smiled sadly. "You exist to deal with men like Lord Callis and the uprisings that will occur as a result. You are the might of Lazarus. The spear that reminds the people why rebellions are unwise, and that should we be attacked—you can handle it. You can keep them safe."

"But Lazarus said—"

"Lazarus knew what he was doing when he took you in, Quinn. He understood the ramifications of bringing on a vassal with so much power, for better or worse." She brushed a stray lock of hair from Quinn's face. "He might not be happy with your actions today, but so long as you remain loyal at his side and are willing to quell the rumors that arise—you're doing exactly what the right-hand should."

Quinn's lips pinched together as she said, "His council won't see it that way."

Lorraine snorted once. "His council isn't half as loyal as you, and he knows that—the late Lord among them." A flinty expression crossed Lorraine's face before it was gone.

"If they're not loyal, why aren't they dead?" Quinn asked.

Lorraine chuckled, her hand dropping away. "Loyalty is not something that can be given without reason and time. If Lazarus killed every man before they could prove their worth, none of us would be here—you included."

Quinn blinked, the corners of her lips turning down. "But if they support the blood heirs—"

"If they truly support them, then Lazarus will handle those lords when the time is right. However, some men might be swayed in the coming weeks when the heirs themselves finally make an appearance." Lorraine turned for the door and said, "I will be back in a moment with water for a bath."

She slipped out of the door, her footsteps quietly padding down the hall while Quinn waited for her. With stiff fingers, she reached up and tugged at the drawstrings of her cloak, letting it fall to the ground beneath her.

Several minutes later, Lorraine returned carrying two buckets of water. She hauled them over to the bath in the corner of her room and took care to dump them in without spilling a drop. Only when the water was in the tub did Lorraine motion for her to come over. Quinn walked softly, pulling her top from her breasts and tossing it on the floor beside her. She unlaced her trousers and bent to handle her boots.

"How do you know when the time is right to kill someone?" Quinn asked, pulling one of her boots off.

Lorraine didn't even blink at the question. "How did you decide when it was time to kill your family?"

Quinn thought on that for a moment as she stripped away the rest of her clothes and stepped into the tepid water. She sat down, settling back against the rim. Lorraine handed her a chunk of soap, and she began to wash.

"I killed them when they outlived their purpose, or their deaths served to further my cause."

Lorraine nodded. "Lazarus will do the same." The older woman pulled out a chair and took a seat while Quinn continued washing. Plumes of brown thickened in the water so quickly, it was no longer clear by the time she got to her hair. Quinn reached around and undid the leather tie, running her fingers through her tresses to break up the stiff chunks where blood had dried.

"Lord Callis hadn't served his purpose," Quinn said, breaking the silence once more.

"No, he hadn't," Lorraine agreed, sighing deeply.

"But I killed him anyways. Does that make what I did wrong?" She leaned forward to dip the lower half of her hair in the water.

"Right and wrong don't matter," Lorraine told her. "Morals are for better men and women than those that follow Lazarus. Each of us has blackened our soul in some way that led us here, and we will blacken it further before the dark realm welcomes us."

Quinn scowled at the water and then leaned back to dunk her head twice before she scrubbed at the top of her head. The wet strands lathered, and their slippery feel mimicked blood.

"I enjoyed killing him. Draeven is furious with me for it, and Lazarus is concerned about the fallout with the council, but I don't regret it." Quinn lifted her gaze from the murky water to see Lorraine nodding.

"I can't say I would either from what you've told me."

Quinn frowned, her eyebrows drawing together. "You don't seem to be condemning me for this."

"I'm not," Lorraine replied. "It's not my place. Not anymore. You're a grown woman, and a Maji in your own right. You've earned your place in Lazarus' inner circle, and while the timing of this particular death is inconvenient," she paused, looking Quinn over. "I don't believe it is insurmountable."

Quinn dunked her head several more times, washing the suds from her hair. Only when she was clean as she could be did she stand, again noticing how the rivulets of water and blood were not so different when they ran freely.

The older woman held up a towel, and Quinn took it, drying herself. Even in the dim light, it came away smudged a reddish-brown in the corners. She grimaced, but said nothing as she dropped it on the floor beside her clothes. Lorraine pulled open the drawers of her armoire and plucked several swaths of fabric. Quinn stepped out of the bath and took them from her, dressing without much regard to what she wore.

"If you're wrong," she started. Quinn swallowed again, this particular question not sitting well with her. "Do you think Lazarus will kill me?"

The other woman paused. She didn't turn or move as she stared straight ahead, as if seeing something Quinn could not. Then, in a voice so quiet Quinn almost missed it, Lorraine said, "I don't think he can."

They cleaned up the floor and tossed Quinn's dirty clothes in the water bin to be washed. Together they worked in silence, until almost all evidence of her actions were gone, save the cloak and the body. The confession of her words hung between them.

Only when the light of an early dawn started to peek through the window did she turn for the door to return to her rooms before morning.

"Lorraine," she said softly, hesitating at the door.

"Yes, Quinn?" the other woman said. Her voice betrayed nothing.

"I hope you're right."

A pause. Then, "You and me both, dear."

Chains of Time

"Secrets and rumors are not the same. One is bound by the lips of society and the other will always, eventually, be set free."
— *Lazarus Fierté, soul eater, King of Norcasta*

There was surely a special place in Mazzulah's realm for Lord Artan Callis, Lazarus knew. The man had been nothing but a pain to deal with. Difficult to appease, to say the least—always wanting this or that. Wheedling away at his time. And for what? Hunting? Flirting with the palace ladies and maids. Lazarus scowled as he stared through the windowpane of his office, watching the morning sun rise and stretch its long orange-red fingers across the sky.

He could not deny that seeing the man dead, and at Quinn's hand no less, gave him some small measure of amusement. But that amusement had been quickly overtaken by the realization of what she'd done. Her actions had damned him. The death of the lord was not one that could be handled lightly. No. It had to be handled with care.

"She is on her way," Draeven informed him as the man came to stand at his side.

"And Dominicus?" Lazarus inquired, but he needn't have. The man in question slid into the private study a moment later, his face drawn and dark circles marking the undersides of his eyes. Lazarus' weapons master looked at him and nodded an acknowledgement of the unspoken question. It was done. The mess that he should have predicted had been cleaned up and the evidence of Callis' demise washed away as though he had never been.

Lazarus' lips twisted cruelly as he strode back across the room to his desk and took a seat, weaving his fingers together and propping his arms on the mahogany as he considered his thoughts. The chains of time tightened in an invisible noose around his neck as he contemplated what they were to do now. Quinn's actions were going to cost him—that much was clear—but how long could he postpone paying the price of her misdeed?

A knock sounded on the door and Dominicus

reached for the knob, turning and holding the door open for those beyond to enter. Quinn—having been cleaned of the night's bloodshed—stood before him, her eyes dimmed and her face strained. Lorraine stepped up to her side. They were all there.

"Close the door and lock it," Lazarus commanded. Dominicus nodded and did as he was bid. As soon as it was done, he turned his eyes back to Quinn and held them for a moment before he sighed and addressed the room. "No one beyond these walls is to know what happened this night," he said. "As you know, Lord Callis is dead." Quinn stiffened, but he ignored her. Yes, he was angry with her—positively furious—but at the same time, he understood. The man was bound to wind up at the end of his life's path in a violent and bloodied manner. The way he lived—fast and hurried, with slaves and mistresses everywhere he went, had definitely seen to that. The timing and method, however, could not have been worse. "I've gathered you all here because there is no way that announcing the man's death will have anything but a negative impact upon my reign. It cannot be put off forever, of course, but a temporary solution is needed."

Draeven nodded, turning to the others. "Before your arrival, Lazarus and I discussed the possibility of telling the other lords that Callis had been called away or sent on an excursion of the highest secrecy. He—"

"That won't work," Quinn announced. Lazarus' eyes landed on hers, and he released his hands, gesturing for her to continue. She took that as her cue and nodded, turning back to Draeven as she spoke despite the fact that this was a suggestion that Draeven and Lazarus had colluded together. "What will happen when he's gone for too long?" Quinn asked. And before Draeven could respond she pushed onward. "Will he die on this top-secret mission? Of course, because he's already dead. But then people will wonder where you sent him and if you didn't have him sent to wherever he supposedly went just so he could be killed. That rumor will only come back on *you*, Lazarus." She paused, her focus switching its target as those cerulean eyes of hers bore into his dark gaze. "And that's what you want to avoid, right? The backlash?"

"Then what do you suggest?" Lazarus asked, curious to see how the woman might come up with some way to rectify her mistake. No, perhaps killing the man hadn't been a mistake, but doing so too early was definitely a blunder—on both of their parts.

Quinn's lips pressed together, and he watched, curious despite himself, as the thoughts raced through her mind. When she realized he was fixating on her so intently, her expression closed down with the same effect of slamming a door. He fought against the curling of her lips as she straightened and glared at him.

"If your only goal is to buy time, then I suggest an illusion."

"An illusion?" Lazarus' thoughts echoed Lorraine's words as the older woman looked at Quinn in confusion. "What kind of illu—oh you mean . . . " Lorraine trailed off, worry falling over her face. "That seems a bit dangerous. The last time you—"

"That was not the last time, Lorraine," Quinn said, correcting the woman. It was clear that Lorraine only recalled Quinn's unleashing an illusion from the battle outside of Tritol in Ilvas. But as both Lazarus and Quinn knew, Quinn's illusions had other uses. "I can create an illusion of something small. Something —or someone, in this case—that everyone would see, and think was there," Quinn said.

Lazarus nodded. "An illusion might work," he concluded. "The only one who wouldn't be affected by it would be—"

"—Me," Lorraine finished for him.

Lazarus nodded. "Nulls wouldn't be affected due to their magical immunities." He turned to Draeven. "Do we have any other nulls in the palace?"

Draeven shook his head. "No, sir. None that are known."

Lazarus narrowed his eyes and then abruptly turned to Dominicus. "I want you to ensure that there are no nulls—known or otherwise—in the palace. Should you find any, have them removed. Quietly."

"You want them killed?" Dominicus asked.

Lazarus leveled the man with a hard look. "That isn't necessary. Simply have them go on an extended leave of absence—with pay, if need be—until after the blood heirs leave."

"Is that the timeline for this delay?" Quinn asked suddenly.

"Yes," Lazarus replied. "We cannot hide the truth forever. It always has a way of getting free. I simply want to keep this contained until such a time as I can use the death of Callis to my best advantage."

Everyone in the room nodded—everyone, that is, except for Quinn, who simply stood there, staring at him as though she were trying to crawl into his mind from across the room. Beneath his skin, a soft fluttering of his souls began to vibrate. He clenched his fists on top of the desk and turned his chin.

"An illusion will do, then?" It was Draeven who asked the question, and Lazarus looked to the man, watching as a pucker formed between his brows.

Lazarus inclined his head. "It works better than setting about a rumor about his unintended departure from court. The man was a glutton for court life. Something major would have had to have drawn him away for the others in his flock to believe it."

"Won't they be suspicious if his attitude changes and he's not seen at as many parties and gatherings?" Draeven pointed out.

"The illusion will only work when I'm in the room," Quinn agreed. "But the attitude of his persona won't change." She grimaced. "I talked with the man enough times that I'm sure my illusion will work well enough. And as we've already said—this isn't a long-term solution, Draeven." She lifted one elegant eyebrow at him. "This is short term. Worrying about suspicions now will only ensure that we're looking for people to be suspicious."

Lazarus agreed with her. "So long as everyone acts appropriately, everything will be fine. We only need to keep up the ruse until the blood heirs leave. Lorraine," Lazarus turned his attention to his stewardess. Lorraine's eyes widened, and she straightened, meeting his gaze. "I'll need you to go to Lord Callis' estate and ensure that things there are running smoothly until his death is announced and a suitable replacement can be appointed."

"Yes, sir," she agreed readily, but then frowned as she tilted her head to the side. "I'll not be able to do it all on my own, Your Grace," she continued. "There are still preparations to be made for the events of Axe's birthday."

Lazarus clenched his teeth, stifling a growl of frustration as he bent his head in acknowledgement. "Fine. Take Gulliver and have him assist you and Dominicus, as you must—but only if absolutely needed."

"Of course, Your Grace," she said.

"As for you, Draeven," Lazarus said, switching his attentions. "Lord Callis had a bevy of duties in the palace as well. I'll need you to ensure that they are done." Draeven's lips tightened in pure displeasure, but he merely nodded and kept any and all objections silent. Lazarus pivoted back to the rest of the room, his eyes scanning them. "That's all," he finally said. "You're dismissed."

Dominicus was at the door in a heartbeat, opening it and holding it for Lorraine as she curtsied and left. Draeven circled the desk and bypassed Quinn, trailing out just behind them.

Lazarus lifted his head and met her unreadable expression head-on and waited.

And then he waited some more. Still, Quinn didn't say anything. She simply looked at him. Watched him for the longest time, her eyes roving over his own expression. He got the feeling that she was attempting to dissect him for information. But there was nothing for her to find. Lazarus kept his emotions in check, under lock and key, and when she finally felt she had looked enough, she turned and strode from his study, letting the door click softly at her back.

Lazarus leaned back in his chair and once again turned his eyes to the rising sun. It glinted off something on one of his many shelves. Some of which held books written by kings and nobles past. Others held trinkets and gifts from foreign dignitaries.

Lazarus' eyes fell on a simple hourglass. A large one by the looks of it. He stood and strode across the room, his shadow blocking out the sun that reflected against the clear surface of the trinket's curved shape.

There was only so much time left, he thought to himself as he lifted the object and turned it, setting it back in place. Sand fell as they all awaited the impending storm.

Temperamental Magic

"There is a first time for everything, even emotions."
— *Mariska "Risk" Darkova, beast tamer*

T*ick.*
    Tock.
Tick.
Tock.

Risk glanced at the grandfather clock, a slight frown gracing her lips. She reached for the door for the third time, considering walking alone when a knock came. Soft. Swift. Two raps. That could only be one person.

She opened the door, blinking her surprise instead of speaking it aloud.

"You're late," she said. Not a rebuke, but a statement instead. Draeven pushed the sandy-blond hair from his eyes and sighed heavily. The dark circles that lined them seemed to have come out of nowhere these past days, steadily deepening to a light plum color. It made the violet of his irises appear even more vivid than usual.

"My apologies, Risk. I was held up dealing with —" He broke off, his mouth open, but no words coming out. There was an extended pause, and then he continued, "well, it doesn't matter. I'll try not to be late again. Shall we?" He stepped away from the door and motioned for her to join him. Risk squinted a little, not sure what to make of his odd behavior. She stepped out and closed the door. Neiss wrapped tighter around her. Draeven didn't even look at the creature.

They walked down the halls in a comfortable silence, from a comfortable distance. While she didn't despise the young lord as she did most men, she still struggled with interaction in all ways. The ebb and flow of conversations were odd to her. Forced. She didn't understand small talk, as Quinn had called it. She had no desire to be pretty and smile. If anything she wanted to be . . . well, she didn't know. A lady of this court, however, was not it.

As they crossed the courtyard, the guards kept their distance, but anytime she made eye contact, one of them would nod as if she were one of their own. It was silly, and though she had no desire to be a guard or part of anything, the notion made her feel better, if only marginally. It gave her the illusion of safety, like she was above these men's notice as a woman and that her horns mattered not. She knew that wasn't true, but it made it easier to leave her room and go to these lessons. The anxiety she felt around any but Quinn was slowly beginning to fade, or perhaps—if not fade —then at least not control her so wholly.

They slipped through the palm fronds, coming to stand in the garden. In the center, sitting on the same flat stone she saw him on each day, was her mentor, Haspati. The old man didn't open his clouded eyes, but he stopped humming as the baboon turned its head.

"Hello, Risk," he said in that deep booming voice. It might have scared her, had it not come out of such a small man. "Draeven," he nodded as a show of respect, and the young lord did the same. Lifting his gnarled walking staff, he tapped the rock across from him, motioning for her to sit.

As Risk settled in and began to close her eyes to get in touch with the world around her, a stick cracked. Her eyes snapped open, and she whipped her head around to look behind her. A guard lifted his hands in surrender. In one was a piece of stationary folded over and sealed with the symbol she'd seen on Quinn's brass knuckles. It was Lazarus' seal, which meant a letter from the King. Draeven waved him over and the soldier tried to stealthily walk by, casting an apologetic glance at Risk. She waited until he'd handed the letter off and left entirely to turn back around.

Her eyes slipped closed. Tilting her head back, she inhaled deeply, focusing on the actual feel of the magic in her veins and how it connected to the living creatures around her. She tried to empty her mind of the thoughts and anxieties and worries that plagued her day and night. Here she was a beast tamer learning to control her magic. Quinn had arranged for her to have a trainer, and she wasn't going to let her sister down, or herself for that matter. Not when she wanted so desperately to get it—to understand it—and ultimately, to control it.

A soft wind blew and the trees rustled, allowing her to sink further into the trance. She again inhaled deeply, opening herself to th—heavy footsteps tromping through the undergrowth were like an arrow through her glass heart. Her concentration snapped, and she let loose a frustrated growl, more animal than human. Risk turned around to level a guard with a glare.

The new guard looked between her and Draeven, who was seated on the other side of the clearing, letters scattered about him. He gave her a half-hearted smile that she thought was supposed to be a silent apology as he continued walking toward the lord and handed him a letter. Draeven didn't even look up as he took it and muttered his thanks. The guard turned and walked away as if it never happened.

Risk turned back around, glowering at the puffs of fur that had broken out across her arms. Her nails had sharpened, but not fully distended. Risk clenched her jaw as she settled in once more. With a heavy exhale, she worked to calm the magic as she would an animal. It wasn't the easiest thing, given the magic itself seemed to be sentient in a way but also connected to her own emotions. She practiced her breathing before letting her eyes fall closed once more.

She didn't even have time to slip into the blissful peace of nature before another set of boots set her already frayed nerves aflame. Her claws fully extended, and she felt a heaviness in her back as the skin stretched over her spine and shoulder blades, warning her that wings were attempting to form even as she turned back once more. Her mouth opened to tell him to leave when the rough brush of wood against her knee made her pause.

Risk glanced back at Haspati, who was grinning like a fool.

"Calm yourself, child," he told her. "You've learned quickly how to feel the world around you, but you've yet to curb your animalistic instincts to run or fight when you feel intruded upon. The young lord has things he needs to attend to. Let's use this distraction as a learning point in patience and focus." He smiled, withdrawing his staff and setting it over his lap. Neiss slipped from her shoulders and settled over the heated surface beside her, his head inclined lazily as he basked in the sun.

"Traitor," she thought toward him. If the serpent could smile, he would have.

"There is wisdom in the old man's words," he replied with an incline of his head before promptly falling asleep. Risk lifted an eyebrow at him, but he didn't speak to her any further. With a huff, she settled in once more, but found it impossible to close her eyes when there was movement behind her.

Teeth clenched and pressing together, her muscles tensed under every motion she couldn't see, but still heard. Haspati chuckled. "You won't get in touch with much more than the ache you'll cause in your own head if you continue tensing so much."

Risk wiped away a damp lock of silver hair, careful not to snag it on her horns. She cast him a nonplussed glance. "I cannot focus with them moving behind me."

"And why is that?"

Her eyebrows drew together, as if it were obvious. "I don't know them. I don't trust them. I can't see them. How am I to know what they're going to do?" she asked, ignoring the way Draeven looked up from across the garden.

Haspati smiled. "You feel them," he said simply. "They are animals, just as you or I or the basilisk. Sense them with your magic, and you will know where they come and go, and then you need not worry about what the eyes can't see." He grinned widely and motioned for her try it.

Risk narrowed her eyes at him, which only served to make the old man laugh.

"You enjoy this far too much," she muttered.

She pretended not to hear when he said, "You're right; I do."

Risk focused on releasing the tension in her shoulders as she loosened her jaw. Her hands came to rest on both her knees in an effort to keep from fisting them as the continued movements hacked at her senses. For every deep breath she took, an unnatural sound that interrupted her thoughts made Risk tense once more.

She tried to open her mind to the world beyond, but that wasn't near so easy when it wasn't just nature she was opening it to, but also the sounds disjointing it. She gnashed her teeth with every footstep and muttered conversation someone had with Draeven, but at a certain point, she grew to expect it. Instead of sinking into the deep nothingness of her magic where they were one and the world felt whole, Risk kept herself grounded to this plane and instead sought them out. While she couldn't see the guards, she could still feel their souls—at least she assumed that's what it was that allowed her to get in touch with animals and men alike.

They entered and exited the garden every few

moments, and Risk pushed herself to feel them past the expected. Unlike how she sank into the magic by simply lowering her conscious mind into it. Here, she hunted them. She pursued them. She tracked them out of the gardens and into the courtyard. She felt them climb the steps of the palace as if she herself were doing so, and sensed every roll in emotion as they went about their business. She opened up the mental network of her mind, and it wasn't the peaceful bliss of nature and silence, but the feeling of power in watching them as a hunter did prey. The forced concentration was all-consuming in that not sound nor sight could pull her from it because she'd homed in on their movements so thoroughly that it was almost as if she were outside herself.

The movements slowed until the guards stopped coming altogether, and only when the courtyard had largely cleared did she come back to herself.

Risk opened her eyes, and it was dark outside.

The moon shined down on them, casting the garden in a silver glow. Risk blinked twice, wondering if she'd somehow drifted off and imagined it all when the white of Haspati's teeth flashed. Even in the night they stood out; a smile in the shadows of nothing.

"You did well, child," he said in praise. Risk stared, not sure how to respond.

"I . . . I don't know what exactly I did," she said softly. "I started to follow them instead of sinking into the magic."

"What you did is called a field of vision," Haspati said. "Every Maji has one, and it is different for each person, regardless of their gift." She leaned forward and winced. After sitting so long in the same position, her muscles had stiffened and grown tense. She twisted around, extending both arms behind her in a series of cracks.

"It was harder to get into, but once I did, I fell into it," she said.

He nodded. "You got in touch with the magic that exists in the world around you instead of relying on your own reserves. Breaking away from your own will be difficult at first, but the power at your disposal when you do is greater than any one soul could hope to harness." Her stomach grumbled, and Risk looked down. Her cheeks heated, not that the old man would be able to see in the dark, even with his familiars. "We'll end your lesson on that today."

Risk nodded, hopping up from the rock she sat on. She leaned over and extended one hand for Neiss to wind his way around her. "That would be good," she said. "Draeven?"

"I'm here." Risk glanced over at the young lord who was now standing and off to the side, watching her completely. "Let's get you back to your rooms. I'll send Lorraine up with dinner if she hasn't brought it already."

They turned and made their way back through the garden in silence, and as she'd seen, the courtyard was near empty when they reached it. Save for the few guards on patrol and the bats she knew to be hanging from beneath the third-floor window, there was no one.

"I'm sorry the messengers were distracting you earlier. I'll try to be better about handling my business around your lessons," Draeven said as they climbed the steps to the palace.

Risk shrugged. "Them being there ended up helping me in the end. Besides, judging by how many of them there were, I doubt it could have waited."

He nodded grimly and ran a hand over his jaw, through the slight growth. "The blood heirs will be here soon. I don't know how I'm going to manage keeping track of them and your sister at the same time." He sighed, shaking his head.

"Well, good luck with that. She's rather clever at making herself scarce when she wants to be," Risk said with a smile. Her lesson today made her wonder about Quinn's own field of vision. She'd have to ask her about that when she saw her next.

"Don't I know it," Draeven said with a chuckle. Risk couldn't help noticing how strained the sound was in her ears as they strolled to a stop outside her door.

"You know," she started. "I can walk myself to my lessons now. I don't want my training to be a burden on you when you've already got so much going on."

His face blanched as his lips parted. The hesitation was only for a moment before he stepped forward. She tensed, and he noticed immediately, stepping back once more with an apologetic smile. "I don't mind taking you to your lessons, Risk. I actually enjoy it. It's a nice reprieve in an otherwise very long day of tasks and appointments."

"You look tired," she said.

"I am," he agreed. "But I still enjoy it. If you'll allow me to continue going despite the intrusions, that is . . ." He lifted a brow, asking permission. Risk swallowed and blinked.

"I . . ." She trailed off. "I think that would be alright."

He smiled, and for some reason she liked the look of it. When men usually smiled, Risk wanted to hide. When Quinn smiled, she feared what her sister was thinking. But when Draeven smiled, it was different.

Good different.

She didn't know what it meant. She couldn't understand for the life of her why she found it nice to look at it, but she did.

"Very well," he said. "I'll see you tomorrow for your lesson."

The young lord walked away, and Risk watched him go, not understanding why for the first time she didn't feel the need to flee in the presence of a man.

Rumors and Riots

"Take care with assumptions, for they can be the greatest of weapons."
— *Quinn Darkova, fear twister, right-hand to the King of Norcasta*

"Lorraine!" Quinn cracked one eye open. The shout sounded from the hallway. She growled under her breath and shoved a pillow over her head to mute out the sound of Axe's voice, but it did little good when she continued to shout. "Lorraine! Look what I just got! It's a letter!"

"I see that, dear," Lorraine's voice infiltrated from just outside Quinn's door and a moment later, a knock sounded.

"I think they're here for you," Risk said from somewhere across the room. Out of sight.

Quinn lifted her head, noting the brightness filtering in from the windows. She'd barely gotten any sleep. An hour or two at most. Quinn flung back the coverings before stomping toward the door, bypassing her sister seated in one of the chairs with a book in hand.

"—comin' for my birthday. Can you believe it? She must be almost here because Madara said —Quinn! Good, you're up. Let's go, then." Quinn blinked down at Axe as the girl cut herself off from the tirade of chattering to shove her way into the room. "Risk, you're comin' too, right?"

"Coming? Where are we going?" Risk's tone suggested hesitation, but not outright refusal. Quinn turned, glaring at the red-headed spitfire before straightening and giving an apologetic turn of her lips to Lorraine.

"I know you probably haven't gotten any sleep since returning, but Axe's celebration of birth is coming up and I wanted to go into the city to put in a few orders for the palace. I thought you and your sister might like to join us?"

Quinn grit her teeth as something crashed behind her. "If we're going, I'll have to get dressed," she finally said.

"Take your time. I've sent Vaughn to get the

horses ready. He'll be waiting out in the courtyard," Lorraine replied.

"What?" Axe's head popped up on the other side of the bed as Risk was attempting to put a candle holder back on one of the nightstands along with the book she'd been reading. "No! He can't come."

Quinn's lips twisted as she headed for the wardrobe and removed a new pair of leather trousers. Donning them under the long white bed shirt, she tied the laces as Lorraine tsked at her charge. "Vaughn's coming to keep you from getting into trouble. Unless you'd rather stay here . . . "

"He's an idiot," Axe snapped. "He'll stick to my side like a barnacle, the giant, dull-brained——" Axe flipped to Ilvan and began to curse violently as she got to her feet and began to stomp about the room.

"Yes . . . well, that's the point," Lorraine replied. "For him to stick to your side, that is."

Quinn whipped off her shirt and attached a leather band back around her breasts before sliding a vest of fur over that as well. Buckling her dagger around her waist, Quinn reached for her staff and nodded for Risk to follow as the four of them made their way out into the hall.

Axe growled when she realized that no one was really paying her any mind, and she snatched up Risk's arm to tug her along. "If he's really gonna be there, you'll have to stay with me," the young girl decided. "Better to have someone that ain't a brainless boulder or," she paused and gave Quinn a sneaky grin over her shoulder, "a hussy."

Quinn glared, but that seemed to only spur the annoying girl on. Axe threw her head back and cackled as she pulled Risk along behind her, leaving them to follow at a much slower pace.

Outside, in the courtyard, Vaughn awaited with four horses. He blinked when he saw the women approach. "Little pirate, who is this?" he asked, nodding to Risk, who stiffened at seeing the broad man. While gentle as a flower to most, Vaughn was tall and sturdily built. His fair complexion wouldn't endear him to her, not when her abusers had also been fair built men with pale skin and eyes.

Moving forward, Quinn extracted Risk's arm from Axe as the girl jerked forward and smashed her finger into Vaughn's chest. "She's my friend, ya ox. Don't look at her."

Quinn shook her head as she steered Risk toward one of the horses. Together, they began mounting. Axe, Lorraine, and Vaughn on each of their own horses and Quinn and Risk together on the last.

"Shall we be going, then?" Lorraine asked, lifting the reins of her beast and leading it toward the gated exit.

Quinn looked up as guards hurried to open the palace gates, her eyes narrowing as several avoided looking her way. The men were quick about their jobs, turning the cranks that lifted the heavy iron wall, holding until they were all clear before turning it once more until the iron gate fell behind them with a thump. A plume of dust billowed in the stagnant heat.

At their backs was a wall of palm trees and thick underbrush that Quinn knew from her ride to the Callis estate stretched far beyond the palace. The route they took into Leone was different; more barren in essence. Along one side of the pathway was a collection of rock and sand, broken chunks of adobe bricks, and stale, yellowed weeds jutting out from cracks in the ground. On the other side ran a single stream of water that flowed from the oasis upon which the palace and several estates had been built— and it led them to the edge of the city.

The sun beat down, unforgiving on their faces, and soon, sweat began to slick Quinn's back. The leather around her chest tightened under the onslaught of heat, and she cursed her stupidity, stripping the fur from her shoulders and shoving it into one of the bags attached to the horse's side.

Lorraine shot her a sympathetic glance. "I should've warned you about the heat," she said. "There should be a white shawl in one of your saddlebags. We each have one in case of emergency."

Quinn handed Risk the reins and awkwardly maneuvered until she could reach the bag again, digging through it until she found the shawl. Quinn wrapped the thin white cloth around her chest and shoulders, and then tucked it up over her hair so that it protected as much of her pale skin as possible. Risk handed her the reins back as soon as she was done.

"Why does it feel hotter out here than in the palace courtyard?" Quinn asked as she clicked her heels and urged the steed beneath her to meet the stride of Lorraine's horse.

Lorraine shrugged. "I suppose it has something to do with the oasis."

Quinn scowled and then glanced back at Risk. "Are you alright?" she asked.

Risk nodded. Unlike Quinn, she'd dressed in an oversized white shirt made of the same material as the shawl.

"Look, there it is!" Axe called from ahead of them. With a swift kick, Axe sent her horse galloping forward—heading straight for the towers of clay that made up the Norcastan capital, the city of Leone.

Some of the buildings were dome-shaped and others squared with straw and wood planks for rooftops. Quinn steered her horse toward a stable at the edge of the city; the place where Axe was already waiting. As soon as Quinn swung down, with Risk not far behind—the little urchin darted forward, snagging her sister's arm once more. She dragged her toward the streets filled with people.

"Axe," Quinn barked. "Slow down." Risk didn't appear to be afraid—merely unsure as the younger girl towed her along.

"I shall follow them," Vaughn said sharply,

dismounting from his horse and dropping the reins into a waiting stable boy's hands.

Lorraine sighed and quickly slid down from her own mount. Quinn huffed with annoyance toward Axe as Risk was tugged into the throng of people. Lorraine tapped her on the shoulder and gestured toward the Cisean mountain man.

"She'll be fine with Vaughn watching over her."

"It's not Axe I'm worried about," Quinn replied.

"She's got to learn to handle being without you if she's to thrive one day," Lorraine said gently.

Pursing her lips, Quinn finally gave in with a shake of her head. "If Risk wants to leave, she will. She knows her way back to the palace."

"She's getting much better," Lorraine noted as she retrieved a folded piece of parchment from one of her horse's saddlebags before handing her reins over as everyone else had done before her. "Is it perhaps to do with your travels?"

Quinn followed Lorraine as she headed toward the market stalls. "I think it helped," she said after some consideration. "We were on the road for most of it, but we did stop in a few cities along the way. While she's not completely used to crowds—she's much better than she was."

"Where did you go?" Lorraine asked curiously. "We've never talked about your travels. I'm curious."

"We traveled along the west," Quinn admitted.

"Jibreal. Bangratas. The Sari Sari Islands—they're quite nice in the spring."

"Goodness." Lorraine's eyes widened. "I've never even heard of anyone traveling to the Sari Sari Islands, much less returning in one piece. I've been told it's akin to the Crystal Continent in more ways than one." She clucked her tongue worriedly.

"I can't speak for the Crystal Continent, but the islands are quite safe," Quinn replied, her lips turning in amusement. "They spread the rumors to keep unwanted visitors away."

"It's worked," Lorraine said. "I assumed them to be cannibals."

Lifting her head, Quinn surveyed the crowd as they moved. Small children darted between the skirts of women and the long pants of men. Many of the market goers were cloaked in a similar fashion as Quinn with stretches of fabric covering their upper halves. Some women wore hoods fashioned from shawls and a few men wore wrapped turbans. "Not cannibals, just people that want to be left in peace. I believe Risk liked the islands more than Jibreal for that reason. They were less inhabited, and the folk were kinder. Simpler. It wasn't like the sprawling cities of Vusut or even Zyburn."

They came to a stop before a butcher's stall.

Quinn wrinkled her nose at the short, squat man that greeted them, leering at Quinn's figure beneath her wrap. "What can I do for you ladies?" the man asked excitedly. Quinn bared her teeth at him in warning, and the man blinked, his excitement dimming a bit as a wariness settled in his eyes.

"We'll take two dozen orders of your finest slabs," Lorraine said, pulling a coin purse from the satchel at her side. "We'll want it delivered to the palace by the end of the day, if you please."

The man's eyes widened and snapped to Lorraine. "Yes, yes, of course," he replied, bowing his head slightly—his cheeks reddening.

Quinn watched as Lorraine paid the man and then moved on. For several minutes, she flitted from one stall to the next, Quinn constantly at her side. "Tell me more about your travels," Lorraine said as she inspected a cart with brightly colored fruits from all across the continent.

"There's really nothing to tell," she said, shrugging.

"Of course there is," Lorraine argued, her eyes sliding past the red dappa fruit in hand to Quinn's face. "All I know of these places are the tales I've heard from merchants and men. You've been to them. Seen what is true and what is story. I'd like to know about it."

Quinn urged the other woman out of the way as a cart swung past them and several people rushed after it, nearly stampeding the both of them in their wake. "The Sari Sari are nomadic peoples that move from island to island on boats made from trees and held together with palm fronds. Contrary to the cannibal rumor, they don't even eat meat." Quinn chuckled at that. "In its own way, their lives are pleasant. Easy. Risk would have enjoyed staying there, were it written in our fate."

"And you?" Lorraine asked. "Where did you prefer?"

Quinn looked out over the throng of people, seeing a land far away. "Jibreal was vast and opulent. We did well in our time there because of the coliseum," Quinn said distractedly, dodging the question. Several shouts sounded around the corner, and taking Lorraine's arm, she steered them toward it.

"I've heard of it," Lorraine replied grimly. "Ghastly act that it is, the bloodshed does please many a lord. Were you a gladiator there?"

"Yes," she answered. "I was one of the best too, by the end of it."

Lorraine tsked, but didn't rebuke her as she once might have. "I don't doubt it. You quite enjoy violence as much as any lord. More so even, I think."

Shooting the woman a dubious look, Quinn arched a brow. "That I do, I suppose. Then again, that's why I am the right-hand and you the stewardess."

Lorraine peered up at her, her thin lips curving upward. She opened her mouth to speak when a loud booming crash jolted the ground and ran through their bones.

"Oh no . . . " Lorraine's hand hovered over her lips as the familiar sound of rowdy laughter greeted their ears.

"Axe," Quinn growled just before she broke into a sprint.

What in the dark realm had the girl gotten up to now?

A Contest of Deception

"Beware of deranged, axe-wielding red-heads."
— Mariska "Risk" Darkova, beast tamer

"Are you sure we should not stay with the others?" Risk very much wanted to go back. She felt the crush of people on either side of her, and her skin had grown tight. Her back ached where wings threatened to protrude, and her nails sharpened. Thankfully, no spots or fur had cropped up, but Risk couldn't be sure how long that would last.

"Nah," Axe objected. "We'll be fine. Besides, yer hussy of a sister probably don't let ya out to have much fun."

"I—"

"Oh look, a tavern." Risk was cut off and dragged

to the side as Axe spotted a swinging sign over a darkened entryway. "Good. I was dyin' of thirst."

"You were?" Risk frowned as she finally managed to finagle her arm from the smaller girl's grip. For such a small thing, she had quite a bit of strength.

Axe didn't bother to answer as she bounded into the building, leaving Risk standing just outside. Risk bit her lip, contemplating leaving the girl and going back to Quinn, but the gruff sounds coming from inside made her worry for the younger girl. With a stiff back, Risk took a step forward and found herself in the darkened interior of the tavern.

It took a moment for her eyes to adjust to the dim lighting; a stark contrast to the bright sunlight outside. Risk avoided touching as much as possible, skirting the edges of the crowd as she searched out Axe's whereabouts.

"Two pints, please," Axe called over the horde. Risk moved toward her, growling as she had to slip between several people. Her chest tightened when someone pushed by her. Risk rounded on them, hissing wildly, but whoever it was had already moved on. She swallowed hard before resuming her attempt to reach Axe.

Risk found her at the tavern's bar, wielding two mugs of what appeared to be ale in each hand. "Here ya go," Axe said, jamming one into Risk's palm before slamming down her own.

Risk sighed and took the mug, lifting it slightly to

take a drink and promptly coughing as fire seized her throat. "What the—" Risk coughed and hacked as she set the mug down, tears coming to her eyes as she struggled to breathe around the burning. "That's . . . not . . . ale. . . ." she managed to get out around her gasping breath.

Axe frowned at her as the girl licked her lips. "Of course it's not," she said as though it were obvious. "It's spirits."

"What . . . spirits? I . . . don't . . . drink . . . " The fire hadn't gone out yet, but it was clear that Axe knew what Risk was trying to say as the girl rolled her eyes, slammed her now empty mug on the bar, and snatched up Risk's discarded drink and downed that as well.

"That'll be two copper each," the barkeep said as Axe polished off the drink.

Risk shook her head as the burning in her throat and lungs was finally beginning to recede. "Oh." Risk stiffened and turned slowly as Axe uttered that one word.

"What do you mean 'oh'?" the barkeep snarled. "You drink it, you buy it."

"Don't suppose you got any coin on ya?" Axe asked Risk.

Risk shook her head. "I don't carry coin," she admitted. At least, she hadn't since they'd been in Leone, or rather—since they'd arrived at the palace.

"Ya little thief," the barkeep snapped. "I'll have ya hanged!"

The tavern went quiet as the scene unfolded. Several men who'd been drinking heartily and paying them no mind were now focused on the two women—one of them just a girl, really—and the barkeep's loud tone.

"How's 'bout a birthday discount?" Axe asked. Though she sounded hopeful, she said it with a rueful, unapologetic grin.

Risk shook her head at the girl in dismay. Axe was a reckless disaster waiting to happen. *Correction*, Risk amended a moment later as the barkeep lunged over the counter, snatching Axe up by the front of her shirt and dragging her halfway up until her toes barely touched the ground. She already *was* a reckless disaster.

"Now hold up, friend," a firm voice intruded. "I ask that you release the little pirate."

Despite her discomfort around the man still, the sound of Vaughn's voice gave Risk some relief.

"This 'little pirate'," the barkeep snapped, "didn't pay for her drinks. She's a thief and nothing more. I'll teach her a lesson and then give her to the authorities to hang."

"It's true I didn't bring any coin," Axe said nonchalantly. "But I'm sure a wager will do."

"What was that, you little thief?" The barkeep shook Axe back and forth with his outrage, but the girl didn't seem the least bit put off. In fact, his rough treatment appeared to bring a grin to the girl's lips as she twisted them mischievously.

Risk turned to the side as Vaughn moved past her. Though, to be honest, she pressed her back against the bar so that she would no longer feel as vulnerable as she had when there had been people milling about behind her. With her position, she could watch the entire room without much of an issue. And as such, she had a clear view of Vaughn reaching out and clasping the barkeep's hand and squeezing until the other man yelped in pain and released Axe.

Sighing as her mounting anxiety abated when Vaughn reached for his coin purse, Risk had never been more thankful for a man in her life. Surely, he would pay for the drinks and they could be quickly on their way and out of this dark little room.

As Lady Fortuna would have it, that was not what Axe had planned. Risk watched with open-mouthed shock as the girl shoved her way between Vaughn and the barkeep, stood with her hands on her hips, and promptly challenged the barkeep to a competition to see who would pay for the drinks.

"Come again?" the man said, staring down at Axe's upturned face.

She was completely and utterly mad, Risk thought as Axe repeated herself. "You heard me," she said. "Unless yer daft. A friendly contest between the two of us. You and me. Winner pays for the drinks or . . ." Axe's grin widened, "ya give up for free."

"There ain't no way I'll be doing that, girly." The barkeep shook his head.

"Axe," Risk hissed between her teeth. "Let Vaughn pay, and we will leave."

"I think you should listen to your friend there," the barkeep agreed.

Risk's eyes widened as instead of making the wise choice, Axe reached down and withdrew one of her small axes from her side. "See this?" Axe asked, shoving the weapon under the barkeep's nose. The man was two seconds from shoving it away, but his eyes caught on the gold inlaid in the handle, and he paused, looking it over. "It could be all yers if ya can beat me."

The barkeep let out a laugh. "Oh, girly, you gonna wish you hadn't challenged me. I'll take your axe, and you'll pay for your drinks."

"I've got more than one," Axe said confidently.

Unable to help herself, especially as more patrons in the tavern began moving closer, Risk backed away. Vaughn, however, was not as willing as Axe. He leaned forward and snatched Axe by her arm, yanking her against him as the girl squirmed and cursed him.

"That is not needed," Vaughn rumbled in that low thick voice of his. "We will pay and go."

"Now hold up there, son," the barkeep said, lifting a hand. "Let the girl fulfill her challenge."

Axe kicked at Vaughn's shin until the man released her with a huff. He turned and spotted Risk, then nodded across the room. Risk followed his gaze. An empty staircase. Risk nodded back in acknowledgement and waded toward it. The barkeep laughed, and the sound of knives being withdrawn echoed in her ears as the voices of the tavern patrons began to pick up once more.

Coin exchanged hands as Risk found the staircase, climbed it, and turned back to take stock of what was about to happen.

It had apparently been decided Axe would have her throwing contest. People spilled out onto the street toward the entrance to make room, while several others crowded closer to watch with fascination. The barkeep stepped up, wielding a set of cheaply made daggers. He eyed Axe with an amusing condescension that befitted men. Risk had never seen Axe with her axes, but the girl didn't seem worried as the barkeep was selected to go first.

He stepped up and, in a deft motion, sent his daggers flying toward a target on the wall. All but one managed to hit near or dead in the center. Cheers went up, coins were traded again. Risk turned her head, searching for red hair in the crowd. Axe's face was hardly visible even from where Risk perched above the others, but she could see the bright crimson of Axe's hair as the girl strode forward.

The barkeep took his daggers and stood back, a smug grin on his face. Risk moved her attention away from him to where Vaughn stood with a frown fixed on his lips and his arms crossed. She tilted her head to the side, wondering why he didn't simply pay for Axe's drinks, pick the girl up, and cart her out. He had the muscle to do it. Axe could hardly stop him.

Risk was so focused on Vaughn and her thoughts that when the sound of wood being split in two reached her ears, she didn't immediately connect it with what had happened until her eyes turned back to the target and the gaping sound of shocked silence resounded throughout the room.

"I'll take another drink now," Axe said, sounding pleased with herself as the barkeep stumbled to the target and gaped at the way the lower half of the wood had split in two with the sharpened blade of both of Axe's weapons imbedded in the very center.

"You . . ." The man reached up and yanked first one and then the other axe from his target before turning back to her. His face reddened as his grip on the axe handles tightened. "You cheated!"

Risk's skin pulled taut as she stood on the stairwell, ready to either flee or fight. Her heart thudding her ears as the barkeep charged forward before Axe could say anything more. Vaughn stepped in before the man could even reach the girl, sending him sprawling with a heavy fist to the man's stomach. He dropped the weapons, and Axe bent to gently retrieve them and slide them back into place at her hips.

The barkeep didn't stay down for long and was soon back on his feet. Stealing a wooden tray from the bar top, he flung it forward, intending to hit Vaughn. And even Risk could tell where this was going. She watched with wide eyes as Axe climbed over the bar top and poured herself another drink. As the barkeep leapt upon Vaughn, slamming him into several patrons, who then bumped into others—Risk saw it all as if time were slowing to give her the chance to take it all in.

Axe laughed as fists flew. Drinks spilled across the floor and chairs and mugs alike were broken over heads. It felt as though Risk were observing a play rather than an actual scene. She only pulled herself back as she noticed a small red head working her way through the crowd, jumping and dodging blows as she held up her pint.

As soon as Axe reached Risk, the girl took her hand and led her the rest of the way upstairs.

"Where—" Before Risk could finish asking the question, Axe shook her head, mirth dancing in her gaze.

"Just follow me," she said. "Yer not gonna want to miss the show."

"What show?" Risk asked.

Axe snickered. "You'll see."

She led Risk through the empty upstairs rooms—some filled with storage items and others with empty beds—until they found a room that faced out the front. Shoving the window open, Axe leaned out and then gestured for Risk to go ahead. Risk poked her head out next and saw an awning made of wood.

"Climb up," Axe urged. "They'll be the best seats in the house."

Risk couldn't say what made her follow the girl's insanity, but she swung one leg out and then the next. Just as Axe had managed to crawl out next to her, the two of them dangling their legs over the awning, people began pouring out from the tavern—fighting and brawling as though they'd lost their minds to the madness Axe had caused.

Axe laughed again, the sound loud and boisterous. She raised her mug as she took another hefty sip, and Risk turned away, spotting Vaughn amidst the fray. His face was red with effort as he tossed one man after the other—all seeing him and finding him to be their next challenge. Unsurprisingly, all Vaughn had to do was lift and propel them toward whatever hard surface was near. Sometimes, he didn't even look for a surface and merely threw them at another attacker.

"Axe!" Vaughn shouted.

Around the corner, a cart careened with several people following behind. "Uh oh," Axe said, sounding like she was having the time of her life.

Risk couldn't face it. She squeezed her eyes shut.

As she did she heard two distinct voices screaming Axe's name—Vaughn's and Quinn's.

"This is gonna be the best birthday ever," Axe said, laughing as she downed the rest of her spirits.

Risk didn't share the sentiment if the bar brawl was anything to go by.

Cruelty's Consequence

"If you poke a monster, do not be surprised when it pokes back."
— *Quinn Darkova, fear twister, right-hand to the King of Norcasta*

The dull roar of the crowd was beginning to give Quinn a headache.

She motioned with her fingers for a servant walking by with a jug of something clear. The young man turned, his eyes widening, the smile on his face freezing to hide the wariness in his expression. Quinn was too parched to care.

"Is that water?" she asked.

"No, my lady," he answered. "Spirits for the contestants."

Quinn groaned but motioned for him to move on. The servant didn't dally as he turned and disappeared into the throng below. She looked out over the raised platform from which Lazarus and his house sat. Wooden benches and chairs had been brought out for those of House Fierté and its emissaries. Down below, the sheep mingled, watching as—not far off—Axe competed in a climbing competition, along with four other poor fools.

Quinn sighed as she watched the girl use the sharp end of her axes as picks to hold her up. She cradled the beam between her thighs, using the muscle in her legs to shuffle her upwards and the strength in her arms to pull the hatchets from the wood and rebury them two feet above.

"It's really not fair," Quinn said to no one in particular, motioning to the 'competition.'

"What's not?" Draeven answered, coming up to her side.

"This," she waved at the courtyard that had been transformed overnight into one of the biggest parties Leone had likely seen in years. "She asked for competitions and entertainment but so far all I've seen are drunkards and fools. Not a single person has been able to win one of these so-called competitions. It's rubbish."

"Rubbish?" another voice asked. "She wanted a competition. She didn't say how competent the competitors need be." Speaking in heavily accented

Norcastan was Petra Stoneskin, a bastard's daughter but a Maji, nonetheless. She'd come all the way from Ilvas to celebrate the young heir's celebration of birth. Apparently, in the time they'd been gone, Imogen had chosen to clean house, and by doing so, she had eliminated the vast majority of her court. Petra was brought back as her new hand, and as such was the one who came to visit for the occasion.

"It's a farce," Quinn replied. "She wanted a day that made her the center of attention and the chance to win at everything. Who picked the events anyway?"

"I did," Petra grinned. Her teeth were yellowed, but some were gold. "I picked the opponents too."

Quinn rolled her eyes. "Of course you did." She wiped her palm over her sweat-slicked face and through her hair. "As if she needed more reasons to think of herself as almighty."

A walloping battle cry sounded from across the yard where Axe sat atop the wooden beam, both hands raised, axes clenched in her fists as she waved her arms. The crowd cheered, although from the looks of it, half of them didn't even know what they were clapping for.

Nobles, she thought. *All anyone had to say was spirits and party and they would flock from across the continent.*

Quinn glanced over across the platform to find Lazarus already staring at her. His face was tilted toward the nobleman standing in front of him, but his eyes—they focused intently upon her face. She lifted an eyebrow as if to silently ask how much longer she must endure this torture. With the hot sun on her pale skin and the scent of fermented drink in the air, she was feeling a bit . . . unsettled.

Lazarus turned his chin a fraction one way and then another, silently telling her it was not yet time for her to leave.

She pursed her lips, and his gaze hardened, threatening to cut like the edge of a stone should she step out of line. Knowing very well the edge she toed with him, Quinn sighed and turned back to the small group gathered around her.

Petra was still talking, somewhat animatedly given her newly found knowledge of their language. Draeven was holding a cup of something vile. He didn't drink it, but he smiled and nodded politely, every now and then his eyes darting over to Risk. Quinn glanced sideways, and a frown started when she noticed how Risk smiled back whenever he looked her way. It was timid. Shy, even—but it was there.

Quinn looked her up and down once, her eyes narrowing further.

Risk glanced over. "What?"

Quinn stared for a moment more before she said, "Nothing."

Risk cocked an eyebrow, tilting her head. The action annoyed her more than anything because it was her own. "Are you sure about that?" Risk asked. "You don't sound sure."

Very purposefully, Quinn looked over at Draeven and then back to Risk.

Her sister's cheeks reddened. Her brow furrowed and the bow of her lips pushed together. Quinn quirked a brow and tilted her head, almost mockingly. Risk glared, but instead of confronting her, she turned and walked off the platform.

Quinn stood there, staring after her, not understanding the slicing sensation in her chest. She crossed her arms, watching her sister's horns move through the throng of the crowd. While the guards might love her, the nobles still feared her more than anything else. They parted like the wake of a ship through still water.

"Where did Risk go?" Draeven asked, pausing in his conversation with Petra.

"To get some air," Quinn replied, a bit more harshly than she should have, but she didn't care.

"Maybe I should—"

"No need," she interrupted smoothly. "I'll follow her."

She didn't wait for his response as she started forward, taking the steps two at a time. The heat of the mid-afternoon day caused the blood in her veins to pound as she trailed through the crowd. The gold insignia pinned to her leather top drew enough attention to make the sheep scatter, but also take notice as she prowled across the green grass toward the row of tents. Her sister's black horns leading her.

"Excuse me, my la—" The words dried up like food left to spoil in the scorching heat. The tone going from pleasant to silently sour as the man looked upon her. "Quinn Darkova," Lord Northcott said. "What an *unpleasant* surprise."

Her jaw slammed shut. A cold wave washed over her despite the unrelenting, dry heat. Her posture went stiff and still as she replied, "The feeling is mutual, my lord."

Much to her ire, he didn't respond in irritation, but instead scrutiny as he looked down at her. His brown hair had been tied back at the nape, making the lines in his face all the more apparent. "Yes," he replied. "So it seems."

With one last scan over her features, he turned back to the other men he'd been talking to, none of which Quinn recognized. She catalogued their faces in case she needed to remember them later, and continued onward, breathing a little heavier for it.

Something about that man inflamed the darkness that settled deep inside her. It riled it, though she knew she wasn't alone in that. After the last lord she'd killed, though, Quinn was careful to stuff it back down and keep the edge of her temper in check—lest someone's head, or even their heart, go missing.

Quinn walked through the row of tents housing the most exotic of creatures in cages. Axe had wanted entertainment, and Petra had brought them in specially from every corner of the continent. Quinn had expected to see her sister there, but at the end of the row, her dark horns veered left and disappeared from sight. Quinn followed.

"Risk," she called out, raising her voice an octave. The young woman dressed in men's clothes paused and looked back, narrowing her cerulean-colored eyes. "What's wrong?"

"Don't you 'what's wrong' me," Risk snapped, rounding on her as Quinn stepped closer. "That was low—what you did back there."

She looked away—toward the tents, toward the sky. Her cheeks did not flame, and her pulse did not race, but Quinn still felt those restless emotions stirring through her. "What exactly did I do?" Quinn asked, watching a cloud drift by in an otherwise endless blue sky.

"You—you—" Risk's teeth clanked as her mouth snapped shut, and she let out a frustrated sound. Fur spotted on her skin, and her nails began to turn to claws. Her chest rose and fell for several minutes as she squeezed her eyes shut. Only when the fur vanished and the claws retreated did she open her eyes and continue. "You insinuated that there is something between Draeven and I."

"Is there?" Quinn prompted, raising both eyebrows.

"No," Risk snapped. "And there never will be because he's a man."

"You prefer women?" Quinn asked nonchalantly, crossing her arms.

"I prefer no one," Risk snapped. "After spending ten years being defiled every single day—do you really believe I'm going to just be able to move on? To pick up as if nothing happened?" Risk clenched her fists, and Quinn let her arms drop.

"No, of course not—" She reached for Risk. That was the wrong move. Her sister swatted her hand away.

"But you do," she said. "You spent months training me to be around people. Teaching me to run and then to fight and then to kill, so that you could return here, and I could be with you. You taught me to turn panic into strength so that we could return to your southern king like we could pick up where you left off as if nothing happened."

Quinn's lips parted, but she promptly closed them and then swallowed. Her throat felt dry.

"You have to move on at some point, Risk—"

"Don't you think I'm trying!" her sister yelled. The tension in the air shifted as her sister's eyes began to glow. "I go to my lessons. I train every day. I make myself take walks even though they stare at me. I know what they think, and yet I am *trying* to pull together some semblance of a life after all these years, but it is not so *easy* as you seem to think it is." Shrieks started in the background. Footsteps pounded against the barren land as a low series of growls came from the tents.

Quinn lifted both hands in surrender. "I was not trying to upset you."

"Oh, really?" Risk asked, mocking her in turn. "It wasn't your jealousy that rode you to point out that I might smile in the presence of a man? You pointed it out, and now whenever I see him I will think of *you*. I will think of what you insinuated. I will wonder if every look he casts my way is heated. I will question every time he knocks on our door whether he one day plans to hold me down and take his pleasure between my thighs while I scream until my voice is hoarse."

Quinn stepped away as the growls grew louder. More pronounced. Beasts from faraway lands roared, and it was only then that Quinn had noticed the courtyard was silent.

"I might have been jealous, but I did not mean to cause those feelings—" she started, glancing between the tents and her sister.

"No," Risk said. "You don't realize the effect your words have on people. You just think you can be cruel and that everyone will fall in line—"

An ear-splitting screech rang through the air, interrupting whatever she had been about to say next.

Risk turned toward the tents.

Crunching metal was not a sound heard often. It echoed through the courtyard like a hammer striking an anvil. Slowly, both women walked toward the noise.

Just as fast as it had started, the sound stopped.

An eerie quiet settled over the yard just before a tent flap moved.

Out came a griffin. With the body of a lion and the head of an eagle, it turned, looking over the people surrounding it. As it made a single sweep, the gold of its eye caught hers and it paused.

Like a beast that had found its prey, it focused and tensed. Wings of golden feathers unfurled. The griffin looked at Quinn, and then, as if it were possessed . . .

It charged.

Court of Misfits

*"There are beasts and there are tamers, but every now and then
—they are one in the same."*
— *Draeven Adelmar, rage thief, left-hand to the King of
Norcasta*

The wine tasted like piss.

Whoever had brought it clearly hadn't tried it. Still, Draeven held his cup and pretended to be partaking in the festivities, even if his exhaustion went bone-deep. Letter after letter he wrote pretending to be Lord Callis. Lorraine had begun to manage the late lord's estate while Dominicus handled the affairs on the actual property. As it turned out, Callis had had his hands in all sorts of unsavory entertainments; slave hunting was only a drop in the bucket. Going through the old letters, writing the new, managing the cover-up, and continuing with his own duties as Lazarus' left-hand was beginning to truly wear on him.

The one bright spot of it all was a girl with obsidian horns.

The very same girl that was striding away right now, her much more intolerable sister following after.

"I didn't know that House Fierté had a raksasa in their court," Petra said, sipping at the disgusting wine as if it were water.

"It doesn't," Draeven answered stiffly. Petra turned to look over her shoulder and then back at him, lifting a brow.

"She has horns," Petra motioned to her head. "And gray skin. What would you have me call her?"

"For one, she is only half," Draeven said. "For another, she is Quinn's sister."

Petra's brows rose further. "And here I thought things couldn't get more interesting in your court of misfits." She grinned slyly. "Imogen will be very interested to hear that the white raksasa has a tainted sister." Petra looked back over her shoulder where both girls were disappearing behind the tents. "Very interesting indeed."

"So long as you don't call her that again, Imogen can be as interested as she'd like. The girl has a name, you know." Draeven bit his cheek, regretting defending her as soon as Petra's grin turned a shade more impish.

"Oh? Does she now?" She chuckled. "Tell me, what do you call her?"

"Risk," Draeven answered. "That's her chosen name, and so long as you are in our court, you will respect that and not refer to her as tainted or raksasa again." He delivered the words conversationally, but they were anything but nonchalant.

"Very well, my lord," she said. "It doesn't change what she is, though."

"See that you call her by her name, if it's all the same to you," he replied and lifted his wine. She clinked their wooden cups together and downed hers in a single swig.

"I need more wine," she complained. Draeven extended his cup.

"Take mine," he offered. She looked down at the maroon liquid and back to him, then shrugged.

"Don't mind if I do," she said. He handed off his wine and left her to it, retreating into the crowd. Every few steps he took, a lord or lady stopped to say hello. He smiled and nodded through their thinly veiled requests as many attempted to stop him for longer than a moment or two. Some wanted men, others wanted favors, and even still were those that wanted a response to the one question even he did not know the answer to.

What did Lazarus plan to do about slavery?

He dodged the question each time, telling them the King had yet to decide, but the sideways glances and unpleased looks said much. By the time he'd reached the tents where they were keeping the animals until the evening show, Draeven wanted nothing more than to take off the golden pin on his lapel marking him as the go-to man for such questions concerning Lazarus and stick it on a donkey's ass.

He strolled through the tents, glancing in each to see where Risk and Quinn had gone. As he did so, he noticed something odd.

A wariness in the animals.

An aggression that hadn't been there this morning.

They shifted and turned, moving uneasily in their cages. Some started to growl. Others batted at the bars. Dread settled inside him as he moved faster. The closer he got toward the end, the more incensed the beasts became. The air thickened with a tension that became smoldering in the dreaded heat.

"Where are they?" he muttered to himself.

He threw open the tent flap, coming face-to-face with a griffin.

It was the most magnificent of the beasts Petra had brought for Axe's celebration. Golden feathers and sand-colored fur lined its body. The creature turned its head and looked upon Draeven.

It opened its mouth and let out the most blood curdling of shrieks.

Draeven watched, unable to stop himself, as the beast quieted and so did the grounds.

He lifted his hands, but the moment he took a step forward to calm the creature, it struck. Using only the power of its beak, it bit at the iron bars containing it in a frenzy.

A horrible feeling settled in his gut as the iron crunched. He'd heard rumors of the strength with which a griffin could bite. Draeven knew the tales, and still he hadn't thought to worry before now.

He hadn't realized the danger. None of them had until the beast bit the bar clean through.

The griffin threw its weight at the now twisted metal and the cage yielded.

Holding his breath, he lowered his gaze and began to back away. The tent flap touched his back and the griffin started forward. Its paws were the size of his head, and it walked with lethal grace as it strode toward him and then, as if he weren't even there, continued on.

Draeven's heart hammered as the flap opened and then shut. His breath was hard. Panting. He turned and pushed it aside once more, facing the creature as it turned in a circle and then paused.

He followed the golden stare several yards away.

Draeven's blood ran cold.

Risk. The beast was staring at Risk.

The back legs tightened, and a pounding rang in his ears as it charged. Wings unfurled and body coiled tight for a kill—it crossed the space and ran straight for—

Quinn.

His chest loosened just a fraction as he reached for the sword in his belt. The metal blade scraped the inner sheath, but the beast didn't stop. Draeven half wondered if Quinn would survive when a shield appeared out of nothing. Black as shadow and night, it spread before her like a void into another realm.

The beast kept running, and just when it was upon her it slammed into the mass of darkness—of fear. A lightning-loud crack rang through the yard as it hit the barrier and rebounded. The creature bounced nearly ten feet back, its back legs crumpling as it landed hard against the dry soil, rolling in the plume of orangish-brown dust.

Draeven strode forward on one side, and Quinn approached from the other.

She lifted a hand, and he saw the movements of the basilisk as it started to rise—

"Wait."

There were only two people that could make both him and her pause in a kill.

He looked up as Risk approached. She was covered in a fine sheen of orange that made her eyes seem even brighter as she stepped forward. "Don't kill it," she said. "It's not his fault."

"Are you mad?" Quinn asked. "That beast tried to kill me—"

"It's not his fault," Risk repeated. Her fingers trembled. Draeven looked from the griffin that was beginning to stir again to the girl before him. "I was angry. I got upset, and my magic— it . . ."

"Lashed out," he said, finishing her sentence. It wasn't an accusation, but judging by the way her eyes watered she might have taken it as one. Her jaw clenched, but she nodded once.

"Myori's wrath," Quinn muttered, lowering her hand. "Can you control it?"

"I think so," Risk said, starting forward. He wanted to stop her from approaching the beast, no matter how strong her Maji abilities might be. He knew better than most how much she struggled to calm it. Even still, he knew there was nothing he could do short of beheading the creature.

She lowered herself before it as the griffin moved to stand.

Her head inclined forward, and her hands lifted palm up, outstretched, but waiting for permission. The creature lifted its head, and Draeven clenched his fists—waiting—dreading—what it would do.

But the anxiety was for nothing.

It sat like a common house cat and leaned forward, rubbing its feathered head against her open hands. She smiled softly, whispering words he couldn't hear.

He couldn't help but release a shaky breath and smile too, because a girl with horns sat in the dirt and tamed the most savage of creatures before an entire palace of nobles.

But when she looked up, it was not him she looked at. It was Quinn she smiled toward. His brow furrowed as he looked between the two sisters. He suspected it was something she had done to cause Risk to get that upset to begin with, given the beast charged at her and no other.

Unlike the lilac-haired woman, Risk seemed to have let it go as she rose to her feet and escorted the creature back inside the tent. The flap closed behind her.

"Whatever you're thinking, get it out of your head."

He turned. "You have no idea what I'm thinking."

Quinn's eyes dropped to the sword, unsheathed and in hand, and then slowly traveled back up the length of his person. The way she watched him wasn't heated or kind. It was like a predator studying the weaknesses of its prey before it pounced.

"Don't I, though?" she asked.

Draeven fumbled for words, and she smiled coldly. Quinn kept walking past him and entered the tent, closing it behind her.

Too hot to ignore the pounding in his head as his own magic started to eat at him, Draeven took her dismissal as his turn to leave.

She was right, and he loathed her for it.

Games of War

"When you have all the jewels and power that money can buy, the only thing left to bargain with is secrets."
— *Lazarus Fierté, soul eater, the esoteric King of Norcasta*

Lazarus lifted the crystal decanter from his desk and poured himself two fingers worth. In the dim candlelight, the amber was a few shades darker; closer to a walnut brown. He brought the glass to his lips and drank half in one swallow.

It burned on the way down, but his souls quieted, if only for a moment.

He took a seat in the thick-cushioned chair and leaned back, letting out a heavy sigh. Lazarus wanted to believe it was the events of the day that had riled him and put his magic so on edge, but he knew the truth. In two days' time the blood heirs were scheduled to arrive, and with them, a litany of problems. Even overlooking Lord Callis' death, he knew that Quinn was going to be an issue.

Rumors had reached his door about Amelia and her brothers. What they wanted. What they planned to bargain with. What was worse was that Lazarus actually had to consider it. With Callis gone, it was only a matter of time until word got out and the other southern noblemen would hear of it. He'd lose at least one member of his private council—likely more. Not to mention the support of his countrymen. Without them and their lands, Norcasta was divided and war was imminent.

It was Lazarus' duty to prevent that war.

Even if he wanted nothing more than to crush the entitled children beneath his boot and let Quinn have her way with them. All of them.

Lazarus sighed, downing the rest of his drink and placing the glass on the desk. It clanked against the hardwood surface, ringing like death's bell through the empty room. With the burn in his chest and the drowsiness settling in his limbs, Lazarus enjoyed the half hour that glass would give him where his mind and his body were his own . . . and not the beasts within.

Two sharp raps had his muscles tensing again within seconds.

"Who is it?" Lazarus called.

"Petra Stoneskin, Your Grace," came the slightly muffled response. "I'd like a word, on behalf of my queen."

Lazarus scrubbed a hand down his face. "Come in."

The knob turned as the door swung open and in walked the Pirate Queen's hand. Her braided hair swung back and forth, the wooden beads clanking with each step as she came to stand before him. The lock clicked as the door swung shut behind her. Lazarus motioned to one of the chairs across from him, and Petra instead turned and grabbed a second crystal glass from across the room. She brought it over and took the decanter, filling his first and then her own. She took a seat before bringing the glass to her lips. Her expression was closed off and unreadable as she tipped it back and swallowed a mouthful. Her lips pressed together as she lowered the glass.

"Not bad," she said thoughtfully, "but I make better."

Lazarus snorted. "Did you come here to steal and insult my spirits, or was there a purpose to this late evening visit?"

"Can't I stop by to say thank you for the party you threw my niece?"

"No."

Petra hummed, taking another sip. "You keep an interesting court, Lazarus, and that's saying something given the court I come from."

Lazarus leaned back. "The way I've heard it, Imogen has had quite the culling since we last saw her."

Petra nodded, staring in her glass. "I wasn't brought back because I wanted to return. I was brought back because she had no one else she trusted enough to take the job."

Lazarus nodded. "I'd heard that as well."

"And the rumors?" Petra asked, slowly raising her eyes. "Have you heard those too?"

Lazarus regarded her for a moment, noting her strong jaw and harsh features. Her skin was dark and not unused to the sun, but it didn't care for the dryer climate of the south. Her age showed more. Her eyes still held a keenness that saw much and revealed little.

"Depends. Which rumors do you speak of?" Lazarus replied, and she grinned, golden and yellowed teeth both on display.

"I might have been away for a long time, but I know better than to fall for that," she chuckled.

"Well, I'm afraid I cannot confirm or deny without knowing what you speak of," Lazarus said, "so if that's all . . ." He raised an eyebrow, indicating that he wasn't in the mood for more games. Mazzulah knew he played enough because of Quinn.

"The blood heirs," Petra said, the nonchalance dropping from her tone. "What do you know of them?"

Lazarus peered at her over the lip of his cup as he

took a swig, the spirits dulling the souls further. If they were going to have this sort of conversation, he didn't need them acting out for Petra to see.

"Too much," he said at first. "Not enough."

Petra squinted, amusement toying at the corners of her lips. "That doesn't follow."

"Neither does your line of questioning," Lazarus responded. "Imogen's my ally, so why are we speaking in riddles?"

A smile toyed at the edge of her lips as she sucked the air between her two front teeth and leaned forward. It occurred to him where Axe got that habit. He found it less juvenile and more calculated when Petra did it. She was Imogen's first mate for decades before being her hand, simply because she was smart enough to be of use, and tough enough to stay alive.

"Are you aware of the proposition Amelia Reinhart plans to offer you?"

Ice shot through his veins while blood went to his head. Lazarus paused, restraining his reaction as the blissfully dulled edge the spirits had taken off sliced through him once more. The monsters beneath his skin writhed in defiance.

"I am."

"Are you aware of what will happen if you don't accept?"

"I can guess." He pressed his lips together and lowered the glass to the table in a firm clink. Lazarus' eyes were hard as he regarded the woman who sat across from him.

"War, kingling, that's what happens. Norcasta is divided through the middle, and you're forced to call upon your allies for help." Petra drained the last of her glass, never breaking eye contact with him, and then placed it on the desk beside his own.

"If war is the price for me to remake this world, then so be it," he answered.

Petra smiled at him like she expected him to respond as such.

"The problem, kingling, is you're not the only one who wishes to remake it." She gave him a knowing look.

"Imogen—"

"Isn't who I speak of," she cut in, interrupting him. Petra raised both eyebrows, and he grimaced.

"Nero," he said on a heavy sigh.

"Yes," she breathed. "Nero." His name hung in the air like an omen to match death's toll. "Imogen's spies tell us that a soothsayer whispers in Amelia's ear. A man that hails from the south."

Lazarus ran a hand over his stubbled jaw, considering that. "With all due respect to Imogen, not all men are loyal to their place of birth. I know she's had issues with spies ever since Zorel, but—"

"They shot down a sparrow carrying a message. It was written in Trienian."

Lazarus lost a heavy breath. The scar over his left

eye seemed to burn, if only in memories. "He's not entering the game just yet, but he plans to."

"When?" she asked.

Lazarus stared at the water spot on his desk, turning over the possibilities in his mind. The truth was he had only a guess. If Nero truly had his hold on the heirs, then there was only one outcome, and it could happen in a week, in a month, in a year. No matter the attempts at diplomacy—it would happen.

"Soon," he said eventually.

"And when he does enter?"

Lazarus looked at her and answered.

"There's no avoiding it. We go to war and hope it's enough."

Reinharts' Welcome

"Jealousy is a monster in and of itself, but so is fear."
— *Quinn Darkova, fear twister, right-hand to the King of*
Norcasta

L eviticus' eye bore down on them as they waited
for the entourage to arrive. Word had reached
the palace when the heirs' carriage crossed the city
gates. From there it was a mad frenzy to gather the
whole of Lazarus' house to greet the late king's
children.

Quinn sighed, pulling at the leather strap around
her torso where the fabric squeezed her slick skin.
While N'skara was no longer her home, she could do
without the ungodly heat that pervaded Leone for six
months of the year.

"Myori's wrath, what's taking them so long?" Quinn griped. "Is the carriage being pulled by children?"

Beside her, Lorraine stifled a laugh. From down near the bottom of the steps, Draeven turned and shot them a look of annoyance. Quinn stared back, lifting both eyebrows. Wariness entered his features, and he turned back to the open gates, waiting for the royal brats they were all spending far too much time coddling. They should have been spending time assessing the reality of the situation.

"Draeven doesn't seem very pleased with you," Lorraine murmured softly. Her eyes darted to see if any of the advisors standing several feet away took notice.

"When is he ever?" Quinn scoffed, eyes narrowing as the sound of wheels crunching bits of rock drifted from the uneven streets beyond.

Lorraine inclined her head forward. "He's seemed unusually cross since the incident at Axe's party. Did something happen?"

Quinn's lips curved up in a wicked grin. "You could say that. Our dear Lord Sunshine was simply reminded of his place with certain persons."

Lorraine lifted both brows and tilted her head. "You mean with your sister."

"That I do," Quinn said, her eyes narrowing on the gates as an ebony monstrosity came barreling through. The carriage was larger than any at the palace and was pulled by four stallions, sable-haired and slick with sweat. It was no wonder it took them so long to get here from the city gates.

The carriage rolled to a stop; behind it, a contingent of guards riding horses followed in suit. They poured in from the palace gates, and by the time it ceased, Quinn counted no less than fifty armed men. Uneasiness spread through her chest as she took a step forward, the toe of her boot coming to the very edge of the platform. Ten steps and several soldiers below, Lazarus stood waiting as a stout man jumped off of the front of the carriage and ran around the side to open the door.

Quinn flexed her fingers and black tendrils rushed to them, waiting for their master's command. She held tight, waiting to see what would happen.

The first one to step out of the carriage was a small, reedy man. His cheeks were gaunt and his dark hair oily enough it clung together in thick strands that brushed just above his cheek bones. He wasn't skinny, but fortune certainly hadn't favored him with a bolder physique. While he wore the finest fabrics in his house colors, there was no air of importance about him. Nothing interesting, nor unique. Quinn tilted her head as he shook hands with Lazarus, his eyes scanning the stairs in one motion. He paused upon seeing her, and while there was no reaction on his face, she knew this was his job. To be unremarkable and unseen.

"Erwing Reinhart, Your Grace," he said in a surprisingly charismatic voice despite his bland appearance. Quinn pursed her lips, but stayed where she was.

"Welcome, Lord Reinhart," Lazarus said, nodding once.

Behind Erwing, the next person to step out of the carriage was a giant of a man, large enough to dwarf even Vaughn. He was half a head taller than Lazarus and twice as wide. His clothes fit him tighter than they should, making it clear that it was both muscle and fat that accounted for his girth. He had the same dark hair as Erwing, though it was both shorter and cleaner. His eyes glinted red.

Rage thief, Quinn surmised. He lumbered forward, too large to move in a swift or elegant fashion.

"Titus Reinhart," the man said through gritted teeth. Lazarus assessed him with the same closed off glance he'd used with Erwing.

"Please excuse my brother, Your Grace," a lovely, silken voice called from the carriage. "The heat must be getting to him." Quinn narrowed her eyes on the door of the carriage as a dark-haired beauty dressed in spidersilk stepped out. The admiral blue fabric clung to her form, showcasing both curves and the surreptitious swell of her breasts. Smooth, unblemished skin peeked out of the hemline; a shade darker than the desert sands that surrounded them.

She approached Lazarus, pushing a waterfall of

shiny black hair over her shoulder to better showcase her assets. Quinn tilted her head and raised an eyebrow. The fear at her fingers buzzed with excitement, sensing her change in mood.

"You must be Amelia," Lazarus said, his voice gruff.

"That I am, Your Grace," she simpered, dropping into a curtsy.

"Thank you for coming all this way," he continued, his voice thick. Quinn was already moving down the steps before she could reply.

"The pleasure is all ours—" Amelia started, before she was interrupted.

"Quinn Darkova," she announced, coming up beside Lazarus, in between him and Draven. "Right-hand to *the King*."

Lazarus stiffened, and the smile on Amelia's face froze into place as she turned her head. Quinn gave her a smile in return. One that was all teeth. The courtyard seemed to wait in suspense for a moment while Amelia didn't respond.

"Draeven Adelmar," the other man beside her said, stepping forward. "Left-hand to the King"—he leaned forward— "and between you and I, the more pleasurable one to boot."

Quinn regarded him coldly as the courtyard broke out in a chorus of skittering laughs, the tension breaking just as Draeven had intended. "I wasn't aware you were in the business of pleasuring *anyone*,

Lord Sunshine," Quinn quipped, causing Draeven to freeze. He cast her a look of warning even as he took Amelia's hand and pressed a chaste kiss to the back of it.

"For the right woman, a man will do anything," Draeven answered. "Just ask the guards." Behind him another chorus of chuckles sounded, less wary and more at ease than before.

"Forgive my house, Lady Reinhart. They forget themselves at times . . ." Lazarus' voice trailed off, hoarser than before. Quinn turned to regard him for a moment, but he wasn't paying her any mind. His intense eyes were all on Amelia.

A splicing sensation ran through her chest. The temperature of the courtyard dropped as ice took root. The blood in her veins froze as Quinn pushed a sweaty lavender lock from her head. This feeling in her chest—it was dark and ugly. She pulled her eyes away from him and found herself staring into the face of Erwing.

"Would you care to take a walk through the castle with me, Lord Erwing? I know you must be tired from your travels, but. . ." She let the words hang, sensing her victory before he spoke.

"I would love to, Lady Darkova. Care to lead? It has been a while since I've lived here." His words were suave and his motions even smoother as he approached, offering her his arm. Quinn took it, hiding the grimace from touching his sweat-slickened skin as they walked around Draeven and Lazarus, ascending the steps with ease. Erwing was several inches shorter than her, but made up for it in his quick pace. On their way through the double doors, she spotted the worried expression on Lorraine's face, but the older woman did well to hide it as they stepped into the castle.

"I've heard a great deal about you, Lady Darkova. N'skari and right-hand to the King. That must be quite the story to tell," he said lightly, both leading and following as they walked down the marbled halls.

"It's less exciting than it sounds, truth be told," Quinn said.

"What a shame. The rumors were fascinating."

"You know what they say about rumors," Quinn said as they strolled. "There's often just as much truth as there is lie."

Erwing regarded her with a knowing expression. A sly smile curling the corners of his lips. "Do you know the secret in how to tell what is truth from lie?" he asked. Quinn quirked a brow, prompting him onward. "Look for what lines up. If it's the same in every story, there's bound to be at least a grain of truth."

Quinn nodded slowly. "And what did the rumors have to say about me?"

Erwing leaned in, almost conspiratorially. The ale on his breath smelled sour and the sweat dotting his brow dropped from his temple to his chin. Despite his appearance, there was something about his face that told her to watch and pay attention.

"Everywhere you go, fear follows—and destruction is all that remains in your wake." His words were as ominous as they were true.

Quinn didn't reply to him. She simply smiled and kept walking.

Her silence was answer enough.

King of Fools

"Kick a dog once and it will return to the hand that feeds it.
Kick a serpent, and it will strike."
— *Lazarus Fierté, soul eater, the foolish King of Norcasta*

Fire licked through his veins. Heat settled beneath his skin. A traitorous warmth thickened in his groin. The breath hissed between his teeth as want came over him, and there was nothing natural about it.

Lazarus peered down at Amelia, suspecting she was the source.

She smiled back in her ridiculous little dress, and while his face didn't show it—there was *nothing* he found appealing about the way she tried to play his emotions. Not when the woman he actually desired walked away arm in arm with the disgusting creature she called brother.

Lazarus' fist closed, his knuckles turning white as desire rode him.

Amelia's nails trailed down the thick fabric of his sleeve. Biting through just enough he was certain it was her power trying to control him.

A weak passion cleaver. That's what the spies had said.

Lazarus gritted his teeth.

Skeevs. That's what he'd thought them.

An idiot. That's what Quinn would call him when this was all over.

For once, he wouldn't hold it against her.

Few Maji abilities were strong enough to influence him, and Amelia's was one of them. She'd have his entire court eating out of the palm of her hand within three days' time.

He needed to rectify this situation, and the hardness of his cock wasn't going to make it any easier.

"We are so tired after our long travels," the woman's honeyed voice grated his ears. "Would it be alright with Your Grace if we turned into our quarters before any evening festivities?" Her warm palm closed around his wrist and another shot of ecstasy ran through him. Closing his eyes and scrubbing his free hand down his face was all he could do to not groan.

He needed to get away from her. Now.

"Your Grace," Draeven said slowly, pulling Lazarus from his thoughts.

"Excuse me," Lazarus said, pulling away from Amelia. She reluctantly let his arm go, a syrupy sweet smile on her face the entire time. "The heat must be getting to all of us today. Lord Adelmar, would you please escort Lady and Lord Reinhart to their quarters."

Draeven nodded once, his violet eyes squinting slightly as he looked between Lazarus and Amelia. His left-hand was smart enough to know something wasn't right, but also smart enough to not speak of it in front of so many eyes.

"Of course," Draeven said, stepping forward. He gave the Lady his best smile as Lazarus ascended the stairs. He stopped at the top step and beckoned Lorraine forward. His stewardess approached, waiting for a command.

He leaned in and whispered, "Find Quinn and send her to me. I'll be in my chambers."

Lorraine nodded once. "Yes, Your Grace."

She turned and headed for the left wing of the palace; in the direction his fear twister had gone. He followed after to the main hall, pausing to scan the hallways. Even from a distance he could feel Amelia's power edging into him. It pushed at his boundaries and enraged the souls within. When Quinn used her power, it stirred them because they *wanted* her. With Amelia, it was not the same. Not even remotely.

Equal parts rage and lust hammered through him.

He turned and headed for his rooms. The further he got from the courtyard, the more her power eased. It was only when he was in his suite with the door closed that he felt her power slip away entirely. Lazarus extended a hand to the wall and leaned against it, catching his breath.

Gods above. He'd been a fool to invite Amelia and her brothers.

If the rage thief was anywhere near as strong as his sister, this was going to be a problem, and he didn't even know what Erwing could do. The rumors were too muddled where he was concerned.

He moved from the wall, further into the King's suite. Crimson sheets rumpled his bed from the many restless nights. Gold and ruby lounges littered the space, leftover from Claudius' reign when he used to take private audiences in his bedchamber because the sickness robbed him of all energy. The servants had done a fine job changing over every aspect in mere weeks to suit him. His house. His rule.

He'd wanted the crown more than *anything*, and he got it.

It was what he'd worked over half his life for.

So why in the dark realm did the weight of the metal on his head make his fists clench? Why did the sight of his colors make his jaw grind?

Why was it that all he thought about the last six

months was the lavender-haired maruda that haunted his dreams and every waking moment?

Lazarus paced. His breaths came heavy. The tension rolling through him would not be abated. Not this time. Not without her.

A knock came at his door and Lazarus stopped. "Come in."

The door swung open, and the rage the beasts beneath his skin felt at being violated by one woman and not appeased by another reached its peak.

Lorraine stood in the doorway. Alone.

"Your Grace—"

"Where is she?"

"Lazarus," Lorraine sighed.

"Where. Is. She?" he asked again. Lorraine's lips pinched together as she looked away. She inhaled once and faced him again. The truth was written all over her face. "She refused me."

Lorraine nodded. "I tried, Lazarus, I did—"

"She refused me," he repeated, almost dumbfounded. Lazarus turned, sending his fist through a wall. The pain barely registered in his hand even as the brick and mortar crumbled to dust. The strength of a troll. He'd pulled on its power unintentionally and the beast obliged as it shared in his anger with him.

"Lazarus," Lorraine repeated sharply. He blinked, turning to the woman before him. "She refused because you won't make up your mind. She's your right-hand by your choosing, and yet anytime she acts as such you admonish her. You made her what she is, and now you expect her to be something different. Something you can control. I've held my tongue these months with you, but it's not right for you to act this way with her." When she finished, her cheeks were pink, and her chest rising and falling rapidly.

"I'm the King," he replied. "I can act in any way I wish."

"You can," Lorraine nodded. "But don't expect her to bend the knee for a king that can't control himself, let alone her. If you want her as a woman, then you take her as that, regardless of what the lords and ladies might say. If you don't, you don't have the right to be angry when she moves on." She gave him a pointed look, and Lazarus swallowed down some of his ire.

"This has nothing to do with Erwing—" he started.

"If you truly believe that, then Quinn is right. You have become a fool."

His stewardess walked out and closed the door softly behind her. Lazarus stood there, staring at the spot she'd been.

Did she just . . . Yes. Yes she did.

Lazarus looked around, running a hand over his stubbled jaw.

First Quinn and now Lorraine. Next thing Draeven would be here giving him 'advice' and then storming out of his chambers. Lazarus settled back on the edge of the bed, lowering his forehead to his open palm.

The crown slid. It hit the marble floors with a clatter.

Lazarus didn't look. He didn't care.

But for once, he listened.

Lorraine had been right. He either took her as she was, or let her go. Quinn would not change for him. She wouldn't change for anyone. She was savage and brutal and cruel.

She was saevyana, and while he'd do most anything for the crown . . .

The one thing he couldn't do was let her go.

Not as his right-hand.

Nor as his woman.

Quinn Darkova was his, and not even the woman herself would keep him from her.

Dinner's Folly

"Illusions come in many forms. None so great as the illusion of safety."
— Quinn Darkova, fear twister, right-hand to the King of Norcasta

Quinn paused at the end of the hallway and lifted a hand. Inside the formal dining room drunken laughter and unease made its way toward her. She hummed under her breath as the whispers of fear rose from her skin, twining together. An image of Lord Callis appeared. He smiled, and her nose twitched as she frowned slightly, adjusting the image until it exuded enough charisma to fool most people. She didn't even have to try to add that hint of darkness in him. The fear added that all by itself. When she was pleased with the illusion before her, Quinn offered it her arm.

Lord Callis took it, and they strolled into the dining room together.

The previous bouts of laughter died down. A stilted silence settled in as Callis leaned in and whispered something in her ear. She laughed softly, purposefully, like she thought it was funny. Across the room, sitting in an oak chair with gold embellishments, Lazarus looked up at her.

The black of his eyes glinted in the low lights. The edges of a shadow peeked out of his tunic, running along his neck. Quinn might have responded, were Amelia Reinhart not sitting next to him.

She moved toward the seat at the other end of the table, between Titus and Lorraine.

"Lady Darkova," Draeven coughed. She squinted at him, two seats down on Lazarus' other side. He motioned to the empty chair between him and the King. "This one is reserved for you, as the right-hand."

"I see," Quinn said. She turned to Lord Callis and shared a knowing look. Her illusion grinned back at her, and took its seat. She walked woodenly down the long table, passing Titus then Lord Northcott, then Dominicus, and finally coming to a stop just past Draeven. On the other side of the table, Lorraine was seated beside Lord Brameer, followed by Lord Langston, who glared at her for simply being present. "Isn't it odd to save a seat for the right-hand, and not the left?" she said softly, pulling back the popular chair with a stiff back and cushions that were more decorative than comfortable.

"Perhaps," Draeven said lightly from her right. "Exceptions must be made for our honored guests, however." He smiled at Amelia, but Quinn didn't glance in her direction. She'd seen her silky black waves piled on her head. Even from across the table the woman scented too strongly of flowers. Quinn sniffed once and frowned distastefully.

"Mmm," she hummed noncommittally as she reached for the clear glass in front of her. The crystal sparkled as she brought it to her nose.

"Water," Lazarus murmured. Amelia, who had been in the middle of prattling on about some Lord, paused. Quinn brought the glass to her lips and took a small sip before lowering it back to the table.

"Mmm," she hummed again, dancing the line of ignoring him and inciting his wrath. If he wanted to play games with her, she would play. She would win.

She would remind him who and what she was.

"Do we have anything stronger than ale?" her illusion asked, calling attention to his side of the table. "Wine, perhaps?" One of the servants who'd been lingering by the door skittered away to fetch some wine at Lord Callis' request. Quinn lifted her glass once more, hiding her grin behind it.

"So, Lazarus," Amelia drawled, bringing this half of the table's attention back to her.

"King," Quinn interrupted before she could continue.

"Excuse—"

"*King* Lazarus," Quinn said. "It's his title, and you're only a noble Lady now. Not a princess. Not an heir. You should not speak like you're equals."

Amelia's mouth opened and closed twice as she tried and failed to find a response.

"Quinn," Draeven leaned in. "This is—"

"Fact," she said, cutting him off.

"Yes, but—"

"Lady Darkova is right," Lord Callis cut in, coming to her defense. Quinn lifted an eyebrow and gave Draeven a tight smile. His jaw clenched, teeth grinding together.

"Thank you, my lord."

Throughout the conversation she'd yet to look toward Lazarus again, but she could sense him. His darkness called to her own, especially when she inflamed it.

A hand closed around her knee beneath the table.

Even through her leather pants, she felt the heat of his skin burning hers.

Quinn swallowed; her throat suddenly dry. Her knee twitched as she tried to shake him off subtly, but Lazarus wouldn't budge.

"Apologies, Your Grace," Amelia quickly amended. "I did not mean to offend."

"No offense taken," Lazarus replied gruffly, his hand moving up her thigh. Quinn's lips pinched together as she looked at her plate. On the other side of her, Draeven was stewing about being shut down by her illusion.

"I wanted to ask," Erwing started, sitting on the other side of Amelia. "I heard rumors of a raksasa being part of your court."

"She's not a raksasa," Quinn and Draeven said simultaneously. She shot him a sideways glance, which he returned. It seemed that at least in this, they could agree.

Erwing's eyebrows rose. "So the rumors are true . . ."

"The rumors are just that," Quinn said pointedly. "Rumors."

A sick thrill entered Erwing's eye as he leaned forward. "But there is a girl, and she does have raksasa blood, does she not?"

Lazarus' hand beneath the table was rapidly approaching the apex of her thighs, as if trying to distract her. She waved him off using a tendril of fear, and his hand disappeared from her skin.

"There is a girl," Draeven nodded. Quinn's eyebrows rose at the nonchalant way he responded. "She has horns and belongs to this house. She's not to be called a raksasa, however. If you see her, I would advise you not to speak to her at all."

"Oh?" Lord Erwing asked, completely engrossed in the conversation. "Why is that?"

"Because the hand of the King told you not to," Draeven responded. Quinn tilted her head in a slight nod, agreeing with that logic.

"Do you know why Draeven is the left and I am the right?" Quinn asked. When Lord Erwing didn't respond, she looked to Amelia, and then Titus. "No? None of you?"

"I've heard—" Erwing started, but Quinn waved him off.

"I'll enlighten you so there's no confusion going forward about what our roles are in the palace." Quinn leaned forward, resting her elbows on the white tablecloth as she spoke directly to the two Reinharts in front of her. "The left-hand is the hand that feeds. Draeven exists to play nice with lord and ladies of the court. He's the one that the people of Norcasta will come to love because he's kind. He's predictable. Safe."

Draeven snorted once, rolling his eyes. Quinn ignored him.

"And the right?" Erwing prompted.

"Is the hand that strikes," she answered. "Draeven consoles the people, but I ensure they know who is truly in charge and don't question it. That applies to noblemen and women, Lord Erwing." She met

Lorraine's steady gaze at the other end of the table. They were almost the same words she'd told her weeks ago when she'd killed the very Lord she was now impersonating. The other woman smiled a fraction and nodded once.

"And how is it that you 'strike', Lady Darkova?" he asked, a sly smile lit his face. She didn't smile in return as she looked back to him. She simply lifted her glass of water and took a drink.

"Let's hope for your sake that you never find out."

Erwing opened his mouth to respond again, but servants began to pour in from the outer hall. They carried silver platters, piled high with smoked pig, roasted vegetables, braised potatoes, and plum pudding. For a moment, she thought of Axe and her obsession with plum liquor. Neither her nor Vaughn had been invited to dinner. As emissaries, they were required for official functions, but not intimate gatherings with the King and his closest advisors.

"Lydia, isn't it?" Lord Callis spoke from the end of the table. "This looks delicious, Lydia. Do give the kitchen my regards." The servant girl blushed a shade of crimson and hurried out of the dining room with the others, her hips swaying a tad more than when she entered.

"Lord Callis, always such a charmer, he is," Quinn commented merrily while loading her plate with food.

"Lord Callis?" Erwing asked.

"Yes . . ." Quinn trailed off. "That is what I said."

Was he daft?

No. She already knew that to not be the case. If he was, her heart wouldn't have just skipped a beat.

The way he questioned it had a sick sensation thickening in her stomach.

"Yes, I'm simply confused why he was mentioned when he isn't here."

"Brother," Amelia chided. "What are you talking about? The dear man is right there." She motioned toward the end of the table where the illusion lifted its cup of wine before draining it entirely, then turning to clap Titus on the back. The rage thief stiffened.

"Right where?" Erwing asked, looking between his sister, Quinn, and the empty chair.

Myori's wrath, she cursed internally as it occurred to her what was going on. She leaned in subtly and whispered in Draeven's ear, "What are the odds he's a null?"

Draeven stiffened.

"Right there," Amelia motioned, growing frustrated with what she perceived as her brother's antics.

"I'm telling you, Amelia, there's nothing there. The chair is empty." He waved his hand toward it, tossing down his napkin though he'd yet to take a bite. "What in the dark realm is Titus cringing about?"

Quinn quickly directed the illusion to get to his feet.

"I can assure you, I'm right here, Lord Reinhart. Are you sure that the travel hasn't done in—"

Lord Northcott got to his feet. Jaw tense and teeth clenched together. He stood and faced the illusioned lord. "Right before the late king died he brought us to his bedside. You, me, Brameer, and Langston. What did he say?"

It was only through the years of learning to mimic others that she kept her expression confused as Lord Callis looked taken aback. "This is hardly the place for this, Darren—"

"What did he say, Artan?"

Quinn didn't know. "I—" Callis broke off to wipe his forehead and let out a heavy breath. She flushed his cheeks and dilated his pupils, letting the wine they thought he'd consumed show. "I can't say I remember. The wine must be getting to my head."

"Excuse me, but *who* are you talking to?" Erwing said, leaning back in exasperation.

Lord Darren Northcott turned to the table, his face grim. "I don't know, but that man is *not* Artan Callis. The real Artan wouldn't have forgotten Claudius' last words."

"Trust in my chosen heir," Lord Langston said. "For he will pave the way to a brighter future for all of the Sirian continent."

Quinn did a subtle sweep of the table, trying to gage reactions. It was a mistake.

"It's her," Amelia Reinhart stated. "Erwing is a

null. Magic doesn't affect him. Which means whatever it is we're seeing isn't there. Everyone knows there's only one kind of Maji that can create illusions."

All eyes turned to Quinn.

She regarded the woman across from her apathetically.

Quinn had two options right now, to stand down or to stand up. She got to her feet, and with a flourish of her hand, Lord Callis vanished.

"It appears you've caught me."

"If that was only an illusion . . ." Lord Brameer began, already moving on to the truth that they'd specifically tried to keep from him and the other lords.

"Where is he? Where is the real Lord Callis?" Northcott demanded.

Quinn sighed. "He's dead."

True Loyalty

"There are two kinds of kings. Those ruled by men, and those that rule men."
— *Lazarus Fierté, soul eater, the possessive King of Norcasta*

The wooden chairs around the small council table sat unoccupied.

At the far end of the room, Dominicus leaned against the wall, one hand on the hilt of his sword. Not far from him, Quinn stood, unmoving. She didn't pace or mutter as Lord Brameer did. She didn't stew as Langston or Northcott. She simply stood and waited for the eye of the storm to pass, and the lords of his council to rage at them once more. To his right, Draeven had his hands splayed on the oak table, his head hanging as he took a deep breath. The man was exhausted. They all were after they'd spent weeks pretending that Lord Callis had never died.

In some ways, it was a relief to no longer have to keep up the farce. His attention and that of his vassals was better spent on things other than handling the distasteful things the late lord engaged in. True as that might be, though, it didn't prevent the conflict brewing among his own council that was going to reach a head this night.

"My lords," Draeven began.

"Don't 'my lords' us, Draeven Adelmar. By the girl's own admission, she killed Artan and you helped them cover it up," Langston responded. His eyes, while old and gray, were also hard as he regarded Lazarus' left-hand.

"Why should it matter whether we covered it up?" Quinn responded sharply. "If the King chooses to do so, it's not your business."

"And did the King choose for you to kill Lord Callis?" Langston responded acidly toward her.

Her lips twitched. "No."

"Precisely," he responded, turning to Lazarus once more. "You've taken this *child* as your right-hand and allowed her to act however she wants—kill whoever she wants, and then hide it. What does that say about you, Your Grace?"

"What are you implying it says, Langston?" Lazarus asked, a hint of darkness creeping into his tone once more.

"You can't control her."

He wanted to laugh, because in that moment it was painfully clear to him that Langston was right. He couldn't control Quinn. He never had been able to, and if he had his way, he never would. Once he'd dreamed of being the hand that guided her, but over the months he'd had alone with the iron and oak throne, he'd had to face that simple truth.

When she returned, he once more tried to make her bend, and she once more showed him that she doesn't bend. She doesn't yield.

She gives her loyalty freely, but nothing and no one will control her should she not choose it.

It was the very reason she would be his right-hand as long as she chose so.

If he couldn't control her, no one could.

Not the lords or ladies.

Not the heirs currently making a mess of his court.

Not the one down south, who would soon be entering the game.

In a world full of men who were bound by societal law, Quinn was free.

Truly free.

It made her the most dangerous weapon in the world, and the one he desired above all.

"You're right," Lazarus said. "I can't. We're better for it." From her spot in the far corner of the room, Quinn narrowed her eyes at him and tilted her head.

Her pupils expanded, and the shadow of Neiss danced under her skin, close enough to the surface that should the lords see, they'd begin to wonder what she really was. Fear twister? Soul eater? Chaos given form?

"Excuse me?" Lord Brameer said, turning on his heel. "Better for it? Better for your *whore* running around touting the sigil of the crown to keep her from the noose—"

Several things happened at once. The tendrils beneath Quinn's skin turned stark. Her eyes darkened further as fear leapt to the fingertips. He wouldn't have noticed had he not been watching her when the lord made a misstep in thinking he had the same protection that Quinn did. Draeven looked up right as Lazarus' fingers curled around the lord's throat.

He slammed him into the wall with one arm, holding him a foot above the marble floors.

"I'm only going to say this once, so listen carefully, Henri," Lazarus said, stripping him of his title. "Quinn is my vassal. My right-hand. My fear twister. You can call her any of those things, but she is not my *whore*. Say it once more, and I'll let her play with you as she did Callis after he orchestrated a slave hunt."

"He—" Brameer's eyes went wide. His cheeks were already a ruddy color of rouge and steadily turning purple.

"He brought out a boy. A child. He planned for us to hunt him down like a boar. So tell me, Henri, if my council is better off without a man who would hunt down children for sport?"

Sweat dotted the lord's temple as he tried to nod but failed. His fat lips quivered as he whispered, "Y-yes, Your G-grace."

Lazarus released him, and the lord fell to the ground, landing with his legs sprawled and head hanging. He tried to scurry to his feet as soon as Lazarus stepped back.

"If Quinn was acting outside the will of law, so was Artan Callis. The difference is that I know where her loyalties lie. That's more than I can say for you three. Your spies reported that the heirs were weak. That it was only pity and old blood which kept them well housed in the north." Lazarus walked around the table to stand between Quinn and Draeven. "Not only were your reports faulty, but the capitol is now at risk given the magic they possess and the armed men they brought with. I should have listened to my right-hand and master of arms, and now it seems I'll have to find another way to deal with the heirs that are *not* here for a social visit."

"Another way, Your Grace?" Langston asked, his gray eyes narrowing. "Surely you don't mean to turn down Lady Reinhart's proposal, do you?"

On his right, Quinn stiffened, but didn't comment.

"Lady Reinhart's proposal is as empty as your head if you think I'm sharing the crown with the very heirs that have plotted my demise for years now," Lazarus replied coldly.

"How exactly do you expect to find peace if you won't take her hand in marriage and your right-hand has killed one of the only lords that have supported your ascension from the beginning?" Langston responded, his voice gravelly but strong.

"Quite simply, actually," Lazarus said. "If they don't cede to the crown and disband whatever coup they're intending, then Quinn is going to deal with them, and I have a strong suspicion that Lady Amelia does not want to be at the other end of her ministrations."

"Madness," Langston muttered. "This is madness." From his place against the other wall, Lord Brameer swallowed. It was clear he agreed with Langston, but wasn't about to say as much. The only lord who'd yet to speak through all of this was Northcott as he watched it play out with silent lips and guarded eyes. "You mean to bring war on us."

"I mean to rule, and if the lords won't accept it so long as the Reinharts plot against me, then I'll eliminate them from the equation. And if that isn't enough, I'm certain there are farmers who would love to suddenly be the lord of whatever pisshole in Norcasta these men think they own. They will bend, Langston, or they will be cut off at the knees. At this point, it matters not how it's done, as long as they understand their place at the end of the day."

Toward the end of his speech, Lazarus could sense the shift in himself. He'd tried Draeven's way. He catered to the fools. He let them have their parties and play their games.

The lords of Norcasta didn't want to fall in line.

Now he would make them.

War was imminent either way if Nero was pulling the strings. It was better to get a handle on his country now instead of later.

"I think," Draeven cut in, "that we should adjourn for tonight. Emotions are running high and everyone's had their share of wine . . ." He trailed off, likely recalling Quinn's obscene illusion that played Lord Callis perfectly.

It irked Lazarus how brazen the illusion had been. The detail that had gone into it also impressed him on a certain level. It wasn't the sheer power she put behind it, but the attention she must have paid watching him the few times they'd met.

She'd catalogued the smallest nuances in his movements and verbiage.

It should terrify him, but the truth was it only made him want her more.

He blinked, and the lords were already shuffling out. Draeven closed the door behind them. "I don't know what is with you tonight, but I'm going to assume it has to do with the passion cleaver down the hall who tried to get me to join her in her chambers this afternoon."

Lazarus nodded once. "They're not here to make peace. They've brought war to our doorstep. I'm only acting in kind."

Draeven sighed. "The lords are going to be a problem after this evening."

Lazarus shrugged. "They are lesser men. Being born into station has made them lazy and far too willful. I gave the council my decision. If they choose to turn against me, they will come to sorely regret that choice. Word will spread, and Norcasta will fall in line."

"And if they don't?" Draeven asked. "If you're wrong?"

"If I have to choose between love and fear, then I will choose fear."

His left-hand shook his head. "As much as I don't agree with this, you may not have another option after this visit with the Reinharts is over. The lords will never love you; not when she can wrap anyone around her finger with her magic."

From the corner of the room, Dominicus came forward. "I need to make sure Lorraine got back to her chambers after escorting them to theirs, and then I'm taking watch with whatever guard you have posted. I want to know where these bastards are at all times."

Lazarus nodded. "Draeven, please ensure that Vaughn and Axe are both in their rooms and haven't managed to draw too much attention to themselves."

His left-hand looked between Lazarus and Quinn, shaking his head again as if he knew of the King's intentions. "I hope you know what you're doing," he said, and Lazarus knew he wasn't talking about the Reinharts.

"I do."

Draeven watched him for a moment longer before sighing and then leaving at last. The door clicked shut once more. Quinn still hadn't moved or spoken.

"I called on you this afternoon," Lazarus said into the dark room.

"And I refused you," she answered, slowly moving to walk around the table. Her sharp nails trailed over the hard wood.

"I know," he said. "I don't blame you."

She paused, her head tilting once more as she regarded him. "I was beginning to wonder if the man I left in N'skara *stayed* in N'skara."

"No," he moved toward the table, standing directly across from her. "You were gone for a while, and I began to question."

"I came back," she said softly. "Just as I said I would."

"You did," he nodded, running a hand over his stubbled jaw. "I want to make a trade."

"Oh?" she asked, almost coy.

"A truth for a truth," he clarified. Her slanted eyes peering up at him made the souls vie for power. A wicked grin curved up her lips.

"Very well, ask your question."

Lazarus leaned forward, placing his hands on the table. Less than a foot separated them. The scent of damp petals and midnight weeds hit him, and he inhaled sharply. It struck him how similar this was to the night she'd returned.

"Why do you follow me?"

She didn't react at first, seeming content to study his features. Her lavender hair tumbled down her shoulders in a wild mane, framing the sharp angles of her face. Her skin was so pale it was almost translucent. Blue veins ran across her chest and down her arms, and he knew from memory they'd turn black when she channeled fear magic. Right now, though, in the dimly lit room, all he could see was the brightness of her eyes and the curve of her lips. His cock stiffened, already anticipating how this was going to end.

She leaned forward and said quietly, "I would have thought it obvious, but perhaps not. I follow you because you're the only one worth following." She snorted once. "Even when you're being an idiot."

"Why?" he repeated. "Why am I the only one worth following to you?"

"Answer me this," she leaned away. "Do you trust me? Implicitly?"

"Yes."

"And why is that?" His lips pressed together because she wasn't following the rules. She was making up her own. Then again, that's what she often did with most everything.

"Because I understand you. Your darkness. Your drive. I know what makes you tick, and I know that you're only here because you've chosen to be here."

She nodded. "Like calls to like, Lazarus. That's why I follow you, and why I will continue to do so until the dark realm claims me."

Loyalty. This was what true loyalty was.

Not the half-earned trust of pathetic noblemen who would stab him in the back for the next monarch they could place on the throne that would do their bidding.

The only thing Quinn ever wanted was freedom, just as the only thing he sought after was power. In the end, they've both gotten what they wanted through the other. Lazarus leaned back and began to walk around the table. His skin heated as his heart pounded in his chest.

"I want you to be mine. Only mine."

"I belong to no man. You know this," she answered, taking a step toward him. They came toe-to-toe.

"I do, but it changes nothing. I want you. No—" His voice turned gruff as he grabbed her upper arms and turned them, pushing her back toward the table. He kicked the chairs out of the way, and she didn't stop him. "I need you, as much as I need this crown on my head. I need you in my bed and at my side.

You dance with Mazzulah in the darkness and you play with fear. My advisors would say you are the worst woman on the entire Sirian continent to pick, and I don't care anymore. I need you. Lords and ladies and gods all be damned."

Her chest rose and fell softly, but rapidly. Her skin turning almost warm to the touch. The black in her eyes nearly blotted out all blue, and she breathed harder. "I won't marry you," she said. "So if that's what this is—"

"I'm not asking for marriage. I know you don't want to be queen." He leaned forward, crowding her space as his hands loosened just enough to slide up her arms and over her shoulders. One came to wrap around her slender throat possessively, the other moving to her hair.

"Then what is it you're asking for, Lazarus?"

"Choose to be mine in the ways that matter. I promise to never chain you. To never hold you back. I accept you as you are. You could kill a hundred more lords, and it's not going to change this." He took a deep breath. "It's not going to change what I feel. Nothing is. Not the crown. Not Amelia Reinhart and her damned magic. Not even the gods themselves could stop this."

"And if I say no?" she asked.

He had a feeling that this question was important; that his answer would decide hers.

"If you say no, then I plan to spend the next four

years trying to change your mind because like calls to like, *saevyana*. If not now, eventually you will give in to me."

A twisted smile curved up her lips. "My my," she breathed, a hint of winter touched him. "You do learn." She reached behind her and gripped the edge of the table, lifting herself onto it. Quinn parted her legs, keeping her hands where they were. Lazarus stepped into her heat.

"Is this a yes?" he asked, releasing her hair to wrap one arm around her waist. His shaft stiffened further, and he pressed into her.

Quinn groaned. "You really are an idiot some-times." She pushed into him, grinding against his hardness. "I'm yours as much as I can be any man's."

He didn't care that it wasn't necessarily a yes. It was close enough. It was the best she could give, for now.

And for now, it would do.

Lazarus released her waist, running his hand up her supple back. He stopped at her leather binding, fingers pulling at the buckle that kept it clasped. The leather band slackened. He followed the path of the strap around to the front without releasing her throat, and pushed it up, letting her breasts slip free.

Quinn squirmed, her hips rocking into his as she tried to reach her release. Lazarus tsked, pushing her back. His hand on her throat made her have to yield to him. She released her grip on the edge of the table as her back hit the wood. Lazarus leaned over, taking her budded nipple between his teeth and sucking. Quinn moaned. Her legs wrapped around him as she tried to find friction. He grabbed her hip with his free hand, forcing her to the table while he whorled his tongue around her and then sucked once more.

He released her breast, turning to the other. "Unlace your pants," he said gruffly. Quinn didn't argue with him as she reached past her stomach to the laces of her trousers, tugging at them in desperation. "Tug them down," he commanded, nipping at her hardened bud. Her hips jerked. She released the weak hold she had on him with her legs, instead putting the heels of her boots to the edge of the table to lift her butt, leaving her conveniently spread further for him. He lifted his hand from her stomach and brought it up to tweak her abandoned breast while she shifted to try to push her trousers down. She didn't get very far with her legs spread as wide as they were. Lazarus groaned, but released her entirely as he leaned back. He grabbed her calves and pulled them from the edge of the table, then hooked his thumbs in her pants, pulling once. They went halfway down her thighs before stopping, and she grunted in agitation.

"Turn over," Lazarus said gruffly.

"What?" she asked, the toes of her boots knocking his feet because she couldn't quite reach the ground. Lazarus grasped her waist and turned her onto her stomach, then pulled her a few inches closer, letting her bare ass hang over the edge of the table. "What in the dark realm are you—"

Her words turned into a garbled moan as he reached between her only barely parted thighs and thrust two fingers into her wetness. The tips of her boots scratched against the floor, giving her enough purchase to rock her hips back into his hand.

He curled his fingers, tapping on that taut flesh that would make her erupt. She let out a strangled sound abruptly, her channel tightening around him, sucking his fingers greedily. Only when the aftershock died down did he reach for the laces of his own trousers. Not having the patience with them anymore than he did Quinn's, he grabbed both sides and pulled. The laces snapped, causing the others to unravel as his shaft came free. He fisted himself in his hand once, widening his stance so that her body was right in front of him. Lazarus put the head of his cock to her entrance and pushed it through her folds. Quinn let out another moan, and as soon as he breached her opening, he thrust once, feeding the whole of him into her.

Pushed to the hilt, Lazarus grabbed her hips and began thrusting.

A mad desire to dominate her overcame him as he pushed between the tight space of her thighs. The table shook, its legs screeching against the floor with every movement. He reached around with one hand to pinch the bud between her legs. Quinn jerked, and he thrust into her harder. The souls in him let out a victorious roar, threatening to take hold of his very body as their animalistic urges washed over him.

"Lazarus," Quinn moaned. Her channel started to flutter around him, and he sensed she was close.

"Not yet," he said, pulling out. Quinn growled and tendrils of fear jumped from her skin to his. The feel of her magic only riled the souls further as they pushed him to the brink of madness, having near as much control of his body as he did.

"Finish the job, *King*," she hissed.

Lazarus vied with the souls for power. They wanted her however they could get her, and he wanted more. In the end, his hands reached for her smooth backside. Quinn wiggled once, trying to give him the hint. It was only when his thumbs pulled at her cheeks that she froze.

"What are you—"

"Finishing the job," he ground out in a voice more animal than man. The tip of his shaft, still coated in her wetness, pressed to her other hole. He pushed, her slickness only allowing him part of an inch past the barrier before delicious friction pulled at him. "This is going to hurt." He was trying to control himself for her sake. Quinn didn't argue or try to fight. Her body relaxed, the stiffness of her muscles leaving her as she said, "I know. Do it."

Her permission made it all the sweeter as he started to push inside her. He could tell she was gritting her teeth, but she didn't scream or cry. The tightness of this opening hurt in the best possible ways as he forced himself inside her. His tip breached the rim of muscle trying to expel him, and she let out a small moan. He couldn't tell if it was pain or pleasure. Lazarus pushed the rest of the way, seating himself as deep as he could go. Being inside her made the souls' aggression lessen. He was himself enough to ask, "Have you done this before?"

"Several times," she gasped. "When I was too poor to afford the tonic that prevents me getting with child . . ."

"Good, you know what to expect," he grunted, thrusting into her. Her spine curved as she lifted her backside into him. He brought one hand around to her front once more. Breathing raggedly, he used two fingers to rub her clit while fucking her from behind. The table rocked once more, and after several minutes of it, the legs snapped entirely. The thing toppled downward, and he grabbed her waist to prevent her fall. A plume of dust filled the small council chambers before settling. Quinn leaned forward, reaching for the ground. He didn't pull out as he let her down and got on his knees with her. Backside splayed and filled with his shaft, Quinn put her hands on the top of the broken table and widened her legs a fraction. Lazarus pumped harder, the only sound to be heard was the smack of skin meeting bare skin. Wetness flooded his hand as he rubbed her once more. As he sought his release, her channel suddenly tightened, and her muscles sucked at him. He stopped playing with her with his fingers, instead grabbing her hips with both hands and plunging into her rapidly.

"Oh gods, yes," she moaned.

Fire consumed him as his shaft filled and then emptied. He spent his seed inside her, thrusting shallowly while he rode out the wave of euphoria. When the jets of pleasure stopped coming, he stilled, his sweaty body wrapped around hers.

"You're better than the stable boy was," she said lightly.

Despite the heaviness of the day, Lazarus let out a dark chuckle. "You should know by now I'm not done with you." She turned her head to the side, peering back at him. He pulled out, liking the sight of his release on her skin. Lazarus kept that thought to himself as he stood and walked toward the door. "Adjust your clothes. There's a hot bath waiting in my chambers. You're going to join me, and then I'm going to have you again, and so help you, Quinn, if you're not in my chambers in the morning, not even Neiss will keep me from hunting you down."

Quinn grinned slyly as she got to her feet and adjusted her clothes.

"The god or the snake?" she asked lightly as they walked out of the small council room and toward his own chambers.

"Both."

Uneasy Times

"They say people can't change, but that's not true. It's just easier to believe than the alternative; that people can change if given enough motivation—for better and for worse."
— *Mariska "Risk" Darkova, beast tamer*

Risk walked seven steps, paused, and then turned on her heel, repeating the motion. The blood heirs had arrived yesterday. She watched them from her window, watched Quinn as she strode down the steps, so sure of herself. The King had blown her off, and Risk's sister had returned in a rage. Luckily for the guards, she hadn't turned to toying with them, but instead ranted about foolish kings and *Lord Idiot*.

That was before she'd gone to dinner.

The dinner that had been over eleven hours ago.

Quinn still hadn't returned.

Risk turned once more and a shadow in the window made her pause. She approached it slowly. Pulling her thumb away from her mouth, where she'd been biting the nail to the quick, she reached the padded alcove seat and climbed on top of it, kneeling in front of the window. The thick men's pants she wore kept the embroidery from biting into her shins as she leaned forward and unlatched the window. It creaked as she pushed it open a fraction. Sunlight glinted off the smudged windowpanes.

A creature cawed and she peered over the edge.

Something flew under her window, but disappeared out of sight before she could be certain what. It looked like a bird, but moved like a shadow. She blinked twice, examining the rooftops.

The only thing that remained was a single silver feather.

It was drifting north.

Risk shivered, pulling away from the edge and closing the window shut. The metal lock clicked right as a scuffle outside her bedroom door drew Risk's attention. She twisted around so that she was sitting on the edge of the window seat before getting to her feet. She grabbed a dagger from the tableside. Her fingernails turned to claws as she closed her eyes and followed the magic, taking in her field of vision.

Her eyes snapped open as the lock started to turn.

In the doorway stood Quinn. Her sister raised

both eyebrows and nodded toward the dagger. Behind her a pale-haired man was shuffling away quickly, trying to be unseen. Risk strode forward, the hand holding the dagger falling to her side as she reached the doorway and stuck her head out. All the way at the other end of the hall she could make out Draeven as he turned the corner. His clothes were the same as the one's he'd worn at her training the day before.

"What was he doing outside?" she asked.

Quinn sighed, stepping into their chambers. She started to undress while the door was still open. "Guarding your door."

Risk turned, closing the door behind her. "Why?"

"Because," Quinn paused, pulling at the leather strap around her torso to release the tension. "The heirs are here and one of them has taken an interest in you."

"In me?" Risk repeated, her heart beating faster. Tufts of fur broke out along her arms.

Quinn regarded her carefully while pulling the makeshift top over her head and tossing it on the floor. "Yes," she said. "You need to be careful while they're here. I don't want you to end up in a . . . bad situation."

Risk released a tight breath from her lungs. "I need to be careful," she repeated back. "What about you? You never came home last night."

"Yes," Quinn drawled, her expression turning exasperated as it did when she was trying to find a gentler way to explain to Risk whatever trouble she'd gotten into. "Well, the dinner last night got out of hand a bit when we realized Erwing is a null and therefore couldn't see my illusion. The King's council isn't very happy with me right now, but if the Reinharts keep being difficult and they don't fall in line, Lazarus has every intention of letting me—"

"Quinn," Risk said. "Where were you?"

Her sister fell silent for a moment, turning to face a dresser as she unlaced her trousers. With her bare back to Risk, the scars that she carried were so clear in the light of day. So stark. At night the lines softened, but in the day, the truth of what Quinn had undergone was as clear as the lavender hair on her head.

"After the dinner and meeting with the small council, I retired to Lazarus' chambers with him."

Risk stood there at a loss for words.

She knew that Quinn and the King were *involved*. She'd certainly expected it to be brought up at some point. She just hadn't expected it yesterday. Quinn hadn't told her it was going to happen, and so she stayed up all night, worrying about the possibilities of what could have happened.

She didn't know if the feeling of her chest constricting was meant to be pain from her sister's inconsideration. Maybe it was a betrayal of sorts; the way she never thought of others. Or maybe, Risk simply felt stupid.

She'd worried for nothing.

Quinn was off living her life, and Risk was alone in their room once more with only her wild magic and the strange shadow that followed her for company.

"I see," Risk said, placing the dagger on the table side. Her sister shucked her trousers down her long, lean legs. She had to imagine that if there was a perfect form, that Quinn's would be that perfection. Tall and strong and capable of handling herself. Her sister didn't stay up worrying into the night because she could protect herself and make anything that tried to harm her regret it. She'd faced her nightmares and lived to spit in their faces.

Her brazenness with her body was just another extension of her surety of where she belonged in this world.

Risk wondered if she ever would. Then pushed the thought away as soon as it came to her.

"I'm sorry," her sister said as soon as Risk began to turn away. She paused. "You stayed up waiting for me, and I should have let you know that I was alright."

Risk opened her mouth, trying to find the right words to respond with. "You," she paused. "You don't apologize for things."

She looked over her shoulder to find Quinn doing the same. A grin curled around her sister's lips. "I just did."

"But, but," Risk started, motioning with her hands. "Why? I don't understand."

Quinn let out a soft exhale as she pulled on linen pants and a loose flowing shirt. "Someone told me recently that I act cruel because I think I am above consequence. While that is true in most things, some people are worth considering my words with." Quinn lifted a brow, and Risk's jaw snapped shut. She nodded once, and her sister stepped into the wash-room, closing the door behind her.

A warmth spread through her chest as she undressed and redressed for the day, swapping her linen shirt for another and layering it with a thick leather vest. She wrapped a layer of white fabric around her shoulders and hair to help with the heat.

"I'm heading out for training," Risk called. There was a bump on the other side of the door before Quinn thrust it open.

"Are you sure you're okay going alone? Lord Sunshine is indisposed after guard duty last night. If you give me a minute, I can throw on—"

"I'll be okay," Risk said. "Give me Neiss, and if there's any trouble he can handle it." Quinn nodded, rubbing the sleep from her eye as she extended one hand. The mauve reptile crept forward, slithering from beneath her skin. He dropped to the floor, letting out a pleased hiss before making his way to Risk. She bent over, extending one hand for him to coil himself around. The weight of his form settled behind her shoulders made Risk stand straighter. Surer. More like her sister.

"Be careful, even with Neiss," Quinn said, her eyes fell on her familiar. "If there's any trouble, you let me know." Risk swallowed once. Knowing how that would go down. "I'll be here taking a nap before I have to start getting ready for this damned ball Lazarus is throwing."

Quinn was already collapsed in bed and half asleep by the time Risk closed their chamber door behind her. Her soft leather boots clicked lightly as she strode down the hallway. It looked the same as any other day she'd gone to lessons. That was until she reached the foyer. There were the usual guards in red and gold, but joining them were those in blue and silver. They watched her as she walked, scrutinizing her beneath the wrap. Neiss lifted his head and let out a warning hiss to one that stepped too close. The guard in blue stumbled back, muttering to himself about marudas. Risk continued on, keeping her head down until she reached the palm fronds that enclosed the garden. The shade combined with the breeze down here was far less stifling than her room in the palace. Down here there was no silence that sat on her as the hours ticked by, the birds and the breeze and the beasts of Leone didn't allow it.

She stepped out of the trees and a gust of wind carrying sand smacked her in the face. Risk cringed, rubbing the grit from her eyes as she approached

Haspati. Her teacher sat cross-legged on the flat surface of a rock. His tattered robe blew around his thin form. Sightless eyes peered up at her, and he smiled with teeth whiter than bones picked clean.

"Hello, Risk."

"Haspati," she nodded once in respect, taking her place on the rock across from him. Neiss slithered down her body to curl up on the heated rock. She closed her eyes, sinking into the magic almost instantly. It felt like a breath of fresh air after the anxiety she'd been experiencing. The sensation of coming home comforted her.

"Use your field of vision. Tell me where the closest person is," Haspati instructed, his gnarled fingers wrapping and unwrapping around the wooden staff that lay across his lap.

"There's a guard that's close to the edge of the courtyard by the palm fronds. He's following a rotation, though," Risk answered. She could feel so much more than the singular guard and track them all simultaneously, but that wasn't what Haspati asked.

"Call on your magic; make yourself grow talons," he continued. She extended both hands and all it took was a light stroke for the magic to respond. She grew talons.

"Now put them away."

Risk lowered her hands to her lap and took deep, calming breaths to release the tension inside her. The talons shrunk away, back to her bitten fingernails as the magic allowed itself to be lulled into security.

Haspati continued doing this, running through every exercise they'd ever tried. She passed them all and at the end the sun was still high in the sky.

"You've improved a great deal in very little time," her teacher told her.

"I've been practicing," she said. "The drills help the magic . . . settle more. Without using it, my magic feels trapped. It gets riled easily. I do the drills every night and every morning so that the outbursts don't happen as much."

"Soon it won't be enough," he said.

Her lips parted. "I don't understand. I've done everything you've told me——"

"You have," he agreed. "This is through no fault of your own, child. It is the way of the world. The will of the gods."

"Haspati," she said slowly. "What exactly are you talking about?"

He smiled a sad sort of smile. It didn't quite meet the corners of his wrinkled eyes. "Your time draws near. I can sense it."

Risk blinked. "My time?"

"To ascend."

Unveiled Intentions

"Threats and promises are the same thing; the latter is simply a more palatable term."
— *Lazarus Fierté, soul eater, the unforgiving King of Norcasta*

A knock at his office door interrupted Lazarus' meanderings. He lifted the glass of spirits to his lips and drained it. The liquid burned on its way down and the souls settled. He left the glass on his desk corner as he stepped around the side and went to answer the door, already knowing who waited on the other side.

"Your Grace," Lady Reinhart said when it swung open. Lazarus nodded to the guards on either side of her, relieving them of their duty. They both swallowed hard.

"Have a good afternoon, m'lady," one of them said under his breath. Lazarus lifted a brow and the same murmured, "Your Grace."

They both disappeared down the hall, and he opened the door wider.

"Come," he said almost pleasantly. "I think it's time we had a talk."

She smiled coyly, her magic already reaching its sickly tendrils for him. She wanted to be desired. To be worshipped. She wove a spell that would pull most men in, but he was not most men. The only thing it made him do was grit his teeth and think of Quinn.

Where her fear was palatable for him, this sort of wickedness was not.

"You're looking much better today," Amelia commented as he shut the door. She waited for him to walk around to the other side of his desk before taking a seat.

"I'm feeling it," Lazarus answered gruffly, recalling the ways he'd had his fear twister the night before. The way she gave herself freely and without expectation was more thrilling than anything he'd experienced with another. It was darker. Deeper.

Something that a title nor a ring could not define.

"Well, that pleases me, my king," she said, like a bird parroting back what its master wanted to hear. Lazarus regarded her for a moment. Her long, dark hair and sultry expression. The tight fabric of her dress and rouge painted on her lips.

"Why are you here?" he asked once, bluntly.

Amelia stiffened for part of a second before recovering. "I'm here to show my support to the crown—"

"Why. Are. You. Here?" Lazarus asked once more. "You can't possibly believe that I'd fall for this charade. Come now, Amelia, you're smarter than that. Your father made sure of it."

The sickly sweet smile slipped from her face, turning her from the picture of false innocence to something more intriguing altogether.

"I've come with a proposition for you. Something that will please the lords of the land and get both you and I what we want."

Lazarus arched an eyebrow. "I have what I want."

"You have a weak claim to my throne. You have no lords' support. You have no people who will stand for you. You're ruling this country in title alone." Amelia laughed once, and it was as practiced at being sensual as the rest of her. "Perhaps if you listened to Lord Adelmar more, you might have had a stronger claim after all these months. As it is, your right-hand has done a fabulous job paving the way for me."

"Ah, Amelia," he sighed. "Men can be bought, both lords and armies. What can't be bought with gold can be bought in other ways. As you seem to know well, given the assets you've been using during this meeting."

She placed a dainty hand to her well-endowed

chest. "Your Grace, whatever do you mean?" she asked, mockingly.

It didn't have the same effect as when Quinn did it. In this case, all it did was serve to grate on his nerves further.

"You're a skilled passion cleaver to be able to strip away one's emotions so that they feel the desired thing you want them to. Clever, really. Quite ingenuous." He leaned back in his chair.

"My king," she purred, "you flatter me."

"I know another woman," he continued. Her expression turned brittle at the change in conversation. "She's also quite good at what she does. Clever too. I've never heard screams quite like what she draws out of men who are more battle hardened than you, Lady Reinhart."

"Is that a threat, Your Grace?"

"Yes."

Amelia leaned forward, resting her forearms on his desk and extending her chest until her breasts sat raised up over the edge. "I can assure you, my king, there's no reason to worry for me. Me and my brothers are quite adept at handling ourselves."

"Perhaps," he said. "If you'd like to test that, keep pushing me. I do enjoy her most when she's at her worst."

Amelia didn't flinch, much to her credit. "I take it you've made up your mind about my proposition already?"

"I have," he nodded, placing his forearms on the armrests and steepling his hands together. "The answer is no."

"That's a shame. We would have made such a lovely pair," she answered, almost wistfully if not for the indifference in her tone.

"You don't make attempts on my life or my vassals and get rewarded for it. You don't come into my house and play games with me. You don't get to set the board and make the rules, Amelia. Your father may have ensured you had the best tutors his money could buy, but you overestimated your own talents." She narrowed her eyes but made no move to interrupt him. "Tell your brothers to fall in line."

"Or?" she asked, challenging him. That single word made his blood boil, though he didn't show it.

"Or I let Quinn out to play. I think you'll find her games less palatable than the ones we've been playing."

An inkling of uncertainty crossed Amelia's expression. She hid it fast, but not fast enough. Lazarus clapped his hands together once before getting to his feet. He walked around his desk and opened the office door, signaling her dismissal.

"The choice is yours. I look forward to seeing you at the ball, Lady Reinhart."

She got to her feet and passed by him. The gauzy material of her gown brushing over his boots. Amelia stared straight ahead; the words nothing more than the script she'd rehearsed. They told him very little. It was the tone that said it all.

"And you as well, my king."

Dangerous Delights

"The only use for a dress is to be worn as a weapon unto itself."
— *Quinn Darkova, fear twister, right-hand to the King of Norcasta*

"I'm not wearing that." Quinn crossed her arms over her chest and tilted her head, looking from the bone and fabric corset to the woman holding it.

"It's all the fashion these days," Lorraine argued.

"I don't care."

"This is an official ball, Quinn. You must look the part—"

"I don't care," she repeated.

Lorraine pursed her lips. "Such a pity," she said,

turning to place it back in the trunk of unmention-
ables she'd had Draeven drag into Quinn's chambers
before shooing him away. "Lazarus would likely find it
very attractive and have a hard time controlling
himself."

Quinn rolled her eyes. "Lazarus already has a
hard time controlling himself. I could be dressed in
rags and it would be no different. Your attempt at
manipulation, while applaudable, isn't going to work
on me."

Lorraine tsked and let out a harrumph. The metal
hangers screeched as she flipped through the hanging
assortment in the wardrobe she'd had Vaughn bring.
"Half these dresses can't be worn without a corset."

"Perhaps," Quinn mused, "I shouldn't wear a
dress then—"

"Oh no," Lorraine said, shaking her head.
"You're wearing a dress. You agreed."

Quinn opened her mouth to reply when the bathroom door flung open, slamming into the wall. Axe
stood in the center wearing a sky-blue eyesore. Her
pale cheeks were pink and her crimson hair sitting like
a mop upon her head. Behind her, Risk grimaced.

"Oh, Axe," Lorraine cooed, turning from the
wardrobe to admire the young girl. "You look—"

"Ridiculous," Quinn finished for her. Lorraine
slapped her arm and shot a glare her way.

"Sublime," Lorraine corrected. "There will be

many young suitors at the ball, and you'll be sure to catch their eye."

Axe's brow furrowed until it was nearly a straight line across her forehead. "Catch their eye?" Axe repeated. "That's not all I'll catch if I wear this fluffy, creme puff, monstrosity. Lorraine," the girl bemoaned. "I won't be able to pick pockets or reach any—"

"That's the point, dear," Lorraine responded chipperly, her smile pointed. "Besides, you look lovely. Risk, what do you think?" Over Axe's puffy blue sleeve, Risk stood with her eyes wide.

"Er," she started, scratching the base of one of her horns before catching herself. A light blush crept up her cheeks as she said, "It looks . . . nice."

"Nice?" Axe repeated. "For once, the hussy's right." She thrust her hand toward Quinn, who lifted a brow. "I look ridiculous."

"Axe," Lorraine chided.

"Nope," the girl said. "I'm not wearing this."

Lorraine sighed, leaving Quinn's side to try and convince the child. "The ball is tonight, Axelle. We haven't got time to hire another seamstress—"

Axe lifted one hand in the air and a hatchet came careening from the other side of the room. An impish glint of delight filled her eyes as Lorraine came to a stop several feet in front of her.

"What in the dark realm are you—"

Axe lifted a fistful of fabric and began hacking at it.

"Axelle!" Lorraine chided sharply. "This is not how a lady acts—"

"Good thin' I'm not a lady. I'm a pirate." The girl cackled, continuing away at destroying the dress Lorraine had custom made for her. The King's stewardess turned to Quinn, and motioned to the problem child, silently asking for help.

"Oh no," Quinn said, backing away with both hands raised. "I'm the right-hand. She's not my problem."

Lorraine's glare deepened as she straightened her back and waited. Meanwhile Axe continued hacking away at the damn thing. "It's going to be your problem if she ruins it and I need someone to go down to the market to find her another one."

Quinn sighed. "She's just going to destroy that one too until you get her something she likes."

"She's right, you know," Axe crooned, pausing in her destruction to see how Lorraine responded. The older woman dipped her head and sighed.

"If I take you to the market to find a dress, you have to promise to behave. No bar fights. No brawls. No stealing. We find you a dress and come right back here—"

"Done," Axe agreed, dropping her axe and rushing back into the bathroom. The sound of fabric tearing made Lorraine cringe, and Quinn grimaced.

"You know, she looks up to you a great deal. If you'd agree with me instead of telling her it looks ridiculous, she likely would have let it go and worn the dress."

Quinn scoffed. "She calls me a hussy. I think you're seeing things that aren't there. Besides, she *did* look ridiculous. This is Leone. That thing would be insufferable to wear all evening in a room full of people."

Lorraine sighed. "Yes, but it likely would have kept her out of trouble."

Quinn squinted. "Like it did right there?" She hooked her thumb toward the spot where the girl had taken an axe to her gown.

"Fair enough," Lorraine groaned. "This doesn't get you off the hook. I need you and Risk to both be dressed appropriately."

Quinn chuckled. "Risk won't wear a dress. You can try convincing her, but I imagine it will go about as poorly as that did."

The bathroom door opened once more. Axe stood in her leathers, the blue dress she'd worn discarded on the floor beside her.

"Ready," she said, stepping out.

"Very well," Lorraine said. "I still expect you to pick something while I'm gone, Quinn."

"I'm aware," Quinn answered dryly. She waited for both Lorraine and Axe to let themselves out before she moved toward the wardrobe and began sifting through the options, only half glancing at each. "You know," she started once it was just her and her sister once more. "You don't have to go tonight if you don't want to."

"I know."

"The party is likely to be boring with talk of 'the newest fashions' for ladies and which lord has what mistress." It was true. Partly. There was also likely to be pleasure slaves in attendance and talk of slavery, not to mention her biggest concern for Risk.

Erwing.

"I'm aware," Risk said. "But I made it through Axe's birthday celebration, and I'd like to see if I can make it through this."

"The heirs are going to be there," Quinn finally said, coming to a stop on one gown in particular. The deep red material, close to the color of actual blood, drew her attention.

"Are you scared?" Risk asked her.

Quinn turned, looking over her shoulder as she pulled the dress from its hanger.

"No," Quinn laid the dress over the back of a chair and began to pull at her tunic. "I don't feel fear. Not as others do, at least." She lifted the tunic over her head and began to unlace her trousers. "One of the heirs has taken an interest in you, though. I don't like that."

"An interest?"

"In your heritage," Quinn replied, shucking her trousers down her legs. She pulled them off entirely and tossed them on the floor.

"I see."

Quinn lifted the red dress and examined it carefully. The merlot fabric slipped between her fingers, unbelievably soft and not stiff in the slightest. She lifted the folds and began to pull it over her head.

"The decision is yours, Risk. You know I won't take that from you. If you're going to go, I want you to be prepared. People are going to stare. They're going to whisper. You've made it a long way, but only you know if you're ready for this type of thing." She pulled the cloth once, and in one swoop it dropped to her waist. She released her fingers and the skirts fell.

She turned once and stepped toward the washroom to look in a mirror.

Quinn took one look at herself and smiled.

Now this was a dress she could wear.

"You look"—Risk paused, searching for the right word— "dangerous."

Quinn lifted a brow. "Dangerous?"

"It's not the dress itself," Risk said. "It's how you wear it. Usually you're dressed in leathers with knives on you. In this you're laid bare before them. It would be vulnerable on other women."

"But not me?" Quinn asked absentmindedly as she turned, letting the slit ride up her pale thigh.

"No, not you." Risk nodded. Her sister tugged at the long sleeves of her shirt without realizing. "The way you wear it makes it clear you don't need weapons. You are the weapon."

Quinn smiled at that, and it was as wicked as it was genuine.

The Red Ball

"The most dangerous of creatures come in the most beautiful packages."
— *Lazarus Fierté, soul eater, King of Norcasta*

Lazarus downed the rest of his wine and handed the cup off to the nameless servant who'd been instructed to keep them coming. Beside him, Draeven leaned in.

"Are you certain you should be drinking this heavily tonight?" his left-hand asked. Lazarus surveyed the throne room steadily. Lords entered the double oak doors with ladies or whores on their arms. From all over the land they'd flocked to be here, though he noted with no small amusement that his own council was absent.

"Absolutely not," Lazarus replied, taking another goblet from the same servant boy. "But the drinks keep the souls at bay when they very much desire to rip her apart."

Draeven's brow furrowed as he lowered his voice. "Rip who apart?" he asked.

Lazarus watched the double doors as a woman dressed in silver came to stand between them. On one side of her was the brute of a brother, who'd said no more than five words in Lazarus' presence. On the other, the bastard that had taken far too much interest in both Quinn and her sister. "Her," Lazarus answered gruffly as desire once more began to overwhelm his senses. It started as a subtle buzz beneath his skin. An awareness that made him take note of every woman in his periphery.

Amelia smiled as she took a glass of wine.

He hoped she choked on it.

"I think she might be a masochist," Draeven noted.

"She's certainly taunting me enough for it," Lazarus replied. Amelia smiled at him, and he didn't return it. "I want the men on guard to be doubled tonight. I don't trust her. Something isn't adding up."

Draeven's neutral expression didn't change as he asked, "What do you mean?"

Lazarus narrowed his eyes as she strode forward into the room, encapsulating it in her power. "We had a meeting yesterday afternoon."

"Oh?" his left-hand said.

"I told her that if she doesn't fall in line I have every intention of sending Quinn after her."

Draeven's expression darkened. "If you send Quinn, the lords will rebel—"

"I'm aware," Lazarus said. "Besides it's not like I can make Quinn do anything. My intention was to scare Amelia and make her reconsider this little farce she's pulling." Draeven handed off his cup of wine and straightened his tunic as she approached.

"Clearly, you miscalculated," Draeven muttered, a smile blooming on his face as soon as they were in hearing distance.

"Clearly," Lazarus answered.

Amelia came to stand before them, her smile as manipulative as it was trite. He grimaced. "Your Grace," she said, curtsying slightly before turning her attentions to Draeven. "My lord," she purred. Draeven stiffened, his Adam's apple bobbing once as he swallowed hard. Lazarus noted the sweat dotting his left-hand's temple and grit his teeth against her open manipulations.

"Lady Reinhart, you look lovely this evening," Draeven said, breathing harder than normal. Amelia giggled like a young girl. Lazarus clenched his teeth.

"Thank you, my lord. You don't look too bad yourself." She leaned forward and placed a hand on Draeven's arm as she lowered her voice to a whisper. Behind her, Titus stared out. His expression clouded by . . . rage? It was hard to discern. His fists were almost always clenched at his side. His expression stoic. Lazarus' gaze slid past him to the other brother.

Erwing wasn't with them anymore. Almost as fast as he'd approached, he'd relieved himself from this conversation and was heading toward the entrance. Just past him stood a lone woman in red.

Lazarus' chest tightened as his eyes feasted on her form. A merlot gown clung to her body, displaying every delectable inch despite the long sleeves and high neck. Slits ran up both sides, revealing her porcelain legs and golden sandals with every step she took. Not a single diamond or gem or piece of jewelry adorned her. Only the sandals and the dress.

Her lavender hair had been plaited into ornate braids that he knew from memory to be a style from her homeland. Her skin was clean of the ridiculous pigments and powders women often liked to paint on themselves. The most striking thing of all was the wicked smile she wore.

Saevyana.

Her crystalline eyes met his from across the room as she brushed off Erwing's attempts to speak with her and continued walking. Her gait was a beat slower than the violins playing in the background. The hairs at the back of his neck stood to attention. Waiting.

"Well, well, well," Quinn said softly. She twisted her fingers and tendrils of fear shot from her hand to the pale limb currently petting Draeven. Amelia stiffened, and Titus shifted, taking attention. "Look what we have here. A disgraced lady that forgets her place. He's spoken for."

Amelia was as skilled at manipulation as Quinn, but there was only so much she could sidestep when Quinn came down on her like a hammer. Lazarus shouldn't enjoy it. He should attempt to stop her now before she truly got going. He should try to intervene for the sake of his people, or his country, or his crown.

And yet . . . he couldn't bring himself to say a word.

It was the other night at dinner all over again, where he wrestled with himself on what to do and in the end—did nothing. It was the most satisfying thing of all.

"Spoken for?" Amelia repeated acidly.

"Mhmm," Quinn hummed, coming to stand in front of her, toe-to-toe. Quinn was a good few inches taller and had to look down. "Our dear Lord Sunshine is a good man. An honest man. You wouldn't pursue a man like that, would you? It would be so . . . unfortunate."

Draeven's eyebrows drew together in confusion before shooting Lazarus a look. The King shrugged. "Unfortunate," Amelia repeated. "How so? I don't see a wedding band on his finger. Nor our king's for that matter . . ." Her voice was lithe and skilled at weaving its web. No one knew webs like Quinn did.

"Some bonds surpass that which a piece of metal

binds. Metal can be bent or melted or removed, after all. But a true bond," she leaned forward. "That can only be found when one's soul recognizes another's."

Amelia let out a nervous laugh. "You talk of soulmates?" Several lords around them also laughed, but Quinn didn't seem perturbed.

"Of course not," she smiled. "Soulmates are for children's stories. I'm talking about when two people meet by chance that understand each other on a level that no other can. There's nothing predestined about it. It's not the gods or fate or star-crossed, as some might say." She appraised the other woman with a darkness in her eyes. "It's simply . . . an understanding of one another that you likely won't find again for a very long time, if at all. Do you know what that's like? To have someone that understands you so intimately beyond what the flesh and heart feels?"

Amelia's mask slipped for a moment. Her lips parted, and her eyes betrayed the truth.

"No," she coughed once, clearing her throat. "I can't say that I do."

Lies . . . the souls whispered. Despite the spirits, they were closer to the surface tonight. Closer than they should be.

"Pity," Quinn said, lifting the corner of her lips in what would be a sad expression were it not mocking. "No wonder you—"

"Muahahaha," the exaggerated laugh rang out. Lazarus frowned. At the double doors stood Axe, the

Pirate Queen's daughter, dressed as a woman of the night. Her corset was ill-fitted and the captain's hat looked ridiculous. She laughed as boisterously as men three times her size and ten times drunker might, all while clapping Quinn's sister on the back.

The girl wasn't as frail as she used to be, but her form was still much more petite than Quinn's. Small-boned and thin by nature, she wore a finely woven tunic in his house colors. It was several sizes too big and the belt at her waist highlighted that. Her leather trousers were also a men's cut, though they fit better. He doubted many would see past her horns to assess her clothing.

His gaze slid back to Quinn, whose lips were pressed together in a hard line.

She clearly wasn't happy with Risk being here.

"Ah," Amelia said lightly. "The raksasa—"

Quinn's hand was lifted, and fear tendrils wrapped around Amelia's throat faster than anyone could respond.

"You do not call her that." The scent of damp petals and fresh snow hit him. A darker light entered her eyes. *So close* . . . the souls within whispered. She was straying the line of dancing with Mazzulah.

Titus stepped forward, and Quinn lifted her other hand, anchoring him to the floor. The crimson of his eyes flared as he tried to take another step and failed. She leaned forward, stopping only a hairsbreadth from the other woman's lips.

"Do I make myself clear?"

Amelia's eyes widened. Her cheeks turned a lovely shade of currant. Her upper lip quivered. She flailed a little, but there was one problem.

It was a farce.

A lie.

He couldn't hear what she was thinking or see what her endgame was. She was missing that edge that true fear held, though. Quinn must have noticed because she released a breath of black smoke and Amelia's eyes rolled in the back of her head. Her body went taut and then limp in a short series of motions. Several moments passed before she regained her footing and opened her eyes. Around them the lords were starting to pause. Beginning to turn. To stare. To take notice.

"Tsk, tsk," Quinn whispered. "You're such a lovely thing. I don't think you realize how much I'd enjoy breaking you." Lazarus' blood heated once more, and it had nothing to do with Amelia's cursed powers. "But alas, I'm supposed to be playing nice. Please be a dear and keep your hands as well as your words to yourself tonight so that I can. The small council wouldn't be pleased if there's another repeat of what happened to Lord Callis."

Someone gasped in shock. Murmurs rippled through the throne room.

"So tell me, are you going to behave yourself tonight?" Quinn asked. "Or are you going to act like a spoiled child whose daddy didn't give her what she wanted so she throws a temper tantrum?" Quinn leaned away and lifted a brow, waiting for an answer.

"Please," Amelia murmured. "I can't . . . breathe . . ." Several women of the court gasped.

"That's unfortunate for you," Quinn replied.

The shade of Amelia's neck and cheeks steadily darkened to plum. Still, she didn't give her what she wanted.

She didn't grovel. She didn't break.

He should have known then that something wasn't right. Not as the guards he'd told Draeven to double flooded into the room. Not as the court grew more frenzied.

Not as he only just realized that one very notable person that they'd already overlooked once was missing.

Lazarus searched above the heads of the crowd.

He didn't have to search long.

A woman's screams tore through the air. Harsh and ragged and filled with fear.

The only problem was they weren't coming from Amelia.

Strength by a Different Name

"Just because one survives something does not mean it is forgotten. Even in the light there are shadows."
— *Mariska Darkova, beast tamer, possible member of House Fierté*

She smoothed her tunic and turned twice in front of the mirror. In her stomach, a coil of dread weighed her down. She wanted to go to the ball. She wanted to stand there and eat pasties and drink mulled wine that tasted awful. She wanted to indulge as much as she could. She wanted to forget. Above all, though, she wanted to prove to herself that she could do it. That she wasn't the same scared, frightened girl that Quinn pulled out of that temple six months ago.

She'd lost control of her magic at Axe's birthday

celebration. Most of the court had overlooked it because she was also the one to soothe the griffin.

But Quinn knew the truth.

So did Draeven.

She needed to show them that she could do this. That even with the infamous heirs, she didn't need to be coddled or treated like a child. She didn't need their protection. She could do this.

"Right," Risk muttered to herself. "You can do this." She stopped turning in front of the mirror and strode toward the door. Her boots squeaked on the polished floors. She reached for the handle, only to pause inches away.

Her chest constricted. She hunched forward. Risk's fingers curled into a fist that fell to her side as she hung her head.

Why can't I seem to do this? Take the leap. Open the door.

She reached forward once more only to once again pause as something held her back. She wanted to do this and be that person so desperately, but the fear that lived within her was just as much alive as that which lived in Quinn.

The only difference was her sister controlled it. Risk was a slave to it.

"Let them love you. Let them hate you. If they try to end you, we'll destroy them all," she whispered under her breath.

She reached for the door, and this time her finger-tips brushed the handle.

Her stomach twisted tighter in knots, as if it knew something she didn't. Or maybe she did, and she simply didn't want to see it for what it was.

Two knocks at the door made her jump. Risk put a hand to her chest. Her heart beat rapidly, like a hummingbird trapped in a cage of bone. The magic stood to attention beneath her skin, waiting to come forth should she need it.

"Who is it?" Risk called out, her voice hoarse.

The doorknob turned, and she stumbled back, grasping the dagger on the nightstand. The door flew open. The magic eased.

A girl with hair like the dawn stood in the doorway wearing a pirate's hat. She had too much ash smudged around her eyes and two axes strapped at her hips. Her dress wasn't a dress, but a corset strapped over a billowy white shirt and dark green skirt that only went to her knees. Beneath it she wore trousers, like Risk, and heavy boots.

"What are you doin' standing there like that?" Axe asked, her eyebrows furrowing. "We got a party to go to. Come on," she hooked her thumb to the side and nodded her head in the same direction. Risk swallowed hard. Her fingers unfurled and the dagger fell to the nightstand behind her.

She released an unsteady breath and stepped forward, following Axe out. Her door swung shut behind them, and she couldn't help the way her stomach twisted one last time.

"I've got a plan," Axe said, pulling Risk from her thoughts.

"A plan?"

"Mmhmmm," the girl nodded, the beads in her hair clanking together. "You see, your hussy sister is really great at distractin' people at these things. She gets mad. Does her whole black magic thin'. And while all those lords and ladies are watchin' her, I make the rounds. You get me?"

Risk frowned. "Get you?"

Axe shook her head. "You'll see. You can be my lookout."

They were approaching the throne room. Risk knew because of the people milling about just outside of it. Guards. So many guards. Most of them were in Lazarus house colors. Several of them nodded to her indifference and took a step back to clear the way. Risk kept walking, still not knowing how to respond.

"Your lookout?" Risk asked. "Last time you had me be a lookout—"

"I know, I know," Axe conceded, gesturing with her hands. "This time will be different though."

They came to stand between the doors. In a single sweep, Risk spotted Quinn in her blood-colored dress. Axe was right about that; she was a sight to see. A spectacle.

Most didn't understand her sister. Many hated her. Very few loved her. If there was one thing that everyone would agree on, it was that Quinn was one of those people that simply had to walk and people took notice. Everything she did was filled with power and confidence. She exuded an air that so few could only hope to breathe in, and maybe they would be strong and powerful too.

She was a rare kind of person that didn't come along very often, but when they did, everyone noticed. For good or bad.

"I see what you mean," Risk murmured. Her sister's eyes locked on her and narrowed a fraction. Risk swallowed. Axe leaned in, patting her shoulder.

"Now, while she's keepin' them busy, I'm going to take a walk and dig through some pockets. Follow me, but not too close. I'll need to drop my stash with you so Lorraine doesn't figure out what's up . . ."

Axe took off into the crowd faster than Risk could object.

"*Potes*," she cursed under her breath, following after. The problem in Axe's plan was that she used her size to her advantage, sidestepping drunken nobles and darting under outstretched arms. She didn't pay mind to the people around her, or more specifically, the men.

The places that Axe squeezed, Risk was unwilling to get within five feet of. She made it about halfway into the room before her feet stopped as if weighed down by lead. An itch rode up her inner arm. A buzzing started in her head.

Risk closed her eyes and took a deep breath, trying to fall into the world around her.

It was near impossible to do when she was in the middle of it, though.

"My lady," a voice said from behind her. Risk whirled around.

A man only a few inches taller than her stood with his hand outstretched. His skin was flaccid and his eyes hungry. She'd seen that look on many a man in her short life.

"I'm not a lady," she bit out, trying to fight the inner panic that was beginning to once more overwhelm her.

"Not a lady?" he repeated. His eyes did a slow perusal of her form. "You certainly look like a lady," he said, still smiling. She didn't like the way he smiled.

It wasn't so different from her sister's, but where Quinn would never hurt her, this man . . . she had a feeling that was exactly what he wanted.

"Leave me alone," she whispered. He stepped closer.

"A lady dressed in men's clothes at a royal ball. You're either a servant or a commoner trying to play pretend—"

"I belong to house Lazarus," she said in a rush. Her heart beat faster.

Faster.

Faster.

She sensed the magic as it danced with her at the edge of her panic threshold.

Risk wanted to scream. She wanted to cry. She wanted to hang her head and pull at her hair for how stupid she was to leave her chambers. She hated this reaction she had. To run. To flee. To stay. To fight.

Why couldn't she be like Quinn?

Why couldn't she be strong and wicked and cruel?

"Are you certain?" he asked softly, stepping closer. "Perhaps we should have a talk somewhere more . . . private. I am quite curious about these." He reached out, and she froze, stiff as a board. A single finger traced her horn and she *felt* it.

A shiver ran up the back of her spine.

To run. To fight. To flee. To stay.

Her options cycled through her mind rapidly, but her feet were stuck to the ground. She couldn't move. She couldn't breathe.

Stop. She wanted to tell him to stop.

But the words wouldn't come out of her mouth.

All she could think of were the other hands that touched her.

The chains that held her.

She was powerless to stop them no matter how hard she tried.

"You seem disoriented. Come. Let's get to somewhere quieter, where there's fewer prying eyes—"

Sweaty fingers grabbed her hand and tugged.

Risk squeezed her eyes shut, and regardless of

what he wanted, she couldn't stop herself. Not even if she tried. The tether that held her motionless and unable to answer snapped as a rage consumed her.

In a fraction of a second her nails turned to claws and her skin to fur. A sharp searing pain ran down her back that she knew to be black, bat-like wings. They tore through her tunic and flapped once, holding her in place even as her feet didn't move.

The man paused.

"What—"

She didn't hear the rest of what he said as blood rushed in her veins and the roaring drowned out all else. Her vision tinted red.

Then it went entirely.

She didn't know how long passed.

She didn't understand what was happening.

Not until it was too late.

As the rage faded and she came back to herself, the roaring turned to screams. She couldn't understand. *Where are they coming from?*

She looked at her hands, not understanding.

Red colored them, as if someone had spilled their wine. It coated the floor too. There was a man there. At least she thought it was a man.

It was hard to tell when the pieces had been severed and pulled apart.

She stared and stared and stared.

It was only when it clicked that she realized the screams were coming from her.

This man, whoever he was . . . she'd killed him.

At the ball.

Her teeth chattered, and her body shook. Her legs threatened to give out. But all at once *she* was there.

Quinn. Her sister.

She wrapped her arms around her and pulled her close.

Risk didn't know what to do. She simply clung to her as the truth slapped her in the face.

She wasn't ready.

"I'm sorry," she said. "I'm sorry. I'm so sorry. I'm so—"

"It's okay," Quinn breathed, holding her tight. "Tell me what happened."

"I just"—Risk stammered—"I just—I don't—I'm sorry—I—" Quinn pulled away. Risk felt cold, but her sister didn't leave her. She didn't abandon her. Quinn never abandoned her. She wrapped her still clawed hands around her sister's wrists, and Quinn didn't flinch as she cupped her face.

"You came to the ball, start there. Go slow. Walk me through what happened." Risk nodded. Her breaths were coming too fast. She couldn't calm herself. She couldn't get the words out.

Quinn inhaled slowly, mimicking her own movements. Risk followed, doing as her sister did.

"In," Quinn said, taking a deep breath. "Out," she repeated, releasing it just as slow. They did it again and again. Until she settled enough to speak.

"I was t-trying to follow Axe," she said in a very small voice. "I got l-lost."

Quinn nodded. "What happened then?" There were voices. Other voices speaking. They pulled at her attention, but Quinn made a tsk noise, pulling her back.

"Attention on me. Only me."

Risk could do that.

"There was a m-man. He stopped me. He wanted to t-talk s-somewhere else." Her teeth were chattering still, and the bone-deep cold was beginning to spread.

"He tried to get you to go somewhere else?" Quinn asked. Her voice held no inflection. No judgement. No empathy, but also no damnation.

"Yes." Risk started to lower her eyes.

"What else happened?" Quinn prompted before she could shut down entirely.

"I—he—" she struggled for words, but Quinn didn't interrupt her. Risk took a deep breath and in a rush said, "He t-touched my horns." Water filled her vision. Her sister's face became blurry. "He grabbed me."

Quinn nodded and pulled her in. "It's going to be okay. I promise."

Risk held onto that even though she didn't believe it. When Quinn made a mistake, it wasn't a mistake. One way or another she got her way because she was Quinn.

Risk wasn't Quinn.

She wasn't strong or brave or cruel.

Perhaps though, she was wicked too.

"Draeven," her sister's voice pulled her in once more. Risk blinked twice, letting the tears fall so she could see. Draeven stood near them. He and Quinn shared a look. Risk didn't understand it, but after a moment passed, her sister said, "He's going to take you back to our room where you will lock the door. You do not open it for anyone except me. Do you understand?" Quinn asked her.

Risk swallowed hard. "Yes."

"Good. Now stay near him. You know him. He won't do anything but protect you. You have my word and his. Doesn't she?"

"Yes," Draeven answered.

"Can you do this?" her sister asked. Risk looked between her and him. His violet eyes blazed, but the fury in them wasn't aimed at her. She recognized it. She understood it.

"I can do this." She nodded.

Quinn kissed her forehead, and Risk couldn't help but feel like it was a goodbye.

Draeven offered her his free hand, in the other he held a sword.

She pressed her lips together and took it.

"Step aside," Quinn demanded. Her voice wasn't loud, but it didn't need to be. Even behind her, Risk could sense the shift. The hairs on her arms stood straight because this wasn't Quinn that was addressing the soldiers that surrounded them.

It was the fear twister.

"That *thing* killed my brother," came another woman's reply. "Her head is mine."

"I am giving you one chance, Amelia." The words coming out of Quinn's mouth were apathetic. The decision of whatever she was about to do already made. "Step aside."

Silence held the throne room by the throat like a noose.

One command, and it would break.

"No."

It was a death sentence.

Paint It Black

"Where there is life, there is fear, and no one can control it, save fear herself."
— *Quinn Darkova, fear twister, right-hand to the King of Norcasta*

O ne of them was not walking away from this tonight.

It had been clear to her for a while that might be the outcome. The truth of it was Norcasta couldn't have two heirs. Let alone four. They'd tried Draeven's way. They'd made an attempt at peace. It hadn't worked.

Now it was her turn.

Quinn lifted both hands. They were empty. The

guards around them exchanged glances. A few sneered.

She smiled at Amelia. Then she called fear.

The row of guards before them fell to their knees. Blood dripped from their ears. Skin turned clammy. Eyes rolled back into their heads. She twisted her hands, and they sang like little songbirds for her. The heralds to her wrath.

Quinn let the effects play out slowly to highlight every excruciating moment of what it meant to die by her hand. It wasn't for her enjoyment; not when Risk was still here. No, she needed to get her sister out before the real show started.

When the last note finally ended, and the throne room fell silent once more, Quinn lowered one hand to the ground.

"Neiss," she beckoned forward. The snake moved from her back, up her spine, over her shoulder, and down her arm. His head rose out of the palm of her hand and let out a hiss. The crowd took several steps back as they began to question, was she a fear twister? Or a soul eater? "Stay with her," she commanded the snake. He didn't respond, instead choosing to go to Risk. Quinn glanced behind her as Risk squatted and extended a shaking hand, still tipped with claws that dripped blood. He wound himself around Risk, his forked tongue grazing her jaw where a stray droplet of blood lingered.

Draeven didn't release her hand, though he hated snakes.

He must really, truly care about her sister.

Maybe one day her sister would care about him too.

"You think to fool me with tricks?" Amelia asked. "Illusions?"

Quinn laughed callously as she faced her once more. "I don't need tricks or illusions to handle you, Amelia. I simply need fear. Luckily for me, we have an audience."

She expanded her power to the whole of the throne room and beckoned it forward.

Tendrils black as smoke began to drift upwards into the air as people started to scream and cry and faint. They begged for her to stop. They pleaded with the gods to spare them.

She wasn't doing much more than stirring them up because she still wasn't ready to do what needed to be done.

Not with Risk here.

Her sister had seen her do many horrible, terrible things.

She didn't want her to see what came next.

She didn't want her caught in the crosshairs.

And she certainly didn't want her to fall prey to Quinn's own power.

With the court on their knees, Lazarus' house became easier to find. At the other end of the hall stood Axe, brandishing her weapons. Next to the door leading to Lazarus' study stood Lorraine, slipping away for the worst of what was to come. At the base of the throne stood Lazarus, watching with a blistering intensity.

A girl that could see magic. A null. A soul eater.

Why they stood was clear. But there were two others who also stood, unperturbed.

Amelia and Titus Reinhart.

"The rumors didn't do you justice," Amelia mused.

"Now, Draeven." Quinn kept her eyes on the heirs. Through her field of vision she sensed them moving.

"You know what else they didn't do justice?" Amelia asked. Her dark eyes glinted with hidden knowledge and power. She lifted one hand and made a fist.

The crying stopped.

The pleading stopped.

The terror began to leak away.

People started to get to their feet. They turned on her. On them. On Risk and Draeven and Lorraine and Axe—and even Lazarus.

"Me."

"Kill her!" they exclaimed. "End her! She's a nightmare—a terror!"

They called for her blood, but Quinn merely lifted

a brow. "A passion cleaver worth a damn." Her voice was nonchalant and unhurried even as her heart started to race. "It's been a long time since I had a challenge."

"Where are they?" she asked Neiss.

"Halfway."

Time. She needed time. For her and for them.

Warm fingers touched her bare wrist. She didn't need to turn to know who it was, but she did anyway. Lazarus' eyes met hers, and he nodded once, like he understood.

Damp petals. Midnight weeds. Fresh snow.

Fire. Ash. Bitter winds.

The scents of magic filled the air as a storm unlike any other brewed over the capitol of Norcasta. An errant wind swept through the throne room, bringing with it the familiar cold.

"A king that can't hold his crown. I've heard whispers about you too, Lazarus. I've yet to see even a hint of that power that they claim you hold. Your white raksasa; she certainly is something. Maybe I'll take her for myself when this is over."

Quinn lifted both brows and looked at her.

"You must be daft."

Insults always worked best to buy time. People felt the need to defend themselves, whether they were true or not. Very few simply didn't care.

Amelia chuckled softly. "Titus, step forward."

Without concern for the dead that lay before

them, he stomped forward. A series of cracks and snaps filled the air as he turned the bodies to mush.

"Lazarus tells me you like to play games, Quinn. I like to play games too. Me and my brother used to play them often—and then one day, I won. You see, a rage thief without anything but rage is rather useful. Pliant even. Stripped of all other emotion, I wonder if you too might be of use."

"How far?" she asked Neiss once more.

"Almost."

Close. They were close. She just needed a little more—

Titus lunged without warning. Quinn flung a tendril of fear at him, but the action did little more than bounce off whatever hold Amelia had over him. Around them, the mob moved from jeering to action. They rushed forward, trampling each other in their artificial anger to get at Quinn and Lazarus.

Titus slammed into Lazarus with such strength that a boom echoed through the throne room. Dust and dirt fell from the ceiling. Sand whorled around them.

But Lazarus remained standing, holding his own.

"Not my friends, you swarmy, git-faced bastards!" Axe yelled. Quinn had to hope that between her and Draeven and Risk's own powers that they would make it out of here because she couldn't wait any longer.

Lords and ladies had turned on them.

Servants had turned on them.

Guards, both their own and the Reinhart's, had turned on them.

There was nothing normal about it. Nothing natural.

Amelia had cleaved away whatever emotions that held them back, turning them into a mindless mob.

"You will die for this," Lazarus said. He pulled at the leather gloves he wore and dropped them. Amelia laughed.

"We'll see, Your Grace," she replied pleasantly.

"Neiss?" Quinn asked once more.

He didn't respond.

"Neiss?" she repeated.

The fear in her veins buzzed with contempt. Surely she would have felt something, anything, if the worst had happened . . .

"Safe," came the whispered response. *"We are safe."*

There was much she wanted to say, but no time at all. So she gave him the only command she could. *"Run."*

And then she let go.

It had been a long time since she felt genuine worry. Longer still that she faced something that could inspire it. She let go of that. Let go of whatever humanity she held.

Risk was gone. It was time.

She was going to enjoy this far too much.

Quinn tossed her head back, a laugh bubbling up within her.

"Why are you laughing?" Amelia asked. Annoyance flitted across her features. Quinn grinned.

"Because," Quinn paused, leaning forward to whisper conspiratorially. "They can love you. They can hate me. In the end, what they feel for you and for me matters not. *I* will crush them all."

Darkness descended over the throne room as every light flickered out of existence.

Masked in shadow and night, Quinn didn't just pull on their fear. She sent her own into them. While few lived in the dark, none could run from it. Threads began to form, crisscrossing across the space. They spun their way to and around the men and women present.

She called spiders and snakes and centipedes forward with only one command.

"Burrow," she breathed.

Light flooded the room once more as the illusion of darkness faded, but not her web.

Quinn's breath turned ragged. Her heart beat rapidly. Sweat coated her skin as she sent figments of herself into each of them.

No one came at her or tried to stop her. They couldn't. They were too busy tearing out their own eyes. They scratched at their skin and pulled at their hair.

Some of these men and women might have been supporters. Some were likely enemies.

In the end, friend or foe didn't matter.

Under Amelia's control she had no choice but to kill all of them.

Her body strained as she funneled deeper and deeper into hundreds of people at once. The stench of blood and piss and dark magic filled the air. She clenched her fists tight, shaking from exertion. A cold sweat washed over her as she let go of one last thing.

Herself.

Creatures burst forth from fleshed bodies. Born from the deaths of many. The carcasses fell to the marble ground, splayed open from the groin to the neck. Bone and muscle jutted out, and where the innards should have been, only rotten flesh remained.

The beasts that came forth were as large as wolves and as real as the ground beneath her feet. They didn't have beating hearts, but instead slivers of a soul. Their bones were harder than diamond and the black muscles stronger than steel.

"What is this magic?" a voice asked. Quinn was too far gone to give anything but the truth.

"My children," she commanded quietly. "It's time to feast."

Were there any people alive, they might have screamed.

In the graveyard she'd created, there were only three people to witness as her creatures consumed the bodies from which they were born. They tore at the flesh and muscle. They broke the bones and ground them into dust. Not an inch of the white marble was visible beneath so much red.

Quinn embraced it all.

When there were no more people to eat, they turned to another source.

That which was still living.

"Tsk, tsk," she murmured in an inhuman trill. "I warned you. You should have walked away."

What happened next was too fast—or perhaps too slow—for Quinn to follow when she was so deep in her magic that it became her.

Lazarus roared, and it was a sound that shook her to her bones, but it did not pull her from the depths in which she lurked. Her soul was no longer in her when it was split into so many pieces. The body was but a vessel; the creatures her true self.

They turned to him as Lazarus grasped the head of the giant. His skin bled gray. Craggy lines appeared as he grew three feet taller. The creatures watched as he held the head of their prey between two hands and squeezed.

Enthralled.

Even in this form, his wickedness lured them.

Titus didn't make a sound as his face turned from the color of sand to the violet dusk and then, after a suspended moment, exploded.

He popped like a grape. His body tumbling from Lazarus' blood-soaked fingers.

The creatures turned to Amelia.

She was the last heir. The lone threat.

They circled her. Their razor-sharp nails of bone scraping against the floor as they did so.

She was terrified. They could tell that much.

But there was something else.

Something they didn't see until it was too late.

"Your power is great, fear twister. I'll admit that mine doesn't compare," she said slowly. The creatures tilted their heads in unison. "But I don't need to hold hundreds. I only need one who can do the job."

They turned as one, and from their eyes Quinn saw her error.

Lazarus stood only inches away. Still wearing the skin of a troll, he reached for her with glazed over eyes. Dread didn't even have time to register. It never occurred to her to feel fear.

Even as he crushed her.

Grave Destiny

"Of all the sins to commit, overconfidence is perhaps the worst of them. For pride comes before the fall."
— *Draeven Adelmar, rage thief, left-hand to the King of Norcasta*

Footsteps pounded down the hallway, echoing in the empty corridors as they tried to outrun the screams coming from the throne room. Risk gripped his hand tighter, wincing with every terrible sound that followed.

No guards had taken after them. The mob had stayed contained, and were more intent on killing Quinn and Lazarus than anything else. It didn't sit right with him that he'd abandoned both his king and his friend, but Draeven also knew better than most what they were truly capable of.

Quinn wanted Risk out of there, no doubt for what she planned to do.

Lazarus hadn't countermanded her.

"We're missin' all the good parts," Axe whined, though she kept pace with them. At the end of the hallway, a figure stepped out of the shadows. Draeven tensed.

"Little pirate?" he called.

"Vaughn?" Axe scrunched her nose. "Where have you been, you giant oaf—"

"Axe," Draeven snapped. Shorter on energy and shorter on time, they couldn't afford her antics.

"I stepped outside to get some air," Vaughn said. "I came back, and she-wolf Quinn was not herself . . ." His voice trailed off, and judging by his expression, Draeven knew exactly what he'd seen that made him decide to leave instead of getting involved.

"Vaughn, you're to take Axe and leave the palace. Head to that place we talked about. Messages need to be sent to Thorne and Imogen about what happened here tonight as soon as you're both safe."

"But—" Axe began.

"No buts," Draeven said sternly. "Go with him. *Now.*"

The young girl's eyes began to water as she turned to Risk. "Make sure to stab some people for me if it gets interestin'."

"For the love of Forseya," Draeven groaned. "We're under attack. There are more important things, Axelle—"

Risk extended her free hand and patted the girl's shoulder awkwardly. "You're strange, but I like you. Please go."

Axe's bottom lip quivered, but she didn't cry. The girl sniffed once and nodded. "Alright."

She turned, and they headed off down the end of the hall, disappearing around the corner. Draeven and Risk picked up their speed, half running by the time they came to a stop in front of her room. Draeven released her hand, and a pang went through his chest in doing so.

"I need to go back," he told her.

"I know."

"Will you be okay?" He swallowed hard. Part of him wanted her to answer no. To give him an excuse to stay. Part of him didn't want to see what became of the throne room. And still, part of him had a duty to fulfill.

"I"—she paused, like she didn't know how to answer—"I don't know, but my sister needs you more than I do right now."

A harsh sigh left him. She was right.

"Go inside and lock the door. If anyone tries to enter—"

"I kill them. I know. Quinn is my sister, after all." She gave him a half attempt at a smile, and it hurt how unbelievably sad it was.

"I've only seen her like that once before. She'll be okay, you know."

Risk reached for the door, then paused. "I hope so. She and the world seem to think she's invincible. But even gods can fall from grace."

She closed the door behind her before he could respond. Draeven stared at it for a moment longer than he should have before pulling himself away.

The throne room had gone silent.

And despite his words of reassurance to Risk, dread crept inside him.

Draeven started to walk and then run as the closer he got, the less he could hear. Before him the double doors were open. They'd left them closed.

He slowed to a halt and took a deep breath before peering inside.

Blood. So much blood. It filled his vision as he combed over the empty throne room.

Not empty of people. Empty of life.

Sweat dotted his temple as his pulse raced. He stepped into the graveyard. His chest clenched so hard, his heart ought to have been crushed.

Then he was running. Running and falling, and desperately trying to see.

Smeared in blood and grime and guts, Lazarus lay prone in his troll form.

Where is she? he asked himself as he fell to his knees

and went to put his head to his king's chest to listen for a heartbeat.

He pulled the man's arms, and the dread within him became a pit.

Lavender hair, soaked with blood.

So much blood . . .

"Help!" he yelled as loud as he could. "I need a healer! I need—" His voice broke because it hit him then.

A healer couldn't fix her.

Not even they could bring back the dead.

Silver Feather

"Even in the darkest of places there is hope, if you choose to find it."
— Mariska "Risk" Darkova, beast tamer

The door shut behind her. She turned the bolt to lock it.

Seconds later, Neiss began to convulse.

Risk froze, not sure whether she should try to unwind him or try to calm him. She chose the latter. "Neiss," she said, reaching up to gently stroke his scales. "Neiss, what's wrong?"

"Quinn," he hissed through her mind.

It was the last thing he said before his body exploded in a shower of ash.

"Neiss?" she asked again, knowing what happened

and what it meant, but unable to stop herself. "Neiss!" she screamed. Her body shook so hard she fell to her knees. "No," she breathed. "No. No. NO!"

She screamed once more, and it came out as a roar that shook the very ground beneath her. Tears streamed down her face. She turned, and scrambled toward the door—reaching for it. She had to go back. She had to find her. She had to—

Tapping. There was tapping coming from the window.

Maybe it was her. Maybe this was some grand illusion. Maybe, just maybe, her sister was playing a cruel trick and Risk was the butt of the joke.

Relief started to fill her as she half convinced herself in the time it took to drag herself across their chambers. She clawed at the cushioned window seat, pulling herself up. The golden latch gleamed in the light. She opened it.

"Quinn?" she asked into the night on a jagged, heavy breath. Hope. She had it for only a split moment—when two golden orbs stared back at her.

"I am not," the words whispered through her mind. She blinked twice, grief and anger coursing through her in equal measure.

"Where is she? Where is my sister?" Risk demanded. She didn't know with whom or what she spoke to. Only that it seemed familiar. Perhaps it was still a trick. Perhaps—

"Quinn is dead."

The words were her undoing. Risk slammed her hands onto the window seat and the wood gave way. "No!" she cried. "She's not dead. She's not." Risk turned and stumbled blindly toward the door once more. She couldn't believe it. She wouldn't. She had to see it for herself.

"Wait," the voice called after her.

She did not wait. Her hand wrapped around the golden handle, crunching the metal as she wrenched it open.

"There is a way," the voice said. *"A way to save her."*

Risk paused. With blood on her hands and tears running down her cheeks she turned back to the voice.

"Who are you?" Risk asked. She would only ask it once.

Those twin orbs of gold came closer and then blinked.

Wings of midnight. Eyes of gold. She knew this creature, even if only from a dream.

"I am Alpis," the bird told her.

"Hope," she said. "You came to me once and told me to hold on. My sister came back to me then. Now you come to me once more."

"There is only one way. You must go now, or it will be too late."

Risk looked from the bird to the open door. Silence. Heavy, terrible, drowning silence consumed the palace.

"Go where?" Risk asked. "To the throne room?"

"*No,*" the bird said. *"You must go back."*

A chill crept up her spine. Her mouth was dry, but she swallowed hard.

"Go back?" she asked.

"Where it all began."

Risk closed her eyes, squeezed them shut against the memories. A familiar bone-deep cold settled in, and when she opened them, fresh tears spilled onto her cheeks.

Despite her fear, she whispered the name of the place she vowed to never return.

"N'skara."

And then, Mariska Darkova disappeared into the night.

Grim Ends

"The line between what is good and what is evil is more muddled than many think. To attempt to walk a path so blurred was a masochism of its own."
— *Draeven Adelmar, rage thief, left-hand to the King of Norcasta*

Two knocks at the door made Draeven look up. The door swung open without waiting for an answer. Three lords filed and came to stand in front of the imposing oak desk. Draeven set aside the quill in hand, still wet with ink. He nodded once to Dominicus and the door closed shut.

"Do you know why you're here?" Draeven asked, resting his elbows on the desk.

"No, Lord Adelmar, I can't say we do," Langston

responded. He was the oldest of the higher lords and Warden of the North, though he'd been gone for quite a long time. Wrinkles lined his face, but there was still a hardness beneath his aged exterior. Something that made him speak first and true.

"Well," Draeven remarked. "It's quite simple really. Your fealty has been called into question after recent events. The crown asks that you commit yourself once more to King Lazarus and aid in the search for Amelia Reinhart so that she may be removed from this situation." There was a time when he might have attempted at being more subtle. Made the offer seem more palatable.

"You mean to hunt down and murder Claudius' last remaining child?" Langston questioned.

The unfortunate truth of the situation was that Draeven had run out of patience to care. "I do." He nodded once, his lips firmly set in a neutral line. Behind him, Lazarus' family crest hung proudly on display. There was a time he believed that symbol would show the world peace.

After all that had happened . . . after all he'd seen . . . Draeven wasn't sure if peace was possible, and either way he knew his king. Quinn was dead. All Lazarus would do until Amelia's head sat on a pike was bring war.

The sooner she was found, the better.

"With all due respect, my lord," Brameer said. "This is—"

"Treason," Draeven said. "What she did in this palace was treason. She came into our house as a guest with ill-intentions and fled into the night as an enemy of the crown."

"Her brother—" Brameer started once more, not taking the hint.

"Died for his actions. Both of them did. Now it is her turn." Draeven scooted back and stood from the ornate chair meant for the King. It was Lazarus' study, after all. Though the man himself had been unconscious for over a day now.

"My lord, I know our king hasn't been himself, but surely now that the whore is no longer whispering in his ear—"

It appeared that Brameer truly did not know when to stop talking. Draeven unsheathed his sword, took two steps, and swung before Brameer found the good sense to move.

His head hit the floor before his body did.

Draeven lowered his sword and looked to the remaining lords of Lazarus' small council.

"You have a choice. It's time to make it," he told them.

Langston stepped forward and got on both knees. Were it not for the way he bared his neck and yet stared defiantly, Draeven might have thought he was choosing to live.

"I cannot agree with the hunting down and

345

slaughter of Amelia Reinhart. Claudius was many things, but he wouldn't have wanted this."

Draeven nodded. "That's admirable, Langston. Truly. But I cannot allow anyone who is in favor of that woman to leave this room."

Langston's upper lip stiffened. The flaccid skin around his Adam's apple bobbed.

"Strike true," the older lord said, facing his death with an unflinching sense of honor.

Draeven took care to behead him as cleanly as possible.

While they had to die, there was no reason to make it painful. He didn't enjoy being the hand that dealt the blow. Without the right, though, the left must make do.

"I value my life, Lord Adelmar," Northcott said. "But even a fool can see that war is imminent. Somehow. Some way. I wish to be Warden of the North in return. I will swear my fealty to House Fierté, to King Lazarus, and when called, I will answer."

"Consider it done. The papers will be delivered this afternoon. All of Langston's lands are yours," Draeven replied. "Your first and—for the moment—only priority is to get every guard the palace can spare and send them after Amelia Reinhart. She's to be brought back, dead or alive. I don't particularly care which."

Northcott looked him in the face and nodded

once. "As you wish." He turned for the door, but Draeven speaking gave him pause.

"Understand, Northcott, that if you give your word and break it, that the left-hand can strike as good as the right."

The man paused and a slight grin curved up one side of his mouth. "No insult meant, Lord Adelmar, but I doubt that very much. However, I also doubt our king needs either hand to deliver a punishment for betrayal. I like my head where it's at."

Draeven nodded. "Fair enough. You're excused."

Northcott let himself out, and Draeven leaned over to wipe his blade on the fine cloth of Brameer's tunic. He deliberated the merits of having Gulliver get rid of this, or doing it himself.

He was still debating when the door opened once more.

"What is it?" Draeven asked, the heaviness of all that had happened weighing on him greatly.

"Lazarus is awake."

He blinked, sheathing his sword. "Define awake."

Dominicus' face revealed nothing. "He's asked for Quinn three times."

Draeven swallowed, looking away. "I'll talk to him."

Something like pity crossed Dominicus' features, but it was gone just as fast. "Are you sure you want to be the one to tell him?"

Draeven laughed once, and it was a terrible sound. "No. Not at all. But someone has to."

"Maybe Raine could talk to him . . ."

"She's stricken with grief herself. Lazarus isn't going to handle this well. It needs to be me." Draeven slipped by him and made it halfway down the hall.

"You know, even with seeing what happened, it's hard to believe she's gone. I never liked her, but I didn't dislike her either in the end . . . " Dominicus' words were a muttered confusion, as if the man himself didn't know how to feel. Draeven understood that well. "I don't think I truly believed she could be killed. She just seemed . . . larger than this life. Than this world."

Draeven thought about responding, but in truth, he didn't know what to say to Dominicus any more than he did Lazarus. Quinn was a complicated person. A bad person, though she was also good in her own ways. She loved and hated in equal measure, and fiercer than anyone he ever knew. Dominicus was right. She was larger than this life.

But she was also dead.

Now it was time to tell the King that.

Grief's Gambit

"While many find comfort in the light, it was the dark that was his own salvation and damnation in equal measure."
— *Lazarus Fierté, soul eater, the broken King of Norcasta*

Blue skies. Not a cloud in sight. It was a beautiful day overshadowed by memories of blood and bone. Visions flashed through his mind. Splinters of what happened.

He remembered a merlot dress, and snake-tongued woman.

It was everything outside of that which was hazy.

The door opened. He noted there was no knock. Lazarus pulled his gaze from the dirty windowpanes to his left-hand.

Disappointment filled him. He sighed.

"How are you feeling?" Draeven asked. Lazarus looked away once more, not really noticing the dark circles under the other man's eyes, or the slump in his shoulders, or the exhaustion that was more than being tired—and how it weighed him down.

"Fine," Lazarus said. "I'd be better if the hand I asked for came."

Draeven sighed. Instead of giving an explanation, he pulled out a chair from the table across the room and dragged it over to the bed. "How much do you remember?" Draeven asked as he sat down, letting his legs sprawl before him.

There was a light splatter of blood over his tunic.

Lazarus didn't comment on it as he said, "Very little."

Draeven nodded as if he expected that answer. "You were drinking heavily . . ." Draeven began.

"The spirits don't usually affect me," Lazarus replied, a hint of ire entering his tone.

"I wasn't finished," Draeven said. There was something about the sharpness of his tone that made Lazarus take note. He motioned for his left-hand to continue. "You were drinking heavily. An altercation broke out, caused by Risk. Erwing didn't heed Quinn's warning, and he paid for it—"

"That's not possible," Lazarus said. "I would remember if that had happened."

"Not if you were being controlled, you wouldn't," came Draeven's reply. "Risk lost control and killed Erwing. Amelia called for blood. Quinn answered."

"Where is she?" Lazarus demanded, moving the covers aside to stand. "I need to speak with her—"

"She waited long enough for Risk and me to get out, and then she killed everyone."

Lazarus' jaw snapped shut. That was impossible. There was no way he'd forget all of this. He shook his head, and those brief flashes of red made his stomach turn. A thought was creeping its way in. "Everyone?"

"All but two."

"How?"

His left-hand blew out a loose breath. "I don't know exactly. I can guess based on what remained of the bodies. When I left, everyone was alive. When I got back, they were all dead and Amelia was gone."

Lazarus stumbled onto his feet and quickly regained his balance. He scrubbed a hand up his face, rubbing his eyes. "That doesn't make sense—"

"That's not all I found," Draeven said. The tone of his voice had changed between one sentence and the next. A note of uncertainty. Of wariness. Of fear.

"Spit it out," Lazarus said, staring the other man down.

Draeven tried and failed to meet his eyes as he said, "You'd called upon the troll. I suspect you used it to defeat Titus, based on the state in which we found him."

Those splinters of memories ran through his

mind. The color red. The scent of decay. The snapping of bones and the screams of—

"I found you unconscious, holding Quinn."

His heartbeat slowed, but the pounding of it filled his ears like a drum.

"Draeven, where is my right-hand?"

This time when Draeven lifted his head to look at him, their eyes met. The splinters started to piece together, little by little. "She's dead, Lazarus."

Everything ceased to exist for a suspended moment.

Draeven was talking, but all he heard was silence.

All he heard was roaring. At a certain point, they were one in the same. He felt too hot and too cold. His heart stopped and then it raced. If it were possible to break apart and come back together again, he would have.

The memories started to stitch together. Every horrifying piece.

The souls had been unruly that night. They'd been wild and near the edge. He'd drowned himself in spirits to try to soothe them, but all it really did was let that infernal woman's power in.

Quinn had been glorious for one brief, beautiful moment.

She was everything he wanted her to be. The entirety of his focus.

Which is why when his feelings of desire turned to rage . . .

The rest of his memory escaped him. Even now. Even as he suspected.

"Bring me her body."

"Lazarus, you don't want to see that—"

"BRING ME HER BODY," he yelled so loud the walls shook and the other side of the palace likely heard it.

Draeven didn't so much as flinch.

"We don't have it," his left-hand murmured.

"What?"

"We don't have—"

"Why?" The word was more guttural than anything. The souls within him were pushing him to the brink once more. When Draeven simply lowered his head, Lazarus demanded, "Why don't you have her body?"

"Because there wasn't enough left."

Those words stopped him cold. He opened his mouth to speak, but a response didn't come. Lazarus turned away.

"I crushed her to death," he uttered. He might never say it again, but just this once . . . "Amelia stripped me of all emotion when she saw Quinn's power. It let me overpower Titus, and when Quinn turned the creatures on her . . . she used me. To save herself."

Lazarus didn't want to see Draeven's face. He didn't want to know what this left-hand thought. Whether he believed him, or—

"It wasn't your fault, Lazarus. Quinn knew the risks. She knew the—"

"Stop," Lazarus interrupted. He turned on the other man and found pity in his eyes. "This was not Quinn's fault. You don't get to try to blame it on her in an attempt to remove my accountability. I am King. I could have denied the heirs their request. I could have ordered them killed when they first toyed with us. I could have drank less that night. I could have," his voice broke for a moment as emotion overwhelmed him. "I could have fought back more."

"If that were true, she would be alive right—"

"Leave me," Lazarus commanded.

Draeven got to his feet and started toward him. "Lazarus, I know how—" One step too close and he couldn't stop himself nor the beasts within from lashing out. He swung once, and Draeven took it to the jaw. He landed, sprawled on the floor—but not unconscious.

"I said leave me," he growled. Draeven hobbled to his feet. A bruise was already forming where he'd been hit.

"You're grieving. I'm not leaving you when—"

A bitter wind blew the door to his rooms open. The wooden panel banged into the walls so hard it stuck. Lazarus pointed a single finger. "If you want to continue being my hand, you will get out and tell every single vassal in this palace that I don't want to see them. I don't want to see any of you. When I do, I will call. Until then, leave me."

Draeven stared at him for a few seconds as if debating, but thought better. "I'll be here when you're ready." Lazarus didn't need to say more. Draeven let himself out, not once looking back. When he was gone, there was only silence and solitude.

Lazarus didn't know what to think. He didn't want to think.

He didn't want to feel.

All he knew was resentment and regret. Bitterness and madness.

The souls within him raged, but they were not the worst monster he held. No. The most terrible thing he held was himself.

It was that monster that threw the decanter of spirits at the wall. It shattered into a million pieces, but still the pain was there. He turned over his dressers and flipped the table. He tore the legs from it and used them to destroy the very bed he'd taken her —and only her—in.

He raged for hours and hours, till the sun went down and the moon came up.

As the new dawn rose, his fury still hadn't ebbed. Not even a fraction.

Because everywhere he looked, it was her face he saw. The darkness had been home, but when he closed his eyes it was all lavender and pale skin. In the shadows of the room he saw tendrils and felt fear and remembered what it was like for his pulse to race.

He remembered what it was like to live.

And he remembered what it was like when she died.

Lazarus went to the balcony that evening. His bare feet stepped through glass, but he barely noticed as he looked at Leviticus' eye as it started its descent below the horizon. He looked to the side. To the south.

Then again to the west.

To Triene.

And he knew in his heart that the game had finally begun.

The sun slipped below the horizon. In the darkness, where he saw only her, Lazarus began to plot his revenge.

He began to plot the end.

An Eye for An Eye

"Everyone is either a pawn or player in the game of power."
— *Nero, Emperor of Triene*

One month later . . .

A soft melody haunted the capitol. Servants scuttered about like rats in an alley. Vassals took care to be as far from the throne room as possible.

Because within it, the emperor was playing.

His nimble fingers danced over strings as he sank into the maddening tune. He'd been at it for hours, and provided he was uninterrupted, it would be hours more.

As fate would have it, that was not the case.

A knock echoed through the hall, interrupting his song. The bow skittered across the strings, a harsh, grating sound. Nero paused.

The door opened. The vassal who had done so hanging their head so that he would not see. A woman came running forward. Her gown a dusty shade of brown and orange.

Desert sand, he deduced. Her darkened hair was a mop of unruly, poorly kept curls.

She fell to his feet and kissed his sandals.

Nero set the violin and bow aside, reaching for his cane instead.

"I'm sorry, my love," the woman exclaimed. He reached down with his free hand and petted her head. "I've failed you. I went to kill the King and only managed to get the girl. I used my power on him, but lost control. He started to turn on me, and with the fear twister dead and unable to distract him, I had no choice but to run. They've sent assassins and guards after me. I can't return to Norcasta now after what I've done. I'm so sorry—"

"Shhh," Nero whispered. "My dear, you haven't failed me in the slightest."

She paused in her groveling and looked up. Tears stained her cheeks, mixing with the dust on her skin.

Her eyes rimmed in red and completely, genuinely apologetic.

He cupped her cheek.

"I haven't?" she asked, not understanding.

"No," he smiled then, and he saw a flicker of fear run through her. "On the contrary, you've done exactly what I hoped you'd do."

She tried to pull away, but his fingers had already ensnared themselves in her hair.

"I don't understand," she said, licking her lips. She wouldn't contradict his hold. She wouldn't whimper or dare pull away.

He'd trained her well.

"Lazarus is my friend, darling," he said. "My only friend." Her bottom lip started to quiver, and she bit down on it.

"I thought he betrayed you," she said, lowering her eyes immediately. He liked that she questioned what she did. That she feared him as much as she adored him.

"He did." Nero nodded. His fingers slid from her hair. A fraction of the tension drained away. Amelia let out the smallest sigh of relief and kept her eyes averted.

She didn't see the cane coming.

Not until it struck her.

Nero had gone for the face first, but softened the blow enough to merely send her sprawling, and not unconscious. She cried out in pain. He hit her again. And again. And again.

The blows rained down on her supple flesh, and his groin thickened. Her blood dripped from the end of his cane, and Nero stifled a groan. She didn't have enough in her to scream. He'd known that already from their intimate time together. But he did love her tears. Part of him wanted to lick them from her face.

In the end, he settled for beating her to death.

It was really too bad that she'd played her part perfectly.

He might not have had to do this.

But alas, the real games had begun.

"You," Nero said, panting hard. He limped toward his throne, leaving a trail of blood behind. "Remove her head. Have it put in a box, and send it."

"Your Excellency," the vassal replied in a deadened voice. "Where to?"

Nero looked down at the girl and grinned.

"My brother."

The servant nodded. "Do you wish to send a message with it?"

Nero ran a blood-slicked hand through his hair. Beyond the stone columns and pristine archways, twilight was upon them. One hand went to his left cheek where a scar that spanned his face had robbed him of his vision in that eye.

"Tell him, an eye for an eye."

The Dark Realm

"Life was not a straight path that you follow to the end, but a cycle that never had an end."
— *Quinn Darkova, fear twister, dead*

I n the darkness there was a creaking sound.

While death had not been as she thought, this was new. Different.

Quinn turned to Mazzulah on the dais where they sat. The god of the dark realm and her honored guest. She wore long, black fabrics devoid of any brightness. The strips of cloth covered very little of her skin. A silver circlet sat at her waist, holding the strips of cloth in place between her legs.

"What is that?" Quinn asked, regarding the god in her feminine form.

Her beauty was as terrible as it was great.

"The door," she answered, a smile curving up her lips. Quinn frowned and stood. She padded forward, the cold tiles stinging the soles of her feet as she went to the very edge.

The stairs that spanned before them were nearly endless. Up here, she was as high as the clouds in the dark sky. Her lavender hair whipped away from her face. Beside her, Neiss came to curl possessively around her ankle.

"Quinn?" Her name echoed from the world below. It was merely a whisper on the wind by the time it reached her, but even in death, she knew that voice.

"Risk?" she said, turning to face Mazzulah once more. The god stood a full head taller than Quinn herself. Her black horns spiraled up, and the gold symbol upon her forehead shone.

Once more, she heard her name being called up from the void.

Mazzulah smiled.

"She's come to bring you home."

To be continued . . .

Quinn and Lazarus story continues in :
Long Live the Soulless
Dark Maji Book Five

Also by Kel Carpenter

Ongoing Series:

—Adult Urban Fantasy—

Demons of New Chicago:

Touched by Fire (Book One)

Haunted by Shadows (Book Two)

Blood be Damned (Book Three)

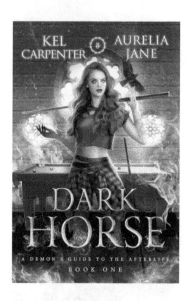

—Adult Reverse Harem Paranormal Romance—

A Demon's Guide to the Afterlife:

Dark Horse (Book One)

Completed Series:

—Young Adult +/New Adult Urban Fantasy—

The Daizlei Academy Series:

Completed Series Boxset

—Adult Reverse Harem Urban Fantasy—

Queen of the Damned Series:

Complete Series Boxset

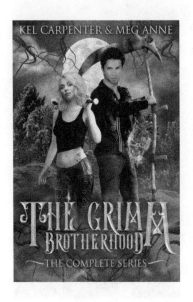

—New Adult Urban Fantasy—

The Grimm Brotherhood Series:

Complete Series Boxset

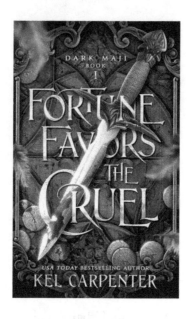

—Adult Dark Fantasy—

The Dark Maji Series:

Fortune Favors the Cruel (Book One)

Blessed be the Wicked (Book Two)

Twisted is the Crown (Book Three)

For King and Corruption (Book Four)

Long Live the Soulless (Book Five)

About Kel Carpenter

Kel Carpenter is a master of werdz. When she's not reading or writing, she's traveling the world, lovingly pestering her editor, and spending time with her husband and fur-babies. She is always on the search for good tacos and the best pizza. She resides in Bethesda, MD and desperately tries to avoid the traffic.

Join Kel's Readers Group!

Acknowledgments

This book was a surprise. It was easy, and yet not. It was told it was great, but I was convinced it was utter garbage. In short, it's a paradox for me.

By the end, I do think that I came to love it. That, however, wouldn't have been possible were it not for Graceley Knox pushing me to finish. She's a hardass, but it's because of her that I finally found my way with this series once more. Thank you, Graceley.

Thank you to Analisa for all your hard work in making this book shine despite my apostrophe problem.

Thank you to all the friends that have supported this series.

And, thank you, dear reader, for following Quinn and Lazarus to whatever ends they may meet.

Printed in the USA
CPSIA information can be obtained
at www.ICGtesting.com
LVHW041533250823
756285LV00039B/336